CORRUPT DOMINION

CORRUPT DOMINION
CHOSEN BY FREYA™
BOOK SIX

MICHAEL ANDERLE

DISRUPTIVE IMAGINATION

DON'T MISS OUR NEW RELEASES

Join the LMBPN email list to be notified of new releases and special promotions (which happen often) by following this link:

http://lmbpn.com/email/

This book is a work of fiction. All of the characters, organizations, and events portrayed in this novel are either products of the author's imagination or are used fictitiously. Sometimes both.

Copyright © 2024 LMBPN Publishing
Cover Art by Jake @ J Caleb Design
http://jcalebdesign.com / jcalebdesign@gmail.com
Cover copyright © LMBPN Publishing
A Michael Anderle Production

LMBPN Publishing supports the right to free expression and the value of copyright. The purpose of copyright is to encourage writers and artists to produce the creative works that enrich our culture.

The distribution of this book without permission is a theft of the author's intellectual property. If you would like permission to use material from the book (other than for review purposes), please contact support@lmbpn.com. Thank you for your support of the author's rights.

LMBPN® Publishing
2375 E. Tropicana Avenue, Suite 8-305
Las Vegas, Nevada 89119 USA

Version 1.00, March 2024
eBook ISBN: 979-8-88878-822-6
Print ISBN: 979-8-88878-823-3

THE CORRUPT DOMINION TEAM

Thanks to the JIT Readers

Dave Hicks
Christopher Gilliard
Diane L. Smith
Dorothy Lloyd

Editor
The SkyFyre Editing Team

CHAPTER ONE

Everyone said Lars was wet behind the ears, and he knew better than to argue. He had been deep-sea fishing plenty of times as a kid, but he could already see his new job was completely different.

"Let's drop the net!" Captain Johansson shouted over the lousy speakers. He was the only person indoors and the only person Lars could really see in the early morning light. It was getting late in the season to be out on the sea, but Johansson and his crew were more than willing to bring in another catch and have a bit more money before winter well and truly set in.

Well, not all of them. But if they had all agreed to come, there would be no room for Lars on the fishing vessel.

"On it!" Lars called back.

Before he could make it across the rocking surface of the boat, Nils was there, operating the controls for the trawler as easily as Lars navigated the internet.

"No offense, little greenhorn, but I'd rather catch some

fish," Nils commented. He was an older man, stringy with muscles and with a stubbly face. Despite Lars having a full beard, seeing Nils always made him feel like a kid.

"If we want to catch some fish, we shouldn't have brought you on at all, Nils!" Bjorn remarked. He was a great, barrel-chested man with a beard bigger than Lars, more gray than brown. He held a large thermos in one hand and several tin cups hanging from a finger in the other.

"Oh, shut up, you fat old man," Nils griped. "Some of us have learned how to do more than operate the coffee machine and the stove."

"I'm sorry, Nils. Did you not want any coffee today? And here I thought it was your day to have the thermos how you like it." He waggled the thermos back and forth. Lars could not hear the contents slosh over the sound of the net releasing, but Nils perked up like he could.

"Extra cream in there?" Nils asked.

"And a pinch of cinnamon," Bjorn added.

"You're not old," Nils muttered.

Bjorn smacked his sizeable belly and laughed. "Fair enough! I would never ask another man to lie to me."

"Just with you?" Nils poked.

"Are you offering?" Bjorn asked, raising an eyebrow at the craggy Nils.

"In your dreams, fat man."

"Wouldn't you like to know," Bjorn returned. He was apparently appeased, though, because he stopped bothering Nils and poured him a cup of coffee.

"Check the propeller!" the captain shouted over the speakers.

"That means you, kid." Bjorn elbowed Lars in the side.

"Oh, right. Sorry!"

"Wait, take a coffee with you!" Bjorn poured Lars two cups of the brew, pale with cream.

Lars actually made it to where he could see the propeller without spilling *too* much of the coffee.

Axel was not impressed. "Bjorn might lick coffee off your fingers, but I'm not so inclined." He took the cup from Lars and frowned at the sticky handle.

"Sorry about that. The sea—"

"The sea does as she wishes, boy. Best not forget it," Axel quipped.

Lars actually liked Axel. He was terrifying to behold, covered in scars and tattoos layered on top of each other, but it was all for show. Axel had paid handsomely for all the tattoos. Upon closer inspection, they were all rare sea creatures, not skulls or monsters.

The scars he'd earned from working as a less-than-cautious mechanic for years. Even now, with the motor chugging along, he was sticking his fingers into it to diagnose it rather than use any of the software that was supposed to tell him the same things.

Lars had come out here to be on the sea and help feed his countrymen, but after meeting Axel, he was reconsidering being a fisherman. Being a mechanic seemed like an interesting career. Constantly solving puzzles and working with machines appealed to Lars. Though he hoped he could figure them out with fewer nicks and burns to his arms than Axel had.

"Is something stuck in the propeller?" Lars asked.

"Sounds like it, but no. Not as far as I can tell," Axel

replied. "The captain can feel the ship being sluggish even though we dropped the net, so he's looking for a problem. That make sense to you?"

"Sure, yeah," Lars agreed.

"But he is looking for problems when I have found the solution," Axel revealed with a wink.

"What's that?" Lars asked, impressed as always that Axel could figure out the inner workings of a machine so quickly.

"They dropped the net, and now the engine is struggling. What could be slowing us down?" Axel asked.

Even greenhorn Lars knew the answer to that one.

"Fish!"

Axel nodded and took out a radio. He yelled something into it that was unintelligible to Lars, but the captain obviously understood. Orders came over the speakers, and other members of the crew emerged, saying good morning or cursing it, as they preferred.

This was Lars' favorite part of the day. When the ship transformed from an object into a sort of super-organism. Everyone went about their jobs, getting into position, opening hatches, readying their cargo hold, battening things down, hell, even pissing off the side of the ship in preparation to bring in another catch. Lars still felt like an extra finger that nobody needed, but after a few weeks at sea, he had at least learned where he could get out of the way.

You really only had to be knocked into a cargo hold filled with fish one time before you made sure never to stand in the way again.

After a moment, the entire crew stilled, ready for the net to come up, but it did not.

Lars looked back at Nils, who was angrily shouting at the controls of the winch.

"I thought it normally took longer to fill a net," Lars remarked.

Axel sucked his teeth and nodded. "Normally, it does. But even a full net shouldn't give the winch this much trouble."

Now that Axel had pointed it out, Lars heard the trawler laboring to pull the net up. He had heard it labor before, but only when the nets were actually *out* of the water. He still couldn't even see the top of the net.

Had they snagged a whale?

Obviously, that was impossible. The nets were designed to avoid catching whales. It was only a fancy in Lars' head because he was, as the others repeatedly told him, a bit green behind the ears. Already, much of the crew was cheering. A huge haul this early in the morning meant they might spend the rest of the day heading back to shore for a larger-than-expected payday. Nothing wrong with that!

But even a larger haul should not have troubled the trawler so. Lars had been working with Axel enough to have some idea what the machine was capable of. It should sound like this only if the line was snagged.

No sooner did Lars think this than he glanced at Axel, who shrugged. "Line's not snagged. Nils may be an old fart, but he knows how to work the machine."

Nils fiddled with the controls, trying to rectify the situation.

Then, suddenly, the trawler resumed moving at normal speed. The boat lurched forward, and the net raced up from the depths of the sea.

The preemptive cheers for a large catch faded as the boat shifted back and forth beneath the seamen's feet. It had been laboring to both move and pull in the net, but now it was moving along fast as ever, the trawler unbothered.

The crew, though, was not so quick to forget. They inched closer to the side of the boat where the net was submerged. Everyone wanted a look at what was going on except Lars. He didn't want to get any closer to whatever had slowed the boat down. He knew he was being paranoid, but he strapped on a life vest. Technically, they were all supposed to wear them whenever they were on deck, but the crew didn't care, and the captain did not enforce the safety rule.

Axel did not use the opportunity to roast young Lars. He watched, as transfixed as the rest of the crew, as the crane arm squeaked and rattled while the cable connected to the net spooled back up.

"I hope no one was dreaming about going home early!" Bjorn shouted from near the side of the boat. "Looks like you'll all be eating lunch and dinner with me again. Hardly enough fish in there for a stew."

There was some grumbling, even though Lars knew most of the crew appreciated Bjorn's cooking. Finally, the net lifted from the water. It held a paltry catch inside, but they lost even that as the net raised and the fish tumbled out.

Lars swallowed and adjusted his life preserver straps.

He had helped hook up the net. It should not have a hole in it. Modern nets took months to wear out, and this one was nearly brand new. Even if it did have a weak spot that no one had noticed, it should have only let a few fish escape. Not the entire catch.

Nils stopped reeling in the line and shouted over his radio. The crane arm operator moved the net over the cargo hatch. No point in opening up the hatch, though. There were no fish in the net. Only a huge hole, too big to be explained by any of the reasons Lars had learned from being out here.

Two crewmen approached the net and inspected it.

"It's been cut!" one of them shouted.

"By what?" the captain returned over the lousy speakers.

"How am I supposed to know? A knife?" the seamen called back.

Lars did not think a knife had cut the net. He also knew it was too strong for something like a great white shark to tear through. There was no logical reason the net should be torn. It had been sturdy and in good shape when Lars had last seen it. And they were too far north to worry about—

Someone screamed from the front of the boat, but a splash cut the sound short.

Lars was in no position to see what had happened, being so close to the back of the boat. Surely that splash had been a coincidence? A dolphin or something, or the sound of a wave crashing against the side of the boat. Right after someone screamed.

Lars was not the only one to hear the scream.

Other crewmen headed to the front of the boat. Lars watched them with a growing sense of dread. Then, a huge wave came up out of nowhere and crashed over the front of the boat.

One of the crewmen screamed again, but at least this one was forming words.

"Man overboard! There's a man overboard!"

Despite not wearing life preservers, the crew did take the risk of drowning seriously. The sea was so cold this far north that even a powerful swimmer's strength would drain in minutes. The crewman grabbed one of the life preservers connected to a rope and tossed it overboard.

But rather than waiting by the rope and helping to haul the man back on board, he let the rope go slack as he stepped away from the front of the boat.

Two other crew members reached him. One grabbed the rope, but rather than pulling, he looked around wildly, searching for a man who was no longer there.

"Where is he?" the other crewman yelled. "Where did he go?"

The first crewman to the scene shook his head.

"Come on, kid," Axel urged.

Axel and Lars left their post near the motor and approached the group, gathering around the obviously shaken crewmen.

"He was taken. Pulled beneath," one muttered, eyes wider than any dose of morning coffee could have made them.

"Pulled beneath by what? The sea?" Axel demanded.

The crewman looked up, horror on his face. "He was devoured by a sea serpent."

"Come on, now. Let's go inside and have something to eat. We can all see things when we lose someone. Come on," Bjorn offered.

"I know what I saw! Check the cameras!"

Lars did not want to know what was happening. He did not want to be on this ship. He should have studied math like his mother always said. He should have stayed in school. The pay was good out here, but what did that matter if they never made it back to port? He wanted nothing to do with any of this, yet he found his feet moving him toward the captain's cabin, along with Axel, Nils, and Bjorn.

"Captain, did you see what happened?" Nils asked.

"It was all pretty fast, but I saw…something."

"A whale?" Bjorn asked.

The captain only bit his lip and gestured to the tablet hooked to the security cameras. The one thing the young Lars was better at than anyone else. He picked up the tablet and pulled up the last few minutes of video taken from the front of the ship.

What he saw made his blood run cold.

He started a few minutes back and waited for the lone wave to appear. Except it wasn't a lone wave. There was something in the water, something huge, white, and sinuous. It churned back and forth, more like an eel than a whale.

More like a snake.

In fact, it looked like an absolutely massive water snake. Its body boiled up from the depths, bringing a giant wave that knocked the seamen overboard. A moment later, when he got his bearings and turned his head back to the man with the life preserver, a giant emerged from the sea, opened wide, and swallowed him.

"That's not possible," Nils stated.

"I don't think Lars doctored the video." Axel snorted.

"But that was a snake," Bjorn insisted. "It looked like the head of a viper. Pits and ridges and slitted eyes."

Indeed, it did. Lars froze the video on the horrible monster's face, and now that Bjorn had said it, there was no denying it appeared to be a snake. But what snake had a head so large it could swallow a man in one bite? Lars knew about the anaconda, which could eat an entire deer, but that took hours. The snake had to unhinge its jaw to stretch it wide enough to consume the entire animal.

That was not what happened. The massive white serpent had opened its mouth and swallowed a man like it was eating sardines.

"I've seen enough," Captain Johansson announced. "We're heading back to port."

He steered the tiller, but before the boat could reverse direction, something struck it and knocked everyone off their feet.

The captain was the first to get back up. He grabbed his microphone and gave orders.

"All crew, prepare to abandon ship! We have run aground on…err…prepare to abandon ship!"

Outside the cabin, people rushed around, grabbing life preservers and inflatable rafts.

Lars found that his sea legs, hard-earned after his first season at sea, were gone. He found he could barely stand on his feet. It felt like everything was tilting to one side, farther and farther.

With the sound of snapping wood, the ship lurched in the other direction. Lars was thrown from his feet and crashed into a wall.

Axel, Nils, and Bjorn hardly did any better. They scrambled to their feet and raced from the cabin while the captain hollered a distress call into the radio. He looked at Lars. "Abandon ship."

Lars ran out of the cabin and onto the deck.

The sun poked over the horizon, turning the clouds purple and orange. It also provided great illumination for the massive white tail that rose from the sea, higher than the deck of the boat, higher than the crane. It reached for the sky as Lars stood there, frozen, then both were in motion as the huge tail descended toward the deck.

Lars' feet carried him away from the huge scaled tail before it smacked the front of the boat with enough force to smash through the deck.

The ship was floundering, taking on water. The back lifted, rendering the motor useless.

"Go back to Hell, you monster!" Axel shouted, flare gun in hand. He didn't shoot it into the air but instead blasted it at a wave.

As the bright ball of light flew, it illuminated the serpent's massive white head. The snake had been about to attack again, but Axel frightened it into the depths.

"What are you still doing here, boy?" Axel demanded. "Get the hell on a raft!"

"What about you?"

"I got another flare."

Then the tail rose from behind Axel and smashed him into the deck, then through it, into the sea.

Lars screamed and stumbled backward.

Meanwhile, Bjorn raced *toward* the tail with a massive meat cleaver. He swung it and took a chunk from the snake's tail, but it was no cause for celebration. The tail flicked and knocked Bjorn through the air as if he weighed nothing.

He splashed into the sea, and the snake submerged. Axel's dead body and Bjorn's living strength were no match for the huge snake. It dove, and they were both sucked beneath the surface.

"Get on a raft, boy," Nils told Lars. "You have to get on a raft."

"What about you?"

"I'm going to catch a fish."

Nils raced toward the crane controls. It was in the center of the ship and not underwater yet, but it would be in minutes. The ship was broken in two places and sinking deeper. Sea water reached the hold, and hundreds of captive fish struggled to swim free, many swimming over his boots. He stumbled backward.

They nearly knocked Lars from his feet, but he managed to reach a raft with two other seamen.

The three of them climbed inside as the crane lurched to life. It swung its boom out over the water. By luck, that was when the snake's head emerged.

Nils was adept at the controls, and he dropped the heavy net on the snake's head. It was torn, but even a torn net could kill a whale. Nils would do everything he could to drive this monster off.

But the snake was not perturbed. It let the net fall on it, then turned and dove.

Nils struggled, trying to let as much cable out as fast as he could, but the machine was no match for the snake. It swam deeper and farther until the cable grew taut, and the boat lurched to the side, pulled over by its own fishing net.

The life raft was tossed from the boat like an afterthought. Lars hung on for dear life as it flew. He'd wrapped his arm around the rope across the top of the raft, but the other two seamen had not. They toppled out, grabbing for the rope, but they missed it and fell into the sea.

The raft hit the water's surface, and Lars was bounced off the inflatable craft and flipped as he held onto the rope. His boots splashed into the water as his chest smacked the air-filled raft wall, but he didn't let go. He hauled himself back into the raft and looked for an oar or a rope to throw to the other two seamen who'd tried to escape with him.

He saw one of them, somehow already distant, splashing against the weight of his clothes and losing. There was no sign of the other seaman.

There came the sound of rending metal as the crane finally gave way. It screeched in protest as it bent further, then snapped from the deck and plunged into the ocean. Lars saw Nils thrown from one side of the control booth to the other. He hit the side too fast, and a smear of blood told Lars all he needed to know.

He choked out a sob. He had been joking around with Nils only minutes ago!

The water churned with life rafts and debris from the boat. Lars couldn't tell how many people made it off the boat or how many were in rafts. The light was strengthening, but the wind was picking up, too, pushing the rafts farther apart. He lost sight of them in the troughs and peaks of the water.

Between the waves, the snake's huge white girth rose from the water and ducked its head under. A minute later, its head rose again, and it crushed a life raft. Then, it vanished beneath the surface.

Tears ran down Lars' cheeks, but he paid them no mind. Instead, he grabbed his oar and paddled. He paddled away from this monster's killing grounds, away from the new life he had intended to start here.

The raft pushed up from beneath him. A huge spine, like a spear made of bone, punctured it. Lars scrambled backward, but he was too slow, and the thing he was escaping too big. He barely made it back before the spine dragged the raft underwater.

The noise of the sinking ship, the ocean, the other people calling for help faded away underwater. Lars threw off his boots and coat and kicked for the surface. He didn't want to see what had pulled him under. He didn't want to see if it was coming back for him. All he wanted was to be back home, to have never left, to still be sipping coffee with Bjorn and Nils and Axel.

He burst through the surface and found himself closer to the hobbled wreck of the ship. It didn't seem to be sinking farther, but truthfully, Lars hardly cared what happened now. He had to get out of the water. The cold would kill him if the—

He saw its face push up through the water.

Its snout with two pits on the front, its long forked tongue, its two eyes, white as the moon and slitted and staring at him. It dove under, and the water churned as it came for the last survivor of the ship it had destroyed.

CHAPTER TWO

Barrow dig site #16 office, Svedjehamm, Finland, Wednesday morning, March

Terra Olsen had hardly been able to contain her excitement as they brought the box from the dig back to the office they had rented in Svedjehamm. "Office" was a generous term. It was a small cottage they used an intermediary to rent, so they would not be followed back here. The Barrow Company had been attacked on multiple dig sites. They had to be cautious.

However, it was starting to feel unnecessary after working on digs all through the fall and winter and not being attacked by anything worse than an overbearing reporter.

"Are you ready?" Leif asked. Obviously, the Asgardian was as eager as Terra. His enchanted spectacles were always perfectly clean, but right now, they sparkled as if catching a ray of the setting sun despite it being morning. His magical skills had improved alongside Terra's since he had come to this world. She wondered exactly what he could see with those spectacles.

"Unwrap it," Terra ordered.

Leif obliged. He placed the wooden crate on the table in the cottage, then used his fingers to pry the top off. That should have been impossible, but *seidr* was augmenting the Asgardian's strength. Was he even aware of how strong he had become? Probably not, considering he sparred with Terra, whose strength far outstripped his.

From the wooden crate, he removed the artifact carefully wrapped in a piece of cloth.

"They found it near a statue." Leif unwrapped the cloth, corner by corner.

"Wild. I didn't think we'd find one of her here. Was there an altar as well?" They had been working on two equally fruitless sites here in Finland. Terra had not uncovered much of anything. More coins. The ruins of a ship. Same old, same old.

"Not really, no. And the statue…well, it was not in as good a shape as the others we've found."

"More like the statue of Loki, then?" Terra asked. All the statues they had found dedicated to Freya had been immaculately preserved masterworks. The one statue of Loki had been equally impressive, but its face had weathered away. A trick, no doubt. A similar weathering here could indicate something else was going on.

"Actually, the Loki statue was in much better shape than this one." He unwrapped the final piece of the cloth to reveal the box holding Freya's final magical artifact.

It was not particularly impressive to behold.

All the other boxes had been ornate things, paneled

with rose gold and carved so masterfully that Terra assumed dwarves had done the work. This box might have looked that way once, but it would have been centuries ago.

It was framed in wood, though the wood could not seem to decide if it was rotting away or petrifying. The metal hinges and lock appeared weakened. Metal pieces attached to the sides seemed to have been worked with some sort of design, but they were now so rusted and corroded that Terra could hardly make out what they were supposed to show. The other boxes had puzzles hidden in the runes on these panels. The only thing the panels on this box could be hiding was tetanus.

"The other pieces were protected from the weathering and erosion of Midgard. This one seems not to have enjoyed those benefits," Leif stated.

"Are you sure it will survive opening it?" Terra asked.

"Honestly, I'm surprised it made it here at all," Leif muttered.

"Well, no time like the present, I guess." Terra gently touched the clasp of the box. It broke away with a tiny puff of rust.

"Tone down the power from the bracers, maybe?" Leif suggested.

"I don't think the bracers did that." Terra tried to be gentler as she opened the lid. Her effort was in vain, though. As soon as she lifted it, the hinges on the back broke.

Inside was nothing more than a few pieces of jewelry and a handful of coins. The jewelry was silver and bronze, so at least it was intact, but it was not particularly impressive. Though Terra knew looks could be deceiving when it came to these artifacts. Freya's ax looked like a simple hand tool but was, in fact, one of the most powerful pieces of the entire arsenal.

Terra touched each piece of jewelry, hoping for a surge of power from one of them but feeling absolutely nothing.

"Well? Is it one of the pieces?" Leif asked, eager with anticipation. "Not much to behold, but it's the magic that matters, not the appearance, right?"

"Except there's no magic," Terra remarked after touching the final piece of jewelry.

"You're sure?"

"Pretty sure this is the Viking equivalent of a knick-knack drawer, but please. Take a look with your magic spectacles and tell me I'm wrong."

Leif peered through the lenses and sucked his teeth. "I'm not seeing anything."

"Damn it!" Terra pounded the table. When she did, the box crumbled further, leaving only the vaguest outline of the artifact intact. "It's been *months,* and we haven't found a thing! I thought this would be our big break." Terra was careful not to sigh on the box of junk. It would likely blow it all to pieces.

"Now, now. That's not the Terra we've all grown to love and be intimidated by. You're normally a paragon of unnecessary optimism. What's wrong?" Leif asked.

"We've been pulling permits and doing digs all winter despite no one in the region wanting to. I feel like we've been busting our butts and have nothing to show for it."

"You weren't so disappointed at our last site," Leif pointed out.

"Because I thought we'd find something at *this* one. Every time we turn up something that even sort of looks like an altar, I get my hopes up. But it's all been a bunch of nothing. Do you think the list we got from the Villon Institute was a fake?"

"I would not be able to guess at the modern methods of subterfuge, but don't these knickknacks prove this site is at least worthy of traditional research?"

Terra smiled. "When did we switch?"

"What do you mean?"

"When you first arrived, all you could focus on was that I was the Chosen of Freya, and you were my guide. The only part of archeology you cared about was how we had gotten so much of it wrong. Now, you're the one pointing out the historical significance of coins while I'm desperate for another artifact."

"Don't beat yourself up about that. Remember, I'm not a mortal of this realm like you are. I have lived what you would call lifetimes. Why, I once spent years looking for a lost scroll! A few months traveling around this world in airplanes and trying all the foods your people have invented has not bored me. I'm sure we'll find the last piece, though. We simply need more time."

"But what if we don't have more time? What if someone already found it, and they're plotting against us even now?"

"Given the history of the people who have attacked us, I would think we would know if someone was working against us. They have not exactly been subtle."

"That's true, I guess. I don't know how much longer I can keep looking and not finding things, though. It's silly. I mean, looking and not finding is part of archeology, but this is different. A discovery might change history, but the wrong person finding one of Freya's artifacts *will* change the future."

"I think that means no one has found the final piece yet. I think we would know. In the meantime, we should keep training and searching."

"Easy for you to say! All it takes for you to be happy is a new kind of junk food."

Leif looked hurt, and Terra immediately regretted it.

"I resent that," Leif clarified. "You of all people should know that sometimes, returning to the same junk food is wonderful!" He laughed, and Terra could not help but snort in amusement despite her bad mood.

"You're thinking about your book, aren't you?"

Leif grinned. "Truthfully? I have begun drafting. There is so much content! I can hardly believe it. The question of how to format the book is looming large in my mind. Do I try to make a chronology of the age? That seems an impossible task. Why, I can hardly watch all the current television shows. How could I make a list of their history?"

"The history of television? Is that seriously the book you're writing?"

"Well, it *could* be! I could also sort the world geographically and try to dig into the similarities and differences of the cultures. I know we've only seen a tiny portion of the modern world, but it *does* happen to be the part of the world the Aesir and Vanir are most familiar with. I think quite a few people would be interested in the difference between pickled fish and Sweden and Norway."

"Oh! So, you *do* eat things besides Doritos? I had no idea."

"We all must suffer in the name of our craft. If it means eating food that's not fortified with the deliciousness that is monosodium glutamate, so be it."

"Is that what you insist on teaching archeologists? Are you trying to make them suffer?"

"I'm imparting real-world knowledge to them!"

Terra snorted. "Maybe it feels that way to you, but you never have any evidence to back it up."

"I *saw* the way people lived in the Viking age! Better than guessing based on what's left of their tools."

"You have to stop telling people that!"

"Oh, it's fine. They all think it's a joke. Doctor LARP, they call me. Whatever that means."

"Doctor LARP, huh? Well, might I remind you we're on this particular dig because of you. Which means you need to explain to the boss that we did all this work for a knick-knack drawer."

"I believe I was clear from the start. My map is not the most precise. It activated when we flew in from Sweden. I had thought it meant we were getting closer here in Finland, but it is not precise."

"You seemed pretty confident before."

Leif smiled with embarrassment before managing a weak shrug. "We had been to every part of modern-day Scandinavia except Finland!"

"So you came for the snacks?"

"Yes? I mean, I really did think Freya might have hidden her pieces all over the former domain of the Vikings. It's not like the ones we have found were clustered together. You are not wrong about the prospect of snacks, though. I…I might have a problem."

"Well, admitting you need help is the first part of getting help. Let's put you on a junk food detox."

"Sure. Of course. Starting tomorrow. There's one more flavor of Taffel Sips I want to try. Cheese flavor! Can you imagine?"

"You understand those things have nothing to do with real cheese, right?"

"I don't fully understand how cheese comes from milk, so do not pester me with concerns of snack food purity."

Terra sighed as Leif pulled out a bag of his precious cheese chips. She stood from the table and stepped outside the front porch of their little cabin.

It afforded them fantastic views of the sea and the many tiny islands the locals called Lappor's Sund. The islands were constantly growing and shrinking as the tides came in and out, so the view was never quite the same. It was always spectacular, however.

Clouds crowded against each other, growing darker and heavier as they reached the horizon. The morning sun at her back created beams of light through the cloud cover, making parts of the sea dazzle with light.

There was movement everywhere. Birds wheeled overhead and dove into the water. The faintest indication of darker spots in the sea blew sprays into the air. Whales, going about their business. The wind came in from the west, so the sea was alive with whitecaps that crested and crashed before hitting the many islands that hemmed in the narrow bay.

Barrow had picked this spot because it gave them a three-hundred-and-sixty-degree view. They did not want anyone sneaking up on them again, and a clear line of sight was the simplest way to achieve that. Leif had also shown Terra how to make warding spells with runes, but they had yet to have an opportunity to test them.

It would be a good thing. Not being attacked by cultists, demigods, or rival archeologists was supposed to make her job easier, but that was not how Terra felt. She sensed her energy frittering away. If she could not use it as it was intended, namely in the glory of battle, she was wasting it.

Leif had tried to assure her this was not the case many times, but she had not embraced it. She did not think he had, either. Leif had changed since coming to Midgard. Maybe not as much as Terra had changed since she met him, but he was not the uninformed, magically challenged person he had been. Why, consider all the different kinds of snacks he had discovered.

"It's beautiful," Leif commented around a mouthful of cheese chips. Terra could smell the flavoring on his breath.

"The view or the chips?"

"Modern wonders. It's funny, but back when the Vikings were spreading the power of the Aesir and Vanir to the world, these views were nothing special. This much sea was something to be crossed, maybe. Forests were nothing more than future boats.

"Now, humans have grown so plentiful that views of the world are quite rare. It's another piece of how this world has changed that I would like to bring back to Asgard. It's amazing how one's view can shift. I think many people there don't view change the way they do here."

A cloud passed over them, casting them into shadow before swallowing the sunshine on the hill leading down to the beach. Without the glare of the sun, Terra's eyes adjusted, and she saw things she hadn't moments before. Seals in the shallows. Fishing boats going about their business.

And the wreckage of a ship washed up on the beach directly below their cabin.

"Oh, no, Leif. Look!" She pointed at the ship.

The shipwreck drew all her attention. It was cracked in half, more a mess of debris bound with ropes and fishing nets than a ship.

There were people on it, too.

Someone pushed himself out of the wreckage, snagged his foot in a bit of fishing net, and crashed to the beach. He barely had the strength to pick himself back up and save himself from drowning. He dragged above the surf onto a piece of craggy rock where the water only splashed water rather than soaked.

"We need to help him!" Terra insisted.

"We need to do no such thing. We are on a mission to find Freya's artifacts! This town will have plenty of people who know how to help those poor men," Leif replied.

"You're right, of course." Terra pulled out her phone, even though what she really wanted to do was teleport down there. She dialed the police. When she explained the situation, they informed her they were already aware and that someone was on their way. When she hung up, she heard sirens.

"Very mature of you," Leif commended.

"Thanks. I do what I can. Now, go wash your hands and grab a jacket. We're headed down there."

"Wait, what?" Leif sputtered chip crumbs from his mouth.

"Do you really think I'm going back to sorting coins and knick-knacks from a broken box when there's a shipwreck down there?"

"That was, in fact, exactly how I thought we'd spend the rest of the day."

"Look at the damage done to that boat! It's been demolished by who knows what. We need to see what did it and find out if we can help those people."

Leif did not protest. He grabbed his jacket and hurried to follow Terra before she teleported and left him alone up here.

CHAPTER THREE

The docks, Svedjehamm, Finland, Wednesday morning
Leif actually managed to persuade Terra *not* to teleport to the shipwreck, which he counted as a small victory. Terra had been growing more restless as of late. Leif did not blame her. It had been nearly six months of painstaking research in the cold of the northern winter, and they had found nothing.

It was amazing what these modern humans could endure to keep their civilization moving along. Not only did Terra keep her head down as she kept unearthing more artifacts from sites around Scandinavia, but so did all the locals. All winter long, people went about their jobs, made their money, and lived their lives.

The Vikings never had such patience. They spent winters planning raids for when the waters were easier to navigate in the summers. Only the excitement of what was to come kept them from turning on each other.

However, it seemed everyone being cooped up had a

similar effect on the locals here. When they made it to the beach, they were not the only people there.

Even after all his time here on Midgard, Leif was surprised by how much humans had changed. A thousand years ago, people would have come to pick through what remained of this ship. However, the locals here did not seem interested in the material wealth they could gain. They were trying to help the few survivors.

"Hey, you're safe now. Is there anything I can get for you?" Terra asked a young man who was so pale with the cold that his complexion could be described as "cadaver."

"Water," the man croaked. He looked stressed and dehydrated, which made him look older. Yet the longer Leif looked at him, the more he thought of him as a boy.

"Sure." Terra scampered off behind a boat. Leif felt the familiar twitch of *seidr* as Terra teleported away, then the same twitch in reverse as she teleported back. She stepped out from behind the boat with a water bottle as if there was a store back there. "Here you go." She handed it to the young man.

The kid could barely open the bottle. His forearms trembled with strain as he twisted the lid.

"What's your name?" Leif asked after he'd sipped the water.

"Lars," he replied.

"How long were you out there, Lars?" Leif asked.

"Something attacked us." Lars struggled to clear his dry throat.

"It's all right," Terra told him. "Have some more water and tell us what happened."

Lars nodded and took another sip, larger this time.

"This was last night or this morning, I guess. Something came out of the water. It attacked us. Pulled men into the water. Then, it came back for the ship."

"What kind of something?" Terra asked. "Was it a boat? A submarine?"

"No," Lars said, shaking his head violently. "It was an *animal*. A serpent." He spoke the last word in Swedish.

"You're sure?" Leif asked, looking at the wreckage more closely.

"It came up out of the sea. Pulled men overboard. Then it smashed the ship. It was large. Very large."

"And it was a serpent?" Leif asked. "You're sure?"

Lars nodded, his attention shifting behind Leif.

A siren whooped as an ambulance rolled to a stop. An EMT stepped out and addressed the group.

"All right, ladies and gentlemen. Thank you for your consideration, but we need to help the survivors, if you please."

"You heard them. Get clear! Bring survivors to them!" a police officer called, emerging from a car behind the ambulance. He spoke Finnish, which Leif understood easily enough, but even stubborn Terra got the gist of what they were saying.

"Feel better, Lars. We're glad you made it here." Terra let an EMT lead him away.

While the police and the EMTs worked on the survivors, Leif took a closer look at the boat. He knew enough of how things worked in this world to understand they would not be able to examine it for long. The authorities would want an official investigation, and they would have no reason to include a pair of archaeologists. If Leif wanted to ascertain whether Lars was telling the truth about the serpent, he had to find out what he could now.

He stepped closer to the wreckage. He didn't know what he was looking for exactly. These modern vessels used a combination of metal, wood, and what Terra told him was called fiberglass, which sounded like a hellish material fashioned by a witch.

Leif knew little of modern craftsmanship, which made it difficult to tell what was wrong with the boat. Surely, some of the damage must have occurred when it had made its way through the narrow bay leading to this beach. But not all of it.

Leif peered through his magical spectacles and noticed places in the wreckage that sparkled with the glow of magic. Some of the metal had been torn as if it were nothing but paper. The hull had sustained punctures as well. They almost looked like spear tips, but Leif doubted a boat full of Vikings had attacked this ship.

He glanced behind them. The police had not yet gotten the survivors clear, but they would soon enough. Then, Leif's time to snoop would end. He had to make every moment count. He leaned closer and saw a series of smaller punctures between two larger ones and a few more extending perpendicularly from the other line of holes.

The shape was almost a mouth. A bite wound. But this was not a shark's mouth filled with razor teeth, nor was it an orca or a mighty sperm whale. It appeared Lars had been telling the truth. It looked like a snake had sunk its fangs into the side of this ship.

Leif glanced back and saw a police officer approaching the wreckage. He waved, but Leif pretended not to see. He turned his back to the officer and continued along, looking for more indication of what had happened.

"Excuse me, sir?" the officer called politely in Finnish.

Leif ignored him and looked at the main bulk of the ship. Some of the metal had been snapped in half as if it were twigs. Leif examined it with his glasses and again saw the signs of magic. It should not have broken like that. Something had done so only because it was a magical being that bent the rules of Midgard.

Jotun did that. They were too large to exist in this world without the help of magic to support their bodies. Something was happening here. Leif didn't know whether it was related to the artifact they were looking for, but magic was involved.

He wondered if Freya had plucked the fated threads of *seidr* to make Terra go outside when she had. Even if his great-grandmother had done no such thing, they might as well behave as if she had.

"Sir. You can't be here," the officer announced in English. His tone had changed slightly. Shorter. Less patient with this English-speaking tourist than he would have been with a local.

"Oh, I'm sorry," Leif answered in Finnish. "I just don't know how this could have gotten to shore with no one noticing."

"You and the rest of us," the police officer replied, his tone friendly again. "Even the survivors are clueless."

"None of them saw anything?" Leif asked.

The officer leaned in, eyes twinkling with gossip he likely should not be spreading. "Oh, they all saw something. A sea monster, if you can believe it!" He chuckled.

"It could not have been a whale?" Leif asked.

"That did all this? I guess if one breached and landed right on top of them, but whales don't do that. I would guess the captain was drinking and ran afoul of some rocks."

"Rocks could do this?" Leif asked.

The officer shrugged. "They've been out there for twelve hours. That's enough time for the tides to go in and out. If they were snagged on a rock, the tides could have easily battered the ship. The monster thing is to cover themselves. If the insurance declares this an act of god, they all get paid. If the captain was drunk, they will be lucky to get anything in court."

"I guess I hope it's a sea monster, then, for their sake," Leif replied.

The officer smirked at that. Then he straightened, and Leif understood this off-the-record conversation was over. Perhaps the officer simply wanted to gossip about drunk ship captains.

Leif wandered away from the boat and toward Terra, who stood within earshot of the men being loaded onto the ambulance.

"Anything interesting?" Leif asked.

Terra had the audacity to shush him.

Leif reddened, thinking of a retort, but then the EMTs closed the back of the ambulance, and Terra took Leif's hand and led him away from the authorities.

"Lars wasn't the only one who claimed to see a monster. Everyone was talking about one. A sea serpent. It couldn't be Jörmungandr, could it?" Terra asked.

It was a logical conclusion if you didn't understand what the world serpent was.

"Impossible, I'm afraid," Leif replied. "Jörmungandr is so large he encircles not only the Earth but all of Midgard. There was a time he swam in the oceans of Earth, but it was long ago. If he had attacked this ship, the entire coastline of Finland would have been destroyed by a tidal wave."

"So it wasn't a monster, then?" Terra asked.

"Well, I wouldn't go *that* far," Leif countered. "I saw the residue of magic on the ship. Something not of this realm attacked it. I think we can be sure of that."

"So it *was* a sea monster!" Terra declared.

Leif allowed himself a smile. "Indeed. And I think it might have been a snake."

"That's what everyone said they saw. A long, pale serpent. None of the police or EMTs believed them, of course."

"The people of your world are quite good at not believing. Odd, considering how fantastical so many of the stories they tell are."

"Why did you think it was a snake?"

"I saw bite marks on the side. I don't know all the creatures of the sea, but it looked like whatever bit the ship had two large fangs and many smaller teeth."

"Sounds like a serpent to me," Terra commented.

"Indeed," Leif agreed.

Terra led him away from the shore. The police were gathering witnesses, and Terra likely wanted to avoid either of them going on the record. She didn't like it when Leif let anything slip about Asgard. Even he could see telling the police about such matters at a scene like this might cause them to pay more attention than most of their workers would.

"So if it's not Jörmungandr, what was it?" Terra asked as they started on the long way back to their cottage.

"It could be another Jotun," Leif suggested. "They can come in many forms. Loki's son is the most famous of those without arms or legs, but there are others. They cannot exist in Midgard, though. Remember Fenrir? He needed something to link him to the other realms to sustain him. Without that source of magic, the Jotun struggle to even breathe in this world."

"Hmm. Could it be some effect of magic? All these artifacts have been reawakened. Maybe one of them is affecting the environment. We know Freya's pieces slowed down the erosion of the statues built to her. Could something else have a larger effect?"

"I suppose that's possible, but I find it doubtful. There would have to be a massive influx of magic all at once, then it would have to spread out. We have not seen that happen with any of the artifacts we've found. For anything to have that kind of an effect, it would have to be in the ocean itself!"

Terra stopped walking and nearly yanked Leif's hand off.

"Oh my god, why didn't I think of that?"

"Think of what?"

"The sea levels are anything but consistent, especially around this part of the world. Heck, some of these countries wouldn't even be here if not for the work they do with dikes and dams."

"I'm not following."

"Something magical came from the sea. You're saying it can't be a Jotun unless there's a source of magic for it to use."

"But that's doubtful."

"Right. The other possibility is that magic made this monster from whatever was already in the sea. Either way, we have to consider the possibility there's an artifact underwater. Maybe even the last artifact of Freya!"

"Midgard has truly changed that much? Even the coasts are not the same?"

Terra snorted. "If things keep going like they are going, the coasts will change quite a bit more."

"Well, how do we look for an underwater site? Your water breathing skills are passable at best."

"We need to get Barrow on the horn. I hope he's saved some of his fortune. This is not going to be cheap."

CHAPTER FOUR

<u>Barrow dig site #16 office, Svedjehamm, Finland, Wednesday afternoon</u>

Harris Barrow picked up the phone after the first ring. Terra knew she should be thankful he answered so quickly, but considering Leif had not let her call until they got back to the cabin and refused to let her teleport, she felt like she had been on hold for twenty minutes.

She put the call on speaker so Leif could participate.

"Terra, how are you?" Barrow asked. He sounded tired, like he had recently woken up. He had not revealed his location to the team for months, but when no further attacks came, he finally confided in them that he was in Canada, near the US border. Terra had not even tried to do the math to figure out the time zones. A quick mental calculation made her think he had been sleeping in.

Still, whatever the time, they had little for formalities.

"Have we considered the possibility that one of Freya's pieces might be underwater?" Terra blurted.

"Err, I take it there has been a development?" Barrow asked.

"A ship washed ashore here in Finland, and the wreck had evidence of magic," Leif inserted.

"Well, that *is* curious," Barrow replied. There came the sound of him snapping his fingers, then a moment later, the sound of paper rustling. "There are some potential underwater findings out there. People have always lived near coasts, you understand. The weather is more consistent, and of course, there's plenty of food there as well.

"One of the trickiest parts of human history is finding these lost, flooded sites. It doesn't take much. A mudslide, a tidal wave, a few feet of sea level rise to lose entire communities."

"I don't see how a few feet of water would be such a problem. You modern humans seem quite capable of doing almost anything you imagine," Leif stated.

"Quite right." Barrow chuckled. "But the forces of the Earth are powerful. Only a few years of wave action can weather artifacts down to nothing. The few discoveries made off coastlines were miraculous in that anything was found at all."

"If there's an artifact underwater, we can probably assume it's been miraculously preserved," Terra put in.

"Well, yes, I suppose so," Barrow agreed. "It would be difficult to get to, though."

"Terra has an underwater spell," Leif announced.

Barrow chuckled. "If you know precisely where the artifact is, that would be quite useful. Is this a piece of knowledge you can share with us?"

"Unfortunately not," Leif admitted. "I thought something was here in Finland, so it can be said I make mistakes."

"That is what I feared," Barrow commented. "If we cannot know where the artifact is before we set off, it will be quite a costly expedition."

"We can do it, though," Terra insisted.

"We *must* do it if the artifact is truly underwater. The trick will be finding it on the first try. One of these expeditions will be difficult enough to finance, and two could bankrupt us. Do you have any idea where to begin?"

"Not exactly, sir. We only know a ship was attacked by some sort of giant sea serpent, and magic was involved. Given the state of things, I think this could fall in our jurisdiction."

Barrow chuckled. "I wish we could claim jurisdiction over these artifacts, but I fear we must be the first to get there, or we'll face trouble yet again. Do you have the file I sent with the Villon sites?"

"I do, sir. Give me a moment to bring it up." Terra opened the file on her laptop. She practically knew it by heart at this point. "All right. I have it up, and we're looking right at it."

"Very good. As you can see, we spent the last six months uncovering most of these sites, but if I could direct you to two sites, twenty-one and twenty-one A."

"I see them," Terra replied. "One is on the coast of Sweden. The other looks different."

"That's because it's speculative. As far as I can tell, the Villon Institute never actually explored any of these underwater sites, but there is evidence people might have once lived there. References to islands or coastal communities that no longer exist."

"So there really might be an altar underwater?" Leif asked.

"It is more than possible. The problem is going to be getting there," Barrow explained. "We would need a submarine and a team of trained professionals. Procedurally, it can be difficult as well. The water clouds when you start to dig, so pumps and vacuums are necessary. Then there's the question of who the site really belongs to. If we get too far out and into international waters, we could attract another type of attention."

"I think it's worth pursuing," Terra claimed. "We made the biggest discovery of the dig today."

"Considering you didn't lead with that, I'm assuming it was not terribly impressive."

"It wasn't. Some coins. Some jewelry. Nothing magic, and nothing new to the archeological world."

"So you wish to move on."

"Yes, sir. I do. We've done our due diligence for months and come up with next to nothing. This is the first thing we've seen to indicate there's something out there besides the remains of long-dead mortals."

"Let's not forget those long-dead mortals keep us in business. I agree an aquatic mission might be worth our time, but it won't be easy to get investors. It's not as if we can tell them we're after the final artifact of Freya. If we had something else to go on, I could lead with that."

Terra and Leif remained silent.

"It's as I thought. That means we'll be financing this thing ourselves. I'm not sure that is possible. The logistics alone are a headache, and we'd have to pay the same amount in hush money."

"What if we give up the pretense of doing an archeological expedition?" Terra asked.

"I'm sorry? After all the work you did over the last few months, I thought that would be the last thing you would suggest!" Barrow exclaimed.

"I think the study of the past is important, don't get me wrong, but you didn't see this ship. Whatever did the damage to it is still out there. If finding the last artifact could stop that, we have to try."

"Frankly, the stakes are larger than that," Leif expounded. "We are assuming, or perhaps I should say hoping, we will find Freya's last piece, but other forces are awakening. If there is some other god now showing interest in Midgard, it would not do to ignore it."

"When did the powers of gods enter my business considerations?" Barrow murmured.

"I know it's a lot, sir, but I think we could start by taking a small group to do a private search. Instead of pulling permits and trying to set up an actual dig site, let's see if we can find anything there first."

"Spoken like a grad student from decades ago!" Barrow declared.

"Plus, well, we're pretty much done here. We didn't find an artifact or much of anything else," Terra added. "This site should be shut down. Opening up something smaller could be a convenient business expense until we figure out where we really need to dig next."

"I suppose, but there are still a great many risks involved. I will not have the two of you going out there by yourselves. That would be true even if there were not a giant sea serpent around."

"What do you have in mind?" Terra asked.

"I'm not quite certain. I haven't looked at an underwater dig in years, but at the minimum, you'll need to charter a boat with a professional captain who knows a thing or two about diving. I suppose a tour guide could work, but I would prefer if they had experience doing offshore maintenance or something like that. We should assume if you are correct, there will be trouble, and I don't want anyone who might panic."

"That makes sense, sir. We can start looking for someone near the site you indicated.'

"In addition to that, I think we'll need more agents with you as a sort of informal insurance. It's not as if I can tell the insurance companies we're looking for a piece of a goddess that's worth more than mortals can comprehend."

"As a former insurance adjuster, I can tell you we probably would offer to insure that sort of voyage, but the price would be outrageous."

"And rightly so. We will not be able to go with financial security, which means I will engage someone more familiar with your own professional idiosyncrasies."

"Who?" Terra asked.

"Make your way to Sweden and find a ship captain with a capable vessel," Barrow replied without answering the question. "I will contact our agent. Don't worry. You know him well enough."

CHAPTER FIVE

<u>Café Del Toro, Barcelona, Spain, Thursday evening</u>

Mads called for more wine, but Romero only shook his head and smiled.

"You don't want more?" Mads asked.

"I didn't say that," Romero countered.

"Well, then, what's the problem?" Mads gestured for the waitress to fill up both their glasses. She did, but before she could leave, Mads asked her to go ahead and leave the bottle.

"And while you're at it, get us some more of those little ham bits, eh?" he asked.

"And some of the squid. That was amazing," Romero added. His Spanish was not as good as Mads', but the waitress seemed appreciative anyway.

As well she should. She might not know it, but she was serving a couple of national heroes!

"Who would have thought you couldn't fake Picassos?" Mads pondered.

Romero chuckled. "I still can't believe the curator was so bold. If he could get fakes looking *that* good, why not sell them like they were real?"

"Because it's not about the art, mate. Not really. It's about knowing they're better than the others. That's why they like to do all that. It's one thing having a Picasso in your house. It's another thing entirely to know everyone in the museum thinks they're looking at the real one while it's actually in your living room."

"You sound like you really understand the rich and greedy. Does that mean you're covering the tab?"

Mads laughed. "The first thing the rich and greedy learn is *never* to pick up the tab. I guess I'll be poor forever, though. I'll cover you, big man."

"In that case, I'm going to get more of that cured ham, too."

"Anything you want, mate!"

"You're in a good mood."

Mads shrugged, but really, he felt great. "I miss these kinds of missions. Following around suspected thieves. Outthinking them, outsmarting them. Using all our cunning and guile. Being subtle as snakes."

"Subtle? You call that subtle?"

"What? That was the very definition of subtle!"

"You pretended to be a rich Norwegian with a *terrible* accent who wanted to buy Picassos for his bathroom! Literally, none of that is subtle."

"Ah, but it worked, didn't it?"

"Something working is not the same as subtle. Look at the machines out of Detroit. Masterworks of engineering. Subtle, they are not."

"If you're calling me a masterwork, I'll take it, mate."

Romero smiled. "I guess I'm surprised. I thought you'd be missing Harris Barrow and all that stuff you were mixed up in. I know we were there for only the one job, but it was pretty wild work."

"Wild doesn't explain the half of it," Mads retorted.

"You can say that again. I never knew artifacts could hold that kind of power. And you two had us going on the tech angle for a while."

"I wish it were all tech," Mads muttered. "That's why I liked working with you on this one. No illusions. No fireballs. Only a fake accent and some forged documents. That other stuff, well, it feels like more than I can handle sometimes."

"Wow. Mads Jostad admitting he can't handle a job? I never thought I'd see the day."

Mads snorted. "I said *feels like,* mate. We're men of the modern era. We're supposed to be chuffed talking about our feelings and all that. Even if I *felt* that way, I still made it through."

"That's why you're here in Spain instead of working with them?"

"They wanted to poke through the mud and dirt of northern Europe all winter long. Why would I want to do that? I'd rather winter in Spain, where the winters don't feel like winter."

"True!"

"I might retire here, really. The payout on this last job wasn't great, but Barrow's been keeping up with inflation. What do you think? A Spanish villa? Or more like a Greek island?"

But Romero wasn't listening. His eyes were glued somewhere over Mads' shoulder.

"I was talking, mate."

"You're always talking."

"Right, but this was actually important stuff. Retirement plans."

Romero was still staring.

Mads turned, expecting to see some sports highlight reel. Instead, it was cellphone footage of a forest. Something was moving around. Something long and scaled with slitted eyes.

The screen cut to a reporter interviewing someone. "It was huge. The biggest snake I ever saw! And mean, too!" the interviewee stated in Spanish.

Mads' heart dropped into his gut as he turned his chair around to watch the rest of the story. It was hard to focus on the Spanish. His heart was pounding so fast. He thought it was over. He thought their hunt for the artifacts, while not complete, might be on pause for a few years.

Now, his gut told him he was wrong.

There were massive snakes in the news, and they had something to do with the world Mads had been sucked into.

Romero smiled wryly at the TV screen. "You know, those effects actually look pretty good. You think they edited that video, or did they make the snake out of rubber or something? Maybe it's a puppet."

"I think it's a lot more than a puppet, mate," Mads countered.

Romero's grin broke wider. "You look pale as anything.

You worried about them being invasive anacondas or something? I didn't think you were the sort who cared that much about the environment."

"I'm not worried about anacondas. I *wish* it were anacondas! Anacondas we could deal with. I'm worried it's people in the shape of anacondas."

"So, rubber suits?" Romero was clearly goading Mads. He understood Mads' position with Barrow encompassed far more than locating artifacts. Or, more specifically, the artifacts they were after were far more than museum pieces.

"Not rubber suits, mate. The powers Beatrice had? Those are just the tip of the proverbial iceberg."

"Interesting. Our mission is done here. You want to go take a stroll in the forest?"

"Not particularly. But I get paid the best to do things I don't want to do." Mads' phone buzzed in his pocket. He was not surprised to see Harris Barrow calling. "You mind settling the tab?" Mads asked, then got up and left the restaurant without waiting for an answer.

He answered the phone. "Dr. Barrow! A pleasure to hear from you. I'm not sure if the curator called you yet, but we got the paintings back to the museum, and the perp is in jail. I sent them an invoice from the Barrow Institute for insurance purposes. Please tell me you're calling because there's some sort of legal dispute."

"Mads Jostad asking for legal trouble? Things must be far wilder in Spain than I thought."

"Just saw a story on the news about giant snakes in a forest. Not exactly the sort of thing that happens around here often. Can't help but wonder at you calling about the same time."

"How curious! Miss Olsen and her partner came across a shipwreck with what they believe to be snake bites."

"Snake bites on a *boat*? I don't like the sound of that."

"Well, that's precisely why I'm calling, Mads. You have proven your skills in navigating these…unusual situations. I believe we need someone of your particular acumen once more."

"Flattery will get you everywhere, I suppose. Should I head there rather than investigate the forest here?"

"For now, yes. We have a few more sites we want to explore. The thinking is that another artifact might have some effect on these serpents. We're chartering a boat, and I'd like you to be on it. As for the forest, we'll have to keep an eye on that."

"We can hope the issue is centered deep in the heart of Scandinavia," Mads offered.

"Hope is what we do best, I suppose. Do you need anything else from me? I assume you still have sufficient funds."

"Yeah, I'm all right on that front. Though if it's not too much to ask, I'd like to bring Romero up north with me."

"Ah, yes, how is our American friend doing?"

"Squaring up with the waitress. I think he likes Dali more than Picasso."

"We can forgive him such transgressions, I suppose."

"Despite his odd taste in art, he's good in a tight spot. And I can't help but think finding another of these pieces might get a bit feisty."

"That does seem to be the pattern. Well, by all means,

bring him along. His fee won't be what breaks this mission."

"You said a boat. We're thinking another island?"

"More like a former island. You do still have a SCUBA certification?"

"It's forged, but it's solid."

"I do believe you'll need the skills more than the paper."

"I've got skills for days, boss. You know that. If we need to take a swim, I'll bring my suit."

"Very good. We'll see you soon. You can make it to Umeå, Sweden?"

"Might have to stop over in Stockholm, but I'm sure I can figure it out."

"Excellent. I always feel better when you're on these missions, Jostad. Thank you for your willingness to continue dealing with all this strangeness."

"Can't really imagine going back to the old ways," Mads replied and realized it was true. Retrieving the Picasso paintings hadn't felt like much of anything. A job about things a couple of rich people thought were worth a fortune. Fine art didn't seem like much compared to the vestments of an actual goddess.

"Well, I do apologize for that," Barrow told him. "I fear I've dragged you into a world from which there is no escape."

"It's all well and good. You pulled me in, and now I'll pull in Romero. We'll be there as soon as we can." Mads hung up.

"Everything all right?" Romero asked, coming out into the street with Mads.

"Got another mission."

"He interested in the snakes?"

"In a manner of speaking. They think another one is up in the Baltic Sea. Took a bite out of a ship. Might be something up there causing these things to take an interest in our world. You want to come along and see what it's all about?"

Romero blinked once, twice, then he smiled. "You're telling me these snakes might not be snakes at all?"

Mads shrugged. "I don't know the rules. Leif will probably have a diagram that shows who their mother is and why she's a royal git, but I just go along and keep the guns loaded. You interested?"

"Oh, yeah," Romero rumbled.

"Great. No time like the present. You mind driving us to the airport?"

"You people don't waste time." Romero headed for his car. The rental was, as usual, a rather large American-made muscle car disguised as a sedan. Romero was a big man and preferred to travel in comfort, even if it meant his vehicle was twice the size of most others on the road.

Mads climbed in. Romero fired up the engine, pulled into traffic, and headed for the airport. While he did, Mads looked for flights on his phone. He was still too paranoid to buy anything online.

After a few minutes of checking flights and another few minutes scrolling through the internet for that little drop of dopamine, Romero cleared his throat.

Mads had known the big man long enough to know something wasn't stuck on the roof of his mouth. He was telling Mads something was wrong.

"What's the situation?" Mads asked, looking up from his

phone but not jerking his head around to avoid drawing attention from the other vehicles.

"We're being tailed," Romero announced.

A glance in the side mirror told Mads everything he needed to know. A rather large SUV was following them, two cars back. It did not take a master of espionage to notice the driver was fixated on Romero's car.

"Not for too long, I hope?"

"Only a few minutes. I moved lanes a few times, and the idiot followed me back and forth. Not exactly the most subtle of thugs."

"Goons, then. The dumber, younger cousins of thugs," Mads suggested.

"What do you want to do about them?" Romero asked.

"Well, I'd say we can let them follow us to the airport and try to get them snagged in security, but considering where we're headed next, I think we need to leave all this mess behind us."

"You think they're with the Picassos?"

"Oh, I'd bet on it. If they had something to do with the next mission, I don't think their vehicle would be running on gas."

Romero said nothing to that, only gripped the steering wheel tighter, then loosened his hold.

"Go ahead and pull over. Let's see if we can pull the vanishing act."

Romero chuckled. "I got this car, knowing how much you like that move."

"Well, then, by all means. Let's get started." Romero moved through traffic to find an exit. He left the highway and stopped on an access road running alongside a field of olive trees.

"Beautiful country," Mads reflected.

Romero nodded, glancing back as the SUV screeched to a stop behind them.

Four men poured from the vehicle, all with handguns and scowls on their faces that said they were not getting paid unless they tied up *every* loose end. Mads almost felt bad for them. He remembered working jobs like that before he had Barrow. Bosses who didn't understand, no holidays, and healthcare that hardly covered the bruises one earned in this kind of work. That didn't mean he'd go easy on the idiots, though.

"Get out of the car!" they shouted when they came up on either side of the vehicle, guns trained on the passenger and driver seats.

Mads could almost see the dumbfounded looks on their faces as their few brain cells struggled to make a connection through the void that was the interior of their skulls.

"What in the—"

Then, Mads and Romero slipped out of the trunk.

Mads forcefully kicked the back of a goon's knee, and the man crumpled. A blow to the back of the head, and the man was out cold. Mads stepped over him and got his hands on the forearm of the other man on the passenger side. He slammed it against the hood of Romero's rental. The force made the goon drop the gun.

Mads cracked him across the temple with his elbow, and he stumbled to the ground, dazed from the blow.

"How did you…" the goon murmured.

Mads glanced at Romero before answering, but the big

man was as quick and dangerous as ever. He had incapacitated both men on his side of the vehicle as easily as Mads had.

"We slipped through the back seat, folded it down, and popped out of the trunk. Rookie mistake, the four of you going for the side windows. I know you don't want to get run over, but it's really best to get one of you in the front to properly assess the situation, then another in the back to avoid this kind of thing."

"I feel bad. I don't want to kill them," Romero called.

"No, no. We're not barbarians." Mads slipped an arm under the dazed man's armpits and dragged him back to his own vehicle. "But we're not saints, either. Let's strip 'em, slash their tires, and take their keys."

Romero chuckled. "You really have been spending too much time with Leif."

Mads shrugged as he yanked off the goon's pants and shirt, then hoisted him into the passenger seat and buckled him in. Romero did the same to the two men on his side of the vehicle. Mads left him to it and approached the trunk of the SUV. He found a bag of weapons and put it in the trunk of their own rental. He wasn't sure if he would try to get it through customs. It would depend on who was on shift and whether Mads had a history with them.

Then, he took out his pocket knife and stabbed the back tires one at a time. The SUV seemed to soften as it sunk onto its rims.

Last but not least, Mads took the car keys and hung them on the branch of an olive tree. It might make it easier for the goons to find. If they saw the keys glinting in the light, they could be attracted to the shiny thing and go check it out. But if they were as dense as Mads believed, they might spend hours looking through the dirt.

"No hard feelings," Mads told the dazed goon. "Tell your boss fair is fair. If you want to mess with me again, you should at least send someone with some kind of subtlety. But as of right now, we've got an appointment with an anaconda."

CHAPTER SIX

The docks, Svedjehamm, Finland, Friday afternoon

"Stroke! Stroke! No, no, not like that!" Leif huffed as he tried to control the back of the canoe.

They had chartered a flight the next morning, but both realized they were less than experienced on the water. Leif claimed he was actually quite skilled, but his skills were proving a bit out of date.

"I did what you told me to!" Terra cried though she could see why Leif was complaining. She had paddled too vigorously, and they were now going to overshoot the dock. "Don't you know how to brake?"

"Put your paddle in the water!" Leif followed his own advice and plunged his paddle in. It struck something submerged, and rather than letting go, Leif clung to it even as it flipped him out of the canoe.

Rather than splashing around gracefully, he grabbed at the edge. It didn't take much to push the lip below the water level. Water poured into the tiny boat, and it sank.

Cold water flooded Terra's clothes as she scrambled

from the craft and into the shallow water. Together, they struggled to tip the canoe upside-down to get the water out, then hoist it onto dry land.

"Not from around here, are ya?" a man asked in accented English. His giant mustache barely concealed his smile.

"Not so much, no," Terra admitted.

"I can help you with the rental." He pushed the boat back into the water off the dock. He was more adept than either Leif or Terra. When he touched it, it didn't automatically sink.

Terra thanked him for his help, trusted him to get the boat back where it belonged, and went on their way.

"I thought a scholar of Viking lore would be better on the water," Terra told Leif when they were off the docks and onto dry land.

"Well, I should say the same about you," Leif replied. "I studied Asgard, which is not known for its inhabitants ferrying them around under their own power. You're the Viking expert. Now, are you going to teleport us back to the cabin, or what?"

"I thought I wasn't supposed to do that around here because someone might see."

"That's true, and it's good to hear you're actually following my advice. But at the moment, I am quite cold, and there is water in my boots. So, if you would be so kind."

Terra grabbed his arm, and in the blink of an eye, they were back in their cabin overlooking the narrow bay.

While Leif went to take a hot shower, Terra changed out of her wet clothes and looked at the shipwreck's remains still on shore. It was cordoned off but otherwise unchanged. It made the official story that came out in the local news much harder to believe. How could waves and the tides have destroyed the boat when they'd hardly moved it from where the police had put caution tape around it?

Before long, Terra was shivering. She pounded on the door to the bathroom.

"Ah, perfect timing!" Leif emerged, swaddled in a fluffy white towel. "There's not much hot water left, but your powers should make quick work of that."

Terra grumbled at him. Truthfully, she didn't mind. She'd hit a plateau with regard to her strength. There was only so much her bones could endure, and she felt like she had come up against that limit.

Her other skills all needed work, though. She was constantly improving the range and capabilities of her teleportation. It was no small thing that she had been able to teleport her and Leif all the way up here. The bracers had always given her more than strength, and it was those skills she'd been spending the most time with.

One of those abilities was creating darts of energy or fireballs. She could use the same ability to heat the water. It would take more control and a longer duration, but the magic was the same.

Of course, in practice, it was not that simple. However, after a few swings between freezing cold and scalding hot, Terra managed to get an acceptably warm temperature for a shower.

Clean and refreshed, she stepped out. With a flick of her wrist, she used a bit of magic to clear the steam from the mirror. She could hardly believe the woman looking back at her was the same Terra she had always been.

Freya's magic had changed her. She was stronger, with well-defined shoulders, arms, thighs, and a six-pack that would make any Pilates instructor jealous. It wasn't only that, though. Her hair had more body than ever and was flecked here and there with lighter browns and ambers as if a touch of Freya's honey locks had infiltrated her dark hair.

Her own face looked back at her, but at the same time, it wasn't. It felt like looking at herself through a filter on her phone. Her eyebrows were more defined, her cheekbones slightly more pronounced, her lips full and luscious despite not having anything on them. Heck, even her neck looked thinner.

Then, there were the changes to her bust and waist. She had not asked for the figure *seidr* had given her, but now that she had it, she was not complaining. Even if it meant putting on a towel made her look far more scandalous than she would have before.

She left the bathroom and found Leif already half-dressed. He, too, was stronger than he had been. His ropy muscles had filled out, though the biggest difference was now he had a farmer's tan. It had persisted through the winter, coloring the back of his neck and forearms a bit pinker than his extremely pale torso. Funny to think they were both being changed by forces from each other's realm.

Terra found her fashion tastes had changed, too. She still wore pants and boots on digs and when they were expecting hostile company, but she was drawn to gowns and dresses like she had never been before. She pulled one on now, admiring how the reds and golds of the fabric contrasted against her fair complexion.

"Like Freya herself," Leif muttered, smiling at her.

Terra rolled her eyes, but she resisted the urge to dismiss the compliment. Freya was a goddess of beauty, after all. It would not do for her to disparage those who appreciated such things.

"You're not looking so bad yourself," Terra replied.

Leif colored. "You're just saying that." He yanked a shirt on. Not everyone had the grace of a goddess of beauty to live up to.

"So we've established Barrow was right, and we need a proper captain. But what about the rest of the mission? Do you know what the last piece of Freya could be?" Terra asked.

"I can't say for certain. We've seen her on her chariot. Otherwise, I would guess that."

"I would think her great-grandson would know."

"Freya has always loved beautiful things. I have seen her wear a hundred necklaces, a thousand rings. Tiaras, crowns, and a dozen hats that would make the kings and queens of this world squirm with jealousy. Some of those objects were magic, while others were not. It could be any number of them."

"Yeah, that makes sense, I guess."

"You sound skeptical."

"I was thinking it would be something else from the old legends."

"The thing about those legends is that not all of them survived to your modern age. There could be any number of the things I've seen her wear with stories attached. Why, one of her rings is actually the belt of a giant! Can you imagine that? A clever bit of smithing, to be sure. You can bet the dwarfs who made that one were quite proud."

"Well, it's not going to be that since it would be the artifact of a giant, not Freya."

Leif chuckled. "Fair point."

"The legend of her chariot made it through the ages, but you already have the eye from one of her cats. I feel like we would have noticed if something was missing there."

"I was not inspecting too closely, but I agree we likely would have seen something if it was amiss. I wish we had Hildisvíni."

"You mean her boar?" Terra asked. "It has golden bristles, right? Could that be it? An effigy or something?"

"Oh, no. I can assure you that Hildisvíni is quite real. And he had quite the sense of smell! If he were here, we'd find the last artifact with no problem. Well, assuming he wasn't hungry and smelling mushrooms. He has quite the penchant for them."

"Huh. What about the helmet? I think it was called battle-boar or something? I think it had something to do with Freya."

Leif shrugged. "I've never seen her wear a helmet. Her hair is too perfect. I suppose it's possible, though. She did quite a lot before I was born. I'm sure there are stories lost even to the libraries of Asgard."

"Wow, that's a crazy thought. So much of our history is unknown here on Earth. I guess I always thought in Asgard, you would have a record of everything."

Leif shrugged. "History is only as good as its keepers.

We have much, but things get misplaced or lost, or someone discovers they were never true in the first place. Our history might be more complete than yours, but only because it's simpler. None of these changing sea levels to deal with. That's my biggest concern, really. I feel confident that if we are in the presence of a piece of Freya, we will know. But what if one is not there?"

"That occurred to me, too." Terra opened her laptop. "The Villon Institute doesn't have much on the site, but they do have notes referencing it as a craftsmen's village. If we find evidence of Vikings working materials there, it would be highly significant."

"You still feel that way? You could be excited if we come up empty yet again?"

"I have to tell myself it's going to satisfy," Terra responded.

Leif nodded, but he did not look convinced, and Terra didn't blame him. She wanted to find the last piece of Freya, complete her quest, and see what the goddess would demand of her next. She had always wanted to be an archeologist, but would that make her happy if they never found the last piece of Freya?

Her mind still prodded at these thoughts as she lay in bed, trying to sleep. Rather than let it continue to run in circles, she pushed herself out of bed and went outside. The nights were still cold, but Terra didn't mind.

The gown she wore was warm enough, and she could blunt the cold of the breeze with the power of the bracers, even if she wasn't wearing them.

Truly, the cold was invigorating. It made her feel alive.

Without really thinking, Terra put on her shoes and went for a walk.

There was a time she would never have dared to walk alone at night wearing nothing but a gown, but this tiny town hardly seemed the sort of place where people got mugged. If someone tried to rob a pedestrian, everyone would know who it was by morning.

And there was her god-like power, of course. She might not be able to survive a bullet to her head, but unless there were snipers here, she deemed herself safe enough.

She felt comfortable enough as she walked down the path from her cabin toward the seashore. She wasn't really going anywhere in particular, but at the same time, there was only one place worth going.

A few minutes later, she found herself standing in front of the wreckage.

She couldn't sense *seidr* any longer, but she didn't doubt Leif's assessment that magic had played a role in the ship's destruction. It was destroyed so thoroughly. Like something massive had been dropped on it. Maybe it was possible it could have been turned upside-down, but given what Terra had lived through the last year, a magical being with anger issues seemed more likely.

She looked out onto the sea. In the moonlight, it almost seemed to glow. The outcroppings of rocks that made the bay so treacherous were dark, void spaces that reflected very little light. Except for one spot.

One of the rocks on the coast glistened in the moonlight as if Vikings had come ashore and dropped a great cache of silver coins. Until it twitched.

Then, it slithered between the two rocks and vanished.

Terra rubbed her eyes. Had she imagined that? If she'd really seen a snake's tail from this distance, it would have had to have been massive.

She headed that way, walking along the shore, wondering at what she had seen. They had a flight in the morning, then a boat setting sail from the east coast of Sweden since it was closest to the Villon site they wanted to investigate. Could whatever had sunk the ship be here, though? Lingering in the bay? The idea should have terrified her, but it only exhilarated her.

She had been on the sidelines all winter long, combating nothing but the cold and wet of northern winters. She did not have any of Freya's artifacts on her at the moment, but that didn't matter. Terra had more than enough magic to teleport if she needed to. If this sea monster was more dangerous than a big eel, she could teleport back to the cabin, grab her gear, and come right back.

And if it was only a sea monster? Well, she could use a bit of a workout.

But as she approached the outcropping of rocks where she thought she had seen the silvery tail, she wondered if it was all in her head. The moon was creating all sorts of shades of silver and white on the sea. Maybe she had seen a stream of water flow back into the sea?

The coast here was complex. Now and then, spots with sand appeared, but most of the shore featured outcrops of rocks with tall grasses growing out onto them. Water surged and splashed on these rocks, creating little streams and pools that constantly refilled and drained, the heartbeat of the sea.

It was so tranquil out here at night, calm and cool and

alone. Terra wondered if this was what the other realms of Yggdrasil were like. Legend said she could not actually understand the other places. Although they were described in human language, they were places that transcended what a human could comprehend. Like when Fenrir had been roaming the lands outside Hel, that might have looked different than Terra's understanding of land.

The shore made her wonder about Muspelheim and Niflheim, the primordial lands of fire and ice. In the beginning, there had only been the primordial void, Ginnungagap, but then, on either edge, the lands of fire and ice arose.

Niflheim, the land of ice, was in the north. From it, wells rose, and rivers ran into the void, forming layers of ice. It was easy enough to see that here. All winter long, the rivers had frozen, dumping out chunks of ice into the frigid sea.

When those freezing rivers flowed far enough, some of them reached Muspelheim, the land of fire and lava. The interaction between the sparks of Muspelheim and the ice of Niflheim made melted drops that formed the sun, moon, and stars, as well as the primordial being of the universe, Ymir.

Terra had always taken the story as an allegory. The ice of winter was ever-present for the Norse-worshipping Vikings. Their existence was based on surviving the harsh winter. It was no wonder they believed life began with ice. They saw their year begin when the ice melted, year after year.

Muspelheim, too, could easily be understood as a force of life. What else but fire could have kept humans alive in the winters of this climate? And why relegate one's source of power to a fire pit or an oven when the icy reaches of the world were everywhere? It made more sense to grant this life-giving warmth a realm of its own.

Some scholars believed these realms had literal geographical correspondences as well. It didn't take a longship much time to sail far enough north to reach a land that was *always* frozen. The volcanoes and hot springs of Iceland must have sounded like an entirely different world to Vikings living in Sweden, Norway, and Denmark.

Seeing the shore made Terra wonder if that entire world could be seen here as well. The icy sea crashing upon the shore could easily be Niflheim interacting with the void. Muspelheim, the spark of life, was the creatures that lived along the shore.

A crab scurried away from her foot.

"Ymir?" Terra murmured at the little creation.

Even after meeting Freya herself, it was easier to believe in these legends as allegory. Freya looked like a human woman, the same as Terra. She liked jewelry and gowns, and she had a stake in the battles of this mortal realm. How could it be that her contemporary Odin had actually created the universe? Could he really have slain Ymir with his brothers Vili and Ve and used the body of this first being to create Midgard?

Terra had met him. He had offered to take Leif to Valhalla when his life had been slipping away. Could that one-eyed wanderer also be responsible for both the icy sea and the first bits of grass poking into spring?

It was like that game, six degrees of separation, taken to the foundation of the universe. Terra might not be able to trace friendships to an Oscar winner, but she had met the man responsible for forming the universe.

Or maybe it was only words Odin had created. The legends also said Odin had given mankind poetry and runes. Could these stories of creation be the literary forms of what really happened? Perhaps Odin had not existed back then in the same way he existed now.

He had formed humans, carving them from driftwood. Could this be the only way humans could understand the forces that had come to inhabit human bodies? Could it be that Odin had not appeared as a man with a beard until he had undertaken the effort of explaining what he was to the mortals he had created?

Maybe it *had* to work that way. After all, Terra was using archeological methods to unearth the past. Those same methods gave archeologists an understanding of the long history of people on Earth.

Homo sapiens had come to replace homo erectus after following them out of Africa. The methods of using layers of strata and carbon dating to understand *that* timeline were the same methods Terra and the Villon Institute used to figure out how old the various Viking finds were. Terra did not, could not, would not believe all of archeological history was a hoax placed there by Odin.

And yet, she had met him.

She had seen beings that defied comprehension.

She had seen the forces of this world changed and warped by the forces of another world along the branches of the world tree.

She wondered if she could ask Freya about all this and what would happen if the goddess answered. Terra put equal stakes on an unsatisfyingly simplistic answer or an awareness so complex that it burst her mind like fireworks.

Better to focus on the shore before her.

She was nearly at the outcropping where she had glimpsed the sliver of silver, but she saw nothing of the sort now. Maybe it had been a trick of the light, rendered obsolete by the different angle.

She had not come this far to turn back, however. She climbed out onto the outcropping. The contrast of jagged features and smooth surfaces worn down by the water was difficult to navigate in the dark, but Terra persevered, moving farther out, looking for some sign of what she had seen.

She reached the end of the outcropping, some fifty feet out into the sea. Only then did she hear something besides the roar of the surf crashing onto the beach.

Something was hissing at her.

She turned, looking in all directions, but saw nothing. Not until she peered into the water through a glimmer of reflected moonlight and saw a sinuous form beneath the surface. It glowed with its own pale light. Then it looked at her, eyes like stars from the deepest night.

Terra backed away, but the giant snake exploded from the water, baring its fangs as it struck.

CHAPTER SEVEN

<u>An outcropping at sea, Svedjehamm, Finland, late Friday night</u>

Terra barely dodged the snake's open mouth as it tried to bite her with its giant fangs.

She moved backward. Her foot found a slick spot on the rock, and she slipped to the ground, bruising her hip. She was thankful she felt *that* and not the snake's venom entering her bloodstream.

Its huge girth landed on the outcropping, and Terra got a sense of how big it was. Bigger than a python or an anaconda, Terra had no doubt it could crush her in its coils and swallow her whole. She might not even show inside it; it was so huge.

Its massive body gripped the rocks, and it raised its head, flicking its tongue and turning to her again.

Terra punched it in the face.

The snake recoiled, shaken from the blow but not injured. It struck again.

Terra caught it on the chin with an uppercut, but that

hardly harmed it. All it did was stop the fangs from stabbing her.

Time to try something besides brute strength.

Terra summoned a dart of magical energy and shot it at the snake's face before it could get a third strike at her. Her aim was good, and the bright energy blasted it in the eye, but the snake hardly slowed. It blinked a transparent eyelid at her that apparently worked equally well on water and magic blasts.

The snake's tail whipped toward her at a blinding speed, but Terra could move faster than light. She teleported out of the way of the whip-like tail and reappeared on the other side of the snake. Then she blasted it with a fireball.

The snake's silvery scales flushed amber and gold, and the fireball was gone, absorbed by this fearsome creature.

"Tricks," the snake hissed, and Terra nearly stumbled backward into the ocean. A magic sea serpent was one thing, but a talking snake was something else entirely.

She wouldn't win this battle as she was. She needed the pieces of Freya and the magic they afforded her.

She stepped back from the snake, readying herself to teleport back to the cabin. Before she could, the snake hissed at her, looking her in the eyes with its pale, slitted pupils. When it did, Terra felt something *shift* inside her.

Suddenly, her ability to teleport was gone.

It was as if the snake had cut off her access to part of her body. The magical component had vanished.

"You will not run," the snake hissed, then lunged at her again.

Instead of trying to dodge, she let the snake come at her

as she reached for its top and bottom jaw. She felt its teeth cut into her hand as she grabbed its jaws and held on.

The snake thrashed, then struggled to close its jaws, but its strength was not in its mouth. Terra was able to hold it open. Then, risking everything, she released the top jaw, grabbed the base of a fang, and rolled out of the way.

The hollow fang, designed to transport venom from the snake's glands to its victim, snapped at the base. Terra came up with the fang in her hand.

The snake hissed as it retreated, shaking its head and spraying a mix of blood and venom that crackled when it hit the water. Terra felt a tiny spattering of droplets hit her forearm, but the burning was nothing. Not enough to let it affect her in this fight.

The snake splashed into the water, but she did not see its pale form retreat into the distance or the depths. Instead, it hugged the edges of the outcropping.

"I see you, serpent!" Terra yelled. "You won't get the drop on me!"

The snake's head rose from the water at the end of the rocks, as pale and luminous as the moon.

"You have no right to my fang," the snake hissed.

"I took it from you. That means it's mine," Terra insisted. Maybe not the best philosophical foot to put forward, but then again, who ever imagined trading ideas with a massive magical sea serpent? She reached for her ability to teleport, but it was still blocked.

"Is that how you became her chosen? You stole the right?" the snake hissed.

"You know who I am?"

"There are not many who don't, Terra Freyasdatter," the

snake replied. Its head had not come any closer, but several rolls of its coils were rising from the water behind it onto the stone outcropping. Terra kept her feet firmly planted on the ground. She had a feeling the snake was only waiting for the right moment to strike.

"Who are you, serpent?" Terra demanded.

"I am nobody. Like you."

"I am not nobody. If I was, you wouldn't know my name."

The snake's coils shivered. Terra didn't know snake body language, but she thought she had pissed it off.

"All of you humans have names. You have names for everything. You are obsessed with them. You have been ever since Odin gave you the ability. Do you not see that he has made a cage around you? A cage in your mind? It is like what he did to my father's father."

"Who is that?"

"A blight upon his kin," the snake hissed, venom spattering from its missing tooth.

"Speak clearly!"

"I am the child of a child. Abandoned by our father who was abandoned by his."

"Our father? You mean you're not the only giant talking snake out there?"

The snake flicked its tongue. Terra thought it might be laughing. "I am small compared to my brother, who grew tired of letting you humans do as you wish in this world. He did as you said. He took what he wished. If that is all it takes to be masters of Midgard, you will be naming us that soon."

"Yeah, I don't think so." Terra had adjusted her grip on

the tooth. She had a feeling if the venom was magic, it would work on the serpent itself. She jumped, raising the fang above her head to drive it through the snake's head. When she did, she felt something around her ankle.

The snake had wrapped the tip of its tail around her ankle while it talked to her. The moment she took to the air, it yanked her downward. The physics were simple. Terra weighed far less than the snake and had no traction in the air. She was whipped downward and smashed into the stone. She barely got her hand up to stop her face from crashing against the rock.

The snake was more than willing to try again, though.

It lifted her back up and whipped her through the air, smashing her back against a jagged piece of stone. It would have killed a mortal. It should have killed her, but the power of Freya's bracers was her own now. She felt pain, but her bones did not break. Her flesh did not rend.

The snake tried to lift her a third time, but Terra struck it with the fang. It yanked her away from its coil instead of into the rocks.

So, the snake did not want to be poked by its own fang. Terra could use that.

If she could stay alive.

The snake seemed set on not letting that happen again.

It still held her firmly by the ankle. It used that hold not to bash her against the rocks but to haul her underwater.

Terra sucked in a breath of air, then was plunged into the icy sea.

The cold was so intense she nearly sucked in a breath of water merely to feel something else. She felt her body shutting down, pulling in her energy, preparing her mind for the long, cold sleep that would come before she was taken to Folkvangr to join Freya if she died in battle.

But she was the Chosen of Freya. She was a warrior of the north, of these very seas. She plucked on the strings of *seidr* and changed her fate. She would not live if her lungs filled with water, so she did not let them. It was not her time to die. She would not freeze to death.

Terra enveloped herself with an extremely thin bubble of air. A bubble she could breathe in that would protect her from the freezing cold sea.

The snake pulled her deeper and deeper. Terra didn't fight it. She let the snake think it had been successful. Then, when she was close enough to the bend in its body that broke the surface, she stabbed it with the fang.

The snake recoiled, yanking its tail from her and releasing her like a wasp trapped in its sweater. It was so big it created currents in the water that pulled her toward it, but Terra was strong. She kicked her legs and distanced herself from the serpent. The gown slowed her in the water, so she sliced through it with the fang to free herself from its long, trailing end.

She kicked away from the snake and toward the rock outcropping. A glance told her the snake was expecting her to surface. She saw much of its body, but its head was above the water.

So, she stayed underwater. The water was twenty feet deep where she was, but there were hidden rocks around the outcropping. Terra swam toward one, then to the backside where she wouldn't be in the snake's direct line of sight. She swam to the top of the rock, then pushed her head above the surface to get a breath of fresh air.

She released the bubble around herself and could smell the sea once more.

Her mind cleared with the fresh rush of oxygen, and the first thought that popped in uninvited was that maybe she should have pursued biology. Archeology could take years to prove a theory, but testing to see if the snake's venom hurt it took only seconds. Seeing it spasm and flee from her was as satisfying as any dig she had been on.

The snake had swum around to the other side of the rocky outcropping. Its huge coils rose above the stone and vanished again, hiding its true length. She realized she still had not seen the entire body. Only its head, its tail, or a coil she stabbed. She didn't know how long it was. Fifty feet? Surely, it couldn't be longer than that.

More important was what it was capable of. It was strong, impervious to the magic she had used, and capable of human speech. It had somehow stopped her from accessing her teleportation powers. She knew its fang had hurt it, but would that be enough? It would be better to teleport out of here and regroup. But when she felt for her ability, it wasn't there.

It felt different than before, though. There was a sort of *pressure* coming from the snake. She watched, her head barely above the water, as it slowly moved along the surface, tasting the air with its tongue, looking for its prey. Every time its tongue flicked, Terra felt a surge of that pressure.

The snake seemed to possess some sort of dampening ability. It had stopped her from escaping, but maybe she could use that. The snake was *consciously* hunting her. If she was clever, she might get it to drop the ability.

However, if it had other similar abilities, it might be able to cancel out her magic bubble and drown her.

She couldn't linger. She had to bring the fight to the snake rather than let it learn what it was capable of doing to her.

Terra climbed further onto the submerged rock until she stood on top of it. The water came halfway up her bare thighs, though her torso, still covered in the soaking wet remnants of the gown, was equally cold. She wasn't at risk of hypothermia, though. She had kept some of the magic intact on her legs. It protected her from the cold, even as it let her feel the sea.

She drew a deep, calming breath and performed a mental check of her body. The snake had slammed her into the rock like a rag doll, and she could feel it. Her back hurt and would likely be nothing but a massive bruise in the morning. It hadn't broken, but could she survive another blow like that? Probably. Could she survive two, though? Or three?

Too late to back out now. The snake had noticed her and vanished beneath the water. Terra had put her plan into motion, whether it was a good one or not. She dove into the water with the fang in hand. Covering herself in the thin bubble of air also let her see underwater like she was inside the world's biggest goggle. She could see the snake on the seafloor, slithering around the bases of the various rocks.

No part of her plan involved fighting a giant sea serpent that could hold its breath for an extended period of time. If it could cancel her bubble the same way it had canceled her teleportation, she was done for.

She swam across the surface, controlling her movements less than was strictly necessary. This creature might be able to speak in human languages, but that did not mean it was human. It had the body of a predator. Hopefully, that meant it also had the instincts of one.

She didn't swim fast enough to out-distance the snake. Terra let it think it had the advantage over its prey. When it got close, she turned and clambered backward onto the rocks, desperately swinging the fang back and forth. Or so she hoped it would appear.

The snake might not have believed her performance, but it kept its distance all the same, not striking with the risk of being stabbed by its own poison.

She climbed completely out of the water and sliced at the sea's surface.

The snake dove back under and vanished.

There was the slimmest chance it had given up on her and was retreating, but Terra would not take that bet. She could still feel the pressure it emitted, tamping down her ability to teleport away. If it was a conscious ability, and it was retreating, why would it bother to keep it going? Terra found it far more likely the snake was still hunting her.

She was counting on it, really.

She couldn't let the snake know, though. She dashed around, looking into the water, trying to find some indication of where the snake was.

For a giant creature that seemed to glow in the moonlight, it was quite good at hiding. Terra hardly noticed it move past her and make for the shore. She kept looking in the water, though. She needed it to believe it could strike her...

It burst from the water. Terra tried to teleport away, but she still couldn't. It was not going to let its prey slip away easily. So, instead of vanishing, she sliced at the snake with the fang.

It yanked its head back, out of range. Terra kicked its huge, girthy body. Punching bags had more give than the snake did. It didn't budge. Instead, it knocked her over with a coil.

Terra tried to push herself out from under its massive weight, but then another coil crashed into her shoulders, and another and another. She tried to pull herself through the knotted mass of the snake, terrified of letting go of the fang. It was the only thing she had that could do anything to the creature.

The snake sensed its opportunity and was willing to risk itself against the fang. It crashed more of its mass against her, burying her.

Terra felt herself pulled into the mass of the snake as it snagged her ankle.

Unable to slip away, she repeatedly pounded it with her elbow until the huge coil slid off. But another was around her waist, her legs, then she was being constricted, the life squeezed from her.

She called on the power of *seidr* to strengthen her, to invigorate her, to not let her story end as snake food on a cold beach in the middle of the night. The best she could do was prevent her ribs from being cracked.

The snake flinched, and Terra felt it pull away from the fang. It had pricked itself, and when it did, it loosened its grip on her. She sucked in a breath of air.

It was too late to slip away, as she should have. The

snake held her by the ankle. It lifted her into the air, and Terra fell face-first into the rock. She caught herself with one hand, using the other to keep her grip on the fang. That was enough to stop her from bashing her brains out on the rock but not enough to prevent a black eye.

Her vision exploded with stars as she hit her face on the rock. Then she was airborne, being dangled by the snake. It whipped her over itself, and she crashed into a rock.

That cracked a rib, but only one.

The snake wasn't done, though.

It whipped her overhead in the other direction, and her shoulder smashed into the slick stone.

She screamed in pain as the snake yanked her in the other direction. She kicked the leg the snake had her by, and it was enough to release her.

Or maybe the snake simply wanted to see its prey fly through the air.

Because that's what Terra was doing.

She careened above the stone outcropping, over the sea, and back toward the rock below. She felt as if she were as high as the cabin, looking down on the battle from above.

Water glinted in the moonlight, and Terra saw a large pool on the natural jetty of dark stone. It was a small thing to twist her body in midair and slightly adjust her angle of descent. She could still feel the pressure of the snake not allowing her to teleport. She could use that. She had to use it.

She slammed into the puddle. It was maybe a few feet deep. Deep enough to let her back-flop onto the water and slow her fall with a massive splash, but not nearly deep enough to prevent her from hitting the bottom of the pool.

She felt rocks, barnacles, and what had to be a crab pincer dig into her back. The pain was intense and excruciating, and she let herself succumb to it.

She let her body go limp as it struck the rock. She let her limbs flop out as if her brain had lost control. She let her eyes flutter closed and stay that way. It was what she wanted, anyway. Not so hard to sell something like that.

She lay there, eyes closed, body in the same twisted position it had ended up in, waiting for the snake to grow close.

She could still feel the pressure of its canceling power, stopping her from being able to get away, even now. But she could also feel it lessening with every flick of the snake's tongue. As it approached, it saw how beaten and broken its prey was.

She kept her eyes closed, but she felt its presence. She could sense it come up from the water, get its body on land, then raise its head as it prepared to strike her with a proper dose of venom and finally end her life.

Then, right before it struck, the pressure it had been exerting on her teleportation dropped away.

Just like Terra thought.

She teleported from the puddle and reappeared in midair, above the snake, broken fang in hand. She brought it down into the back of the snake's head.

It punched through the silvery scale, the top of the skull, and directly through its brain.

Terra jumped clear as the snake, victim to its own venom, thrashed and spasmed.

Its huge body caught her across the waist, and she flew

off the rocks and back into the sea. She splashed into the cold water, but she hardly cared.

She was clear of the snake's violent thrashing, safe from its deadly bite. She could tolerate the cold for a few minutes while the last of its energy left it. It twisted, turned, and splashed, then slowed and finally began to sink.

Terra gritted her teeth, not liking what would come next but also not wanting to leave this place with no evidence of the giant magic snake.

She swam toward the rock outcropping and approached the dead snake. Wanted to take the fang she'd used to kill it, but it was nowhere to be seen. Knocked loose, no doubt. She swam to its head and tried to force its jaw open so she could break off the other tooth, but when she did, the jaw broke clean off.

That might have worked as the formidable souvenir Terra wanted, but no sooner did the jaw come free than it started to crumble. First, the silvery scales fell off, then the flesh came away as if it were no more substantial than wet clay. The jawbone itself broke into pieces in her hands.

With the jaw missing, the snake's head also started degrading. Its teeth fell out and crumbled into sand. Its scales flaked away into pieces no larger than bits of broken shells.

Terra swam out of the muck its flesh was becoming and tried to take one of its ribs, but the rest of the snake was faring no better than the head. It was fading, breaking to pieces, becoming nothing.

Everything except a single, massive scale from the

center of the snake's back. It had caught the surface of the water and was floating there.

Terra grabbed it and swam to shore. She climbed from the water with the scale in hand. Already, it was starting to break down at the edges. Terra got the sense if she dropped it on the rocks, it would shatter to pieces, but for now, she had her souvenir.

It should be enough to show Leif she'd had one hell of a night!

CHAPTER EIGHT

<u>Sikskärsvaken, Umeå, Sweden, Saturday, late morning</u>

Terra only had time to talk to Leif briefly in the morning before they had to catch a flight across the sea to Sweden.

It might have been kinder for her not to say anything about what happened. Though that likely would not have been possible. She had taken another shower after spending most of her night drenched in seawater, and when she had stepped from the bathroom in her towel, Leif had seen the absolutely massive bruise covering her back.

"Did you have the dream where you fell out of bed, but you'd actually teleported a mile in the air?" Leif guffawed.

"I wish. Sounds restful compared to my night," Terra answered enigmatically.

Leif was not able to resist the bait. "And *what*, may I ask, is *that* supposed to mean?" He demanded.

"I went on a stroll. Battled a magic talking sea serpent. Killed it with its own venom. This is all that's left." She really wanted to toss the scale to Leif but was worried that in its current state, it wouldn't survive if Leif missed it. He looked like he would have definitely missed it unless he somehow managed to catch it in his mouth, which was hanging almost as wide open as the snake's jaw before it tried to swallow her.

"You're going to need to explain," Leif said.

"Of course. And I will. After we catch our flight."

That was an empty promise, of course. They were flying across international boundaries with boxes of a few magical artifacts sprinkled in. It was never easy to get through customs without questions. They did all right, though. They had been in Finland long enough and flown in and out of the airport with odd possessions enough times that the security team knew their faces.

They went through the regular process of filling out the declaration forms, explaining the paperwork for all the objects that needed explaining, and finally boarding.

Leif was the one with questions that could not be answered. Terra was not about to take the scale out in the middle of the airport, nor did she wish to discuss what a magical snake attack might mean to their larger mission of securing the armaments of a battle goddess. Leif understood enough of the modern world to know he could not have these conversations in public, but that didn't mean he liked it.

He kept starting to ask questions, then sort of mumbling the second half of them.

"Did you say that the, err…snake was after…erm, never mind."

Or later:

"And your powers were less than effective because of its magic...um, maybe later."

He was hopping back and forth from one foot to the other when they finally disembarked and collected their luggage. It was always a painstaking process, having to check through their things at the airport. They normally preferred to fly privately for this reason. Still, they had not been able to manage that in such a short timeframe and thus needed to make sure all their artifacts, both magical and non-magical, were accounted for.

But no thieves were aboard the flight crew of this particular jet, so they made it out of the airport easily enough.

Even then, they couldn't talk freely, as their hotel was not ready, and they needed a driver. Finally, after picking up lunch and assuring the driver that yes, he could drop them near the docks with all their stuff and that Terra and Leif could lug it to a picnic table in a nearby park, they had their moment alone.

"All right, Leif. Questions?"

"Start with the snake! No. Start with why you were out there at all. Wait, you said it could talk? What did it say?"

Terra smiled and told him how she had spent the previous night while he stared, mouth agape, sandwich going uneaten.

Finally, she finished her tale by recounting how the snake had broken apart and how only the scale had remained. Leif had yet to touch his food, so Terra took the scale out of her bag, unwrapped it, and handed it to Leif.

"Be careful. It's fragile. If you had mustard on your

fingers, I wouldn't have let you touch it. I bet it would corrode away to nothing."

Leif took the scale and slowly turned it back and forth. It was large, nearly the size of a dinner plate, and almost bone white, though with a glint of silver that shone when Leif turned it back and forth in his hands.

He looked visibly relieved, as if not being able to chatter about what happened had been a binding curse upon his soul, and it was finally lifted.

"Well, I think it's safe to say it's not of this realm," he said.

"What part of a snake that could stop me from teleporting, not to mention *talk*, made you think it was from Midgard?" Terra asked.

Leif grinned. "Frankly, I thought this might have been a hoax. Maybe you had fallen last night, earned yourself the bruise, then concocted this story to cover yourself."

"Oh really? So it was the prospect of a hoax that made you twitch so much on the flight that I thought you would pee your pants?"

Leif reddened. "Admittedly, only a small part of me thought this was a trick. I've trained you well. Anything that can do that sort of damage to you would obviously have to be a serious threat."

"Flattery will get you nowhere. I'm only glad you didn't have a heart attack on the flight."

"Yes, it was quite close there, but I made it through. So you said you saw the snake glimmering on the rocks?"

"That's right."

"Could you have seen a portal or a spell, do you think?"

"I don't think so. I know the scale looks kind of ashen right now, but that's only because it's flaking away. It had more of the silvery aspect of it when the snake was still alive."

"Yes, you mentioned its coloration. I'm trying to think how such a creature could have gotten here. There are serpents like this in Jotunheim, but none are capable of traveling to Midgard on their own. If you had seen a spell in action, it might give us a clue about who has sent such a being here."

"Is it really so hard for something to come here? Fenrir made it, and he wasn't exactly a master spellcaster," Terra pointed out.

"True, but Fenrir is a being of unfathomable power. He killed Odin, after all."

"Is that even difficult, though? Odin's origin story is coming back from the dead."

"The gallows god did indeed hang from his neck for nine days before coming back, but that does not mean killing him was an easy feat. Few possess such power. Fenrir killing him was quite significant, even if he did come back from the dead. It was part of Ragnarök."

"I still don't see how the end of the world can be called the end of the world if the world is still going on," Terra stated.

"Ends must come for new beginnings to be made. That is the way of the stories of your world and the very fabric of ours. Fenrir having a place in all that demonstrates how powerful he was."

"Well, what about his brother? Would he have the power to come here? I know Hel could only work through intermediaries but doesn't Jörmungandr technically live in Midgard?" Terra asked.

"The color is correct. I'll give you that. Jörmungandr was known to be pale, but that is not possible. It could not have been the world snake."

"Don't act like it's not because you're jealous that I already defeated it when Odin couldn't."

The air grew chilly, and Leif looked at the sky, displeased with Terra's little joke.

"There is no way what you battled was the son of Loki. The world snake encircles Midgard, but this is the same Midgard made from the body of Ymir. It is not as if there is a large snake in the oceans of the Earth. Jörmungandr encircles this realm, but he exists outside it, in a realm of his own. Like Hel, I suppose."

"Well, where is this other realm? Could he have sent some part of himself here?"

"Midgard is much larger than Earth. You must endeavor to remember this. His plan encircles what you humans would call the Milky Way galaxy. And his realm can grow as you humans continue to define and redefine the limits of your understanding and influence."

"Wow. So, science already grew him as big as the Milky Way? Go us."

"I believe it is because your ancient ancestors could see the Milky Way in the sky before the light pollution of your modern conveniences rendered it invisible, but by all means, be proud of the sciences that the artifacts you wear are undermining."

"The snake said it was the son of the son. Could that mean Jörmungandr was its father?" Terra asked.

"That does make a certain amount of sense. It's only that Jörmungandr has never been terribly interested in Midgard."

"Never been interested, yet he's prophesied to destroy it?"

"As a consequence of his battle with the gods, yes. But destroying the Earth is not a great challenge. Do you stress about destroying ant colonies? Because to him, that's all you are, really. Particularly loud ant colonies with amazing snacks."

"Yeah, I'm sort of doubtful that telling him about the snacks is going to protect us."

"I simply don't see him being particularly interested in this world. He never has been. I know he and Thor never got along, but honestly, who can get along with Thor? He has a belt that grants him twice his regular god-like strength, then he acts like it's odd that no one is as strong as him. It's a joke, really, the way he—"

"Leif, focus. What about a mate? Could the world serpent have found a lady friend?"

"I don't think so. He is a primordial being, stronger than his mother and father by most measures. But I suppose it's possible. The forms of the Jotun are twisted. There could be a mate out there who wished to find power from the world snake. But wouldn't that mean there are more of them around?"

"There are," Terra remarked.

"I think if there were giant white serpents, I would have heard about it."

"Leif, with respect, you spent half of the flight pretending like you weren't desperate to talk to me about all this and the other half asking for snacks from the flight attendant. How exactly would you have heard about anything?"

"I have my ways!" Leif put his hand to his chest in mock outrage.

"Yeah. Like the cell phone in your pocket. But while you were looking for snacks, I used mine to do a little digging. There's been a surprising amount of recent sightings of large white snakes. All around the world, it seems, though never too far from the ocean."

"Oh…well, this might be an issue, then."

"It's definitely an issue! It has magical powers, and we have every reason to think it's not acting alone. Is that enough for you to think it has something to do with Jörmungandr?"

Leif chewed his lip, but he nodded. "I think it is a theory worth investigating, yes."

"But we're about to go on a boat for a few days, well beyond internet service."

"Mmm… a less than ideal place to be. Good thing you've been working on your underwater abilities!"

"Yeah. Good thing," Terra said. She was about to tell him how, despite her prowess, she did not exactly have the strength to clobber one of these snakes underwater, let alone multiple, when her phone rang.

"Hi, Mads! How are you?" Terra asked.

"I'm wondering where the hell you are, for starters!" Mads barked over the phone. "We left beautiful Spain behind with a forest of snakes to investigate, and you two can't make it to the boat on time? Where are you?"

"Oh, we're having a picnic," Terra replied.

The rumbling laughter in the background had to be Romero.

Terra wasn't able to say hi to him over Mads, who was screaming bloody murder.

"A picnic? They're on a picnic! Can you believe this? We suffer through pickled fish and the worst flight of our lives, but it's all right. These two blokes are out having a nice picnic! Well, it sounds nice, I have to admit."

"You're near the docks?"

"Near the docks? We're on the bloody boat! The captain is over here asking me to sign things and check things off and a hundred other things I have no interest in doing. The sooner the pair of you get down here, the better."

"All right, all right, don't get your panties in a bunch, luv. I'll be there soon," Terra said.

It had the effect of making Mads fall completely silent. Terra could only imagine him growing so red that it made any hair dye he was wearing melt away.

She hung up before the yelling really started.

"It's not too long of a walk, even with our stuff. Let's get going."

"Right, sure," Leif replied, lost in thoughts.

They gathered up their bags and started toward the boat.

"Penny for your thoughts, Leif?"

"Just thinking about this serpent you met and what it could mean for this world I've started to love. We found one piece of Freya that Loki had locked away. I wonder if this could be something similar. Perhaps Jörmungandr has commandeered the last piece."

"Well, that would be good, right? At least we'd understand what we're up against."

"Fenrir can be bound. Hel can be banished. The world snake is a step beyond the other two. He was given dominion of the sea because the Aesir and Vanir feared doing anything else to him. When he grew too large, they gave him his own realm. He is a being beyond comprehension. More dangerous than the other two, who could at least be contained. And apparently, there is more than one of him. I fear to guess what that could mean."

"Could it be he's after Freya's power like Fenrir was, and Loki might have been when he put those locks on the last box?"

"It is possible, but if he is, I can only think of one reason he would wish to augment his strength."

"It's not because he wants to look better in a swimsuit, I take it."

"I fear if the world snake has shown that much interest in this world, another Ragnarök may already be on its way."

CHAPTER NINE

The docks, Umeå, Sweden, Saturday, late morning

Terra didn't recognize Mads until she was practically standing next to him. His hair was longer than she had ever seen it, shoulder-length and silver. He wore the sort of well-manicured stubble that looked effortless but truly must have taken at least a few minutes each morning with both a traditional razor and an electric buzzer.

As always, she was surprised by how attractive the thief could be. It seemed no matter how he wore his hair and face, he wore it well. Terra knew better than to compliment him on his looks, though. Despite her being past having any sort of romantic interest in him, Mads was always more than willing to turn their relationship into a 'coworkers with benefits' situation.

It had bothered Terra at first, but now she found it flattering, even if she had no interest in acting on it. She wondered if that was part of Freya's influence on her. The goddess was known for both beauty and fertility.

Romero, in contrast to Mads, stuck out like a sore

thumb. He was one of the few people of color that Terra had seen in Umeå since they had arrived, and in addition to that, he was quite a large man. Many of the Swedish were tall, but none had Romero's hulking shoulders, massive arms, and giant belly.

Normally, he hid much of his girth behind a perfectly tailored suit that made him into a wall of pinstripes or finely checked fabric. He didn't have a suit on now, however. Instead, he wore a blue hoody that said Detroit on the front of it, written in stylized white cursive. Despite the chill, he wore shorts and tennis shoes that were the exact same color as his hoody.

He could not be mistaken for anything other than an American tourist. Standing next to Mads, it looked like seeing a pair of old friends who had split up in their youth and were now reunited to live out a dream they had made together as kids.

Which was perfect because they did not look at all like archeologists searching for a lost island with a temple hidden beneath the sea.

"Mads, you've aged!" Leif commented when he finally recognized the master of disguise.

"It's called hair dye, you dolt. You telling me Odin never puts anything in his beard?"

"Odin?" Romero asked.

"Figure of speech," Mads was quick to say.

"We don't have to do all that with Romero, do we?" Leif asked. "He was there when Beatrice had that wand."

"Lucky to have made it out of there alive," Romero agreed, his deep voice rumbling.

"Thanks for coming, Romero. I'm not sure how much Mads has told you."

"Enough to know there's white snakes coming out of the seas, and they're not exactly regular creatures. And although I came packing, I am hoping you lot have some of that stuff you were calling tech, which I think we all know is not tech. Not from this world, anyway."

"We call them realms, but yes, you more or less got it all," Leif replied.

"Well, all right, then," Romero confirmed.

"How was your dig? Find a bunch of culturally significant treasures and all that?" Mads asked Terra.

"We *did*." Terra tried to sound more enthusiastic than she had felt for the last few months. "Some interesting bits of jewelry, and more coins, which are of course quite useful in further understanding trade routes and the reach of the Vikings. Did you know there's a team working out of California trying to use AI to recreate the Viking trade routes? They're using some of our coins as data points."

"Sounds boring as hell, luv."

Terra laughed. "Honestly, I'm excited to be here."

"So we're not looking for coins," Romero stated.

"We're looking for a shiny worth a bit more than that."

"Coins are pretty common findings in Viking hordes. It wouldn't make sense to charter a boat and try to do an underwater mission for those," Terra explained.

"Sure," Romero allowed. "So what *are* we looking for?"

Terra and Leif shared a glance, and Romero read it clear as day.

"So it's a treasure hunt! Got you."

"We have reason to believe there is an object of great significance out there," Terra explained.

"Another one of these pieces of…tech that let you stand against that crazy witch bitch?" Romero asked.

"That's right," Terra stated. "We don't know the exact shape, but we're hoping that by looking at the context of the location, we can find the artifact in question."

"It was quite significant to my people," Leif put in.

"Mm-hmm," Romero rumbled. "How do you know there's anything there?"

"We have you to thank for that, mate!" Mads thumped the American on the back. "The Villon Institute had a whole list of places where they thought they could find more of these artifacts. These two spent the winter looking for as many of them as they could and coming up empty while you and I worked those stolen paintings in Spain."

"You mean that data we got out of the warehouse?" Romero asked.

"That's why you're back, mate. Instrumental in the whole affair."

"I thought it was because I knew how to shoot a gun and am still talking to you despite the crazy shit that had happened in the basement of that mansion."

"Well, those were factors, as well." Mads winked. "But ahoy! There's our ride! The *Skidbladnir*."

"The *Skidbladnir*? You mean Freyr's magical folding vessel?" Leif looked out over the river.

"It's just a coincidence," Terra remarked. Obviously, it was not the boat of legend but a modern vessel named after it. Still, Terra felt a chill at hearing the name of the boat that belonged to Freya's brother.

A sleek yacht approached from the river running from Umeå out to the sea. It was all smooth lines that tapered to a point at the tip. Alternating layers of white and tinted windows made it look more like a starship than a boat. It had a cabin on the top of the deck and windows lining another compartment beneath the deck.

The back of the yacht had a small crane arm and what Terra hoped was a submersible but looked more like a torpedo. Other than that, nothing was on the deck. The yacht looked like it had been built and put out to sea a day or two ago.

It was moving fast, though two crewmen stood near the front of the boat, looking unconcerned as the ship grew closer and closer to the dock.

Terra braced herself for the sleek vessel to smash apart the dock in a show of unnecessary and unearned bravado, but before the nose of the yacht smashed the dock, the yacht pivoted and smoothly came into place into a berth. The crewmen on either side of the prow finally snapped into action. One hopped off the yacht while the other lifted a rope.

He tossed it to the other crewman, who caught it and adroitly tied it off. He then went to the stern as the other crewman followed him along the dock. After another rope was tossed and caught, they tied the yacht to the dock.

Two lines of shadow appeared in its sleek lines, and a gangway unfolded from the side. The gangway came to a rest on the dock. Standing at the top, smiling as if she knew exactly how impressed her future passengers would be, was the captain.

She wore dark navy pants covered in pockets, a suit

jacket so crisp that she must have only just put it on, and a white hat with a black brim and a bit of gold trim. The only part of her that looked anything but the pinnacle of professionalism was a smudge on the left side of her neck that might have been a tattoo or a birthmark.

"Welcome to the *Skidbladnir!* I'm Captain Joana, and we're pleased to have you all aboard! I was told there would be four of you. Can I assume this is everyone, and we're all packed and ready to embark?"

"We're us, and we are!" Mads replied.

"Very good. If you would allow my crew to help you aboard, we can start the tour and get underway. You mentioned time was of the essence, so we arrived fully fueled and loaded with provisions."

"I like her." Mads winked to Terra and Leif, then sauntered up the gangway, pointedly carrying only one of the bags he had arrived with. Terra noted it was a random, beat-up duffel and not the pieces of luggage she had come to associate with Mads. Something curious in there, then. Maybe a massive cache of weapons.

Terra followed him up, keeping her bag with Freya's ax and the other artifacts in hand. The crew grabbed their other things and followed them aboard.

"The *Skidbladnir* is normally for taking people somewhere fantastic as quickly as possible," Captain Joana explained. "But from what I heard from who I spoke with on the phone, this will be a different sort of excursion?"

"That's right, Captain." Mads fell into stride alongside her. "We're interested in a long-lost city. Well, maybe 'town' is more apropos. All the sightseeing we wish to do will be through goggles."

"Yes, you mentioned you would be diving. It's not like diving in the Caribbean. The cold here is a force of its own. Even with heated suits, it can be dangerous."

"My associate and I are accomplished deep-sea arctic divers," Leif claimed.

Captain Joana turned and looked at Leif, eyebrow raised. Terra noticed the mark on her neck was a tattoo. It looked like a sea plant of some kind. Kelp, perhaps. It was done in blues and greens, no black. Terra found it beautiful. She also wondered how far down it extended.

"Not many people make that claim. Can I ask about your experience?" the captain questioned.

"I've swum in a hundred frozen lakes and used to run across frozen rivers in the spring. The person who could go the farthest won!"

"You mean the farthest without falling in?" Captain Joana asked.

"That would take out all the fun. The winner was always soaking wet when they won their prize."

"And no one lost their life while you played this sport?"

Leif shrugged. "We have a method where I'm from. I've taught it to Terra here as well. It involves rechanneling our energy to keep our inner core warm, and it allows us to stay underwater for quite some time."

"Is that right?"

"Indeed."

"Well, that's very impressive," Joana replied. Terra could not be sure, but she thought the captain of the *Skidbladnir* was already getting wise to Leif. "But in case your... methods prove less than optimal where we're headed, we have SCUBA gear for the four of you and my crew as well.

Heated suits. Video equipment. Radios. It's as comfortable as one can be underwater."

"Excellent news. I, for one, don't ascribe to this polar bear arctic plunge nonsense, so I would appreciate having a fully functional suit with all the bells and whistles."

Joana smiled as she took in the sweep up the curve of her ship. She had led them to the front, and they now looked back, so the boat appeared as a long, narrow hall split in half by the cabin.

"The *Skidbladnir* is twice the speed of most of her sisters in the bay. Modern hybrid engine means we can get to your location in half the time it would take other ships and with half the fuel."

"We'll be there later today, then?" Mads asked.

"Not quite. The times I quoted you were my own, not my slower competitors. We'll be there early tomorrow after resting for tonight."

"We'll be dining with you, then?"

"Yes," Joana confirmed. "The ship is fully stocked with a deep freezer containing some of the best local produce, as well as a pantry of non-perishables. We also keep a month's worth of emergency rations on hand, just in case."

"That's amazing! Most voyages like these have people eating bags of chips and protein bars."

"And some of us were looking forward to that menu." Leif huffed.

Joana gave him an odd look, but she knew better than to openly question the habits of a wealthy or eccentric client. "I fully expect us to eat well for the duration of our voyage. Unless you think two weeks will be insufficient?"

"God, I hope that's plenty," Mads replied.

Terra looked at Leif, who only shrugged.

"We're not quite sure of the full scope of the location, but that should be enough to give us an idea, at the least."

"You said a city? Is it really that large?"

"Quite a sizeable settlement if it has a shrine to Freya!" Leif answered.

"Not by modern standards." Terra elbowed him in the ribs. "We expect a few stone structures but not much beyond that. I would think the water has eroded most of it away."

"Well, not to worry there. We have the most modern instruments for detecting things in the sea, all the way down to the seafloor. We have a full detection suite of instruments, including LiDAR, radar, sonar…all the arrrs." She growled out the last letter like a pirate.

No one laughed.

Joana grinned. "I apologize. You would be shocked how well that joke usually does."

"It really doesn't," one of the crew offered, having returned from stowing their things.

"This is Alfred. The first mate. I keep him around because he is good at his job, not because he has a sense of humor."

"If a good sense of humor were important on the *Skidbladnir*, we would have mutinied."

"Very good, Alfred. You can get back to scrubbing something."

Alfred saluted and went off to polish the gangway.

"In addition to detection equipment, we also have state-of-the-art image generation software, so we can make models of the seafloor. We have not used it to model lost cities, but I'm sure Anna will be up for their challenge. She's our pilot and quite good at her job. There's two more working besides them, and all five of us will be at your disposal for the entirety of the voyage. We all love our jobs here and are looking forward to making your holiday, or mission, I suppose, as wonderful as possible."

"I saw something on the back. Was that a submersible?" Romero asked.

"Indeed. If you'll follow me, I can show you how it works."

They followed Captain Joana from the bow to the stern. She pointed out various safety features and surveillance equipment. The ship really did seem to be a modern marvel.

"What's it made of? Is it sturdy?" Mads asked.

"Fiberglass with a carbon fiber frame. Strong as steel."

"You sure about that?" Romero questioned.

"Dr. Barrow did have some security concerns, and we addressed them as best as we could, but I am curious. Are we expecting to be under attack from pirates?" Joana queried, obviously intending it to be a joke. Again, no one laughed.

"More like sea monsters," Leif replied after a moment.

Joana laughed, but no one joined her. "You're not serious?"

"He's never serious," Mads countered. "But it's good to know the ship is strong as well as fast."

"You don't seem like archeologists," Joana pointed out.

Terra smirked. "It's a rapidly evolving field. You would be amazed."

"That's the submersible, then?" Romero asked now that they had arrived at the odd, tube-like machine.

"It's only large enough for one," Joana stated, eyeing Romero's huge frame. She made no exception for him, and despite her pirate-centric humor, Terra got the sense the captain took her job quite seriously. "However, it's quite maneuverable."

"It looks fun," Romero remarked.

"No weapons, though," Mads pointed out.

"Were we expecting Viking zombies in this city?" Joana asked.

"Getting closer, luv!" Mads chuckled. "Though I think we put them behind us. Left them in Hel, so to speak."

"It doesn't need weapons," Romero decided. "Does a car need a gun on it to be effective at what it does? Do you need to put a missile on a plane for it to be a thing of beauty?"

"Sorry, luv, I apologize for him. He's out of America and a bit gaga for machines. Probably losing it a bit to be on this ship, eh, mate?"

"This has got to be one of the most amazing machines I've ever had the privilege of being aboard, and certainly the most impressive ship."

"Oh, please, you haven't even seen how she works. Would you like to see the engine?"

"I was dying to ask," Romero agreed.

Terra did not try to follow as they headed to examine the engine room. She let them fall into a patter of engine sizes, fuel types, aeration, and heat allotments while she, Leif, and Mads went to the above-deck cabin.

The cockpit was situated in the room, too, but there

were also a few beautifully pale leather couches and a low table bolted to the floor. The pilot was not here at the moment, so for the time being, they had privacy while the crew went about final preparations.

Leif grinned when he saw the sofas. He sauntered over, plopped down, and kicked his feet up.

"You can't be doing that, mate," Mads snapped, gesturing at Leif's boots. "This here's a classy ship. Classier than the likes of us. Least you can do is show it."

"Barrow's footing the bill, isn't he? What does it matter whether I make myself comfortable or not?" Leif complained, but he did take his feet down from the sofa.

"Matters everything, mate. No one can tell a phony quicker than the rich. We're already going to be pulling the wool over Joana's eyes, which I don't think will be easy. Let's try to at least keep her convinced we're of the right status."

"We told her we were archeologists," Terra pointed out. "Which is the truth!"

"No reason to be an animal about it," Mads shrugged as he settled beside Leif. "My god. This is the softest leather I've ever felt! I'd love to take a nap here."

"Napping is for thieves and cats," Leif quipped.

Mads glared at him but only worked himself deeper into the sofa.

"How are we feeling?" Terra asked. "Is this all going to work?"

"The only thing I'm worried about is the pressure," Mads stated.

"I know. If we don't find the piece on this mission, I'm going to lose my mind," Terra replied.

"I meant the pressure of the water," Mads chuckled.

"Oh. Right." Terra blushed.

Leif shrugged. "That shouldn't be too much of an issue. We've been working on a spell for that."

"The underwater bubble?" Terra asked.

"The very same."

Terra nodded. She preferred battle magic, but the bubble had worked against the snake, so she felt at least somewhat confident she could use it.

"I suppose you can put on the wetsuits, then activate that little number to better convince the crew?" Mads suggested.

Terra nodded. "I think that makes the most sense."

"And you two are certain the artifact is out here somewhere?" Mads asked.

"Pretty sure, yes!" Leif declared.

"Pretty sure? I don't think that's good enough."

Leif looked back and forth to make sure no one was around them, then pulled out his map. A tap from his fingers and the piece of leather came alive with pen marks detailing the coastline to which they were currently moored.

"When we flew over the sea, I felt something here." Leif moved his hand over the map. It changed color over the water, glowing slightly redder near the coast, then richer and darker farther out. "I can't be certain, but I've been training with the pieces of Freya alongside Terra, and it felt quite similar."

"I guess a feeling and some inexplicable scribbles on a map is the best I can ever hope for with you two," Mads grumbled.

"Between Leif's senses and the information from the Villon Institute, I think we're on the right track," Terra proclaimed.

"Aye, but weren't you on the right track all winter long?" Mads asked.

Terra wanted to toss him overboard, but she forced herself to nod slowly instead. "It's always the last place you look."

Mads snorted. "Only because once you find it, you stop looking."

"I didn't get any sense of it inland. I think this is it. I really do," Leif reiterated.

"And what is *it*, exactly?" Mads asked.

Terra and Leif shared a look, and Leif laughed.

"We'll know it when we see it!" Terra stated.

"That's what everyone thought about these Picassos I was working on. You'd be surprised how easy it is to be fooled when you're desperate for things to go your way," Mads told them.

"You really think this mission will be a dead end?" Terra asked.

Mads shrugged. "Don't let me get you down. I spent the last six months looking at forgeries, so I might be a little more suspicious of everything than I should be. If you two think this is the place, I'm sure it could be. Plus, there's the snakes. I don't think they came from nowhere."

"You heard about that?" Terra asked, reaching into her bag and pulling out the scale.

"There were reports of giant white serpents in a forest near where I was in Spain. Sounded like the kind of thing you two would be involved with. And now it looks like you have a souvenir."

"One of them destroyed a ship near where we were. I went out walking last night and met one as well. It attacked me. Which was a mistake."

"For the snake." Leif chuckled.

Mads looked around. They still had their moment of privacy. He took the scale from Terra and frowned at it.

"It was bigger," she explained. "When I killed it, its entire body dissolved. That scale was the only thing that lasted, and it's smaller than it was."

"I don't know much about fossilization and all that, but I'm pretty sure giant snakes aren't supposed to dissolve when you fight them," Mads offered.

"It wasn't natural. It could talk and had magic. It seemed almost hungry for my magic."

"What about it, Leif? You have some knowledge of this thing?"

"We are working under the assumption that these snakes have something to do with Jörmungandr, the world serpent," Leif explained.

"That sounds…bad."

"Indeed. The world serpent is known for being the one to kill Odin, and will likely kill him again, for that matter. It is able to change the weave of *seidr*. From what I could find, I feel confident that not only can it sense magic, but it might be able to consume it."

"And you're thinking its babies can do the same?" Mads asked.

"It did something to my magic. I couldn't teleport away from it while I was fighting," Terra revealed.

"Whether they actively feed on the magic or simply predate upon it as an energy source is up for debate, but they are certainly aware of it."

"Not great news," Mads stated. "They like magic? Aren't you two technically the most magical beings on the planet?"

Terra thought back to all the beings they had fought and defeated. She had more power than Beatrice had, more than Goodwin possessed, even when he had been an avatar of death for Hel itself. Fenrir had been able to tap into more power than them, but he was so powerful that he had drawn the attention of Thor and been taken from Midgard. Which meant Mads was right. As far as she knew, she really was the most magical being around.

A heady thought.

"Unless a giant has somehow snuck into the realm, or Fenrir is out again, I suppose that is true."

At that moment, their privacy ended when the pilot came back in.

"Damn," Mads surmised. "Good luck getting any sleep."

CHAPTER TEN

The open sea, east of Umeå, Sweden, Saturday evening
Leif was more than pleased to be shown to his quarters. They were small by the standards of shore dwellings but more than ample for lodgings in a boat. Leif had fully expected to sleep on the sofas he had seen. His own room was a luxury he had not been expecting out at sea. He had rarely interacted with Vikings of old, but he had spent one memorable jaunt on a longship, and there had not been anything even remotely resembling privacy.

But here, he was able to change in private. A luxury of the modern world most people took for granted. Demanded, even. It would be something to note in his book how, despite a larger population than ever, humans still found places to be on their own.

He wondered how that affected their views of going to Valhalla or Folkvangr. Considering how few of these modern people were warriors, they were probably not overly concerned with an eternity spent feasting.

It was a small consolation to know if things did go

wrong for them, Leif and Terra would end up in Folkvangr together, eating, drinking, and cavorting with warriors from across the ages. Not a fate the librarian had dreamed of for himself, but now it seemed almost a certainty.

Unless the boat sank, he supposed.

That made him want to return to the top deck to keep an eye on things. He could create a bubble around himself, but not if he was asleep when he was sucked underwater.

Leif left his room and was about to knock on Terra's when he heard gentle snoring through the door. Better to let her sleep, especially considering she had spent the night before battling a giant serpent in the cold of the sea while he had been in bed.

He put on a jacket and went up top.

He made it in time to see the red orb of the sun sink beneath the distant mountains of Sweden. There were plenty of clouds tonight, so the sun painted a majestic sunset, turning the clouds every shade of purple and orange.

They didn't have sunsets like this in Asgard. Something about the eternity of this place made the transience of sunsets function differently. Leif would have liked to address it in his book, but he hardly thought himself capable of describing the colors before him, let alone how it made him feel both thankful to be alive and aware of the fleeting nature of mortality. He was a historian, not a poet.

Mads, a man who was about as far from being a poet as possible, came out onto the deck. He saw Leif and sauntered over.

"Makes you feel like a fly stuck in a painting. You know? Trapped on the surface, unable to appreciate the whole thing, but powerless to resist it all the same," Mads commented, looking at the sunset.

"You continue to surprise me, Mads Jostad. I did not think of you as one to form such profound thoughts over a sunset."

Mads shrugged. "I spent the last six months working with paintings. I guess all that overwrought nonsense rubbed off on me. Kind of like how your time here made you appreciate our cheap snacks."

"You compare my weakness for the delicacies of your world to our mortal condition? I don't know if that's wise or inane."

"That's this whole world, innit? Halfway between wisdom and nonsense. One minute, you can be doing what you think is the most important mission of your life, and the next, you realize you've been going about it all wrong."

"Is that a jab at how Terra and I spent our winter?"

Mads chuckled. "I guess it should have been, but I've been in this archeological artifact business longer than either of you. I know how these things go. Clear roads turn into dead ends, and dead ends reveal ways forward. That's how it is when you're dealing with mysteries and whatnot. Compared to this, hunting down forged art is simple. Funny, I never thought I'd miss the insanity of chasing down these artifacts, but I'm glad I'm back."

"We're glad, too," Leif replied. "I know we've had our differences, but it's nice to have you around. The people of this world sometimes make me feel like I'm always being deceived. It feels like everyone is after something else. With you, at least, I know what I'm dealing with."

"Fair enough, mate. Now, let's say we go down below

and familiarize ourselves with the SCUBA gear? You might have a magic bubble or whatever, but you'll need to know how to put this stuff on."

"After you, Mr. Jostad."

Leif followed Mads downstairs and into another bedroom, converted into some sort of dressing chamber.

"Well, would you look at these?" Leif touched the thick black suits hanging from the wall.

"Those are the wetsuits," Mads explained. "You put them on, and the water that gets in sticks close to your body, keeping you warmer than the sea. Should be especially necessary considering how bony you are."

"Despite my love of snacks, they have had little effect on my physique, it's true," Leif replied.

"You want to try putting one on?" Mads asked.

"I think that would be prudent, yes."

The first suit Leif tried was not even close to the right size. He struggled to get it up his legs, but when he tried to put the arms on, it became clear it would not fit. He had to lay down on the floor and have Mads yank it off his legs, which felt like a less-than-civilized way to further his relationship with the thief-turned-poet.

The second suit fit much better. Leif zipped up the front and grinned, moving about as the material bunched around him. "You modern mortals really have found every way you can to exist without magic."

"You ain't seen nothing yet," Mads told him. "There's an oxygen tank to wear on your back, a mask to see underwater, and something to control your buoyancy."

"Oh dear. Are we sure I cannot simply jump in shirtless, as we used to do in the pools of Asgard?"

"Not unless you want Captain Joana to dive in after you."

Leif found something about the tattooed captain rather intoxicating, but if he were to pursue romantic interests, he did not think encouraging a lack of faith in his skills was the way to go about it. He sighed.

"Can you please show me how the tank works?"

"There's no greater pleasure in life than demonstrating to a know-it-all that they do not, in fact, know everything."

Leif did not enjoy being called a know-it-all. There were entire centuries of history here on Earth that he had yet to learn about. However, that seemed to be as far as Mads wanted to tease him. He led Leif to a pile of curious equipment and demonstrated how to use it all.

Or tried to, anyway.

It was far from common sense. First, there were the flippers. Leif put them on his feet and found that suddenly, he could not walk. He felt like a goose hobbling around on land, but unlike the goose that could take to the air and water, Leif did not feel confident with great big webs extending from his toes.

Next came a rather bulky harness and an air tank that seemed both excessively large and not nearly big enough.

"It's compressed air, so there's a regulator to let it all out. You need to keep an eye on your gauges, so you don't—"

Leif twisted one of the knobs on the tank, and a great rush of air blew from a sort of rubber hose.

"Don't do that. You need it to breathe."

"No, I don't." Leif drew a great, deep breath.

"I mean, you need it to breathe underwater."

"Nuh-uh. I have magic, remember?"

Mads grabbed the rubber hose. "And what happens if you run out of energy because all you ate for lunch was potato chips? What happens if these snakes pull the same trick Terra said they did to her, and you lose that ability?"

"And here I was thinking you didn't really care about me," Leif *almost* said. Instead, he twisted the knob on the oxygen tank so a blast of air shot out into Mads' face.

Mads looked like he wanted to send Leif to the bottom of the sea with nothing but a rock to keep him afloat, but he only gritted his teeth. "You figured it out. Bravo. Next piece of gear is the helmet. It's got a face mask with lights, so you should be able to see down there. That is unless you want to send magical darts all over the snake-infested waters."

"No, no. The electric lights are quite useful." Leif put the helmet on. It had a piece of transparent plastic across the face, a little speaker connected to the radio, and a hole below that must have led to the air tank hose. It was ingenious seeing all these human inventions stacked up on top of each other.

"You should be able to operate the lights from a switch on the—"

Leif pressed a switch on the side of the helmet, and bright lights flared into Mads' face.

"Easy with those!" Mads stuck out a hand to block the light from blinding him.

"With what?" Leif asked, unable to resist looking away. Then, when Mads put his hand down, Leif looked directly into his face and blinded him a second time.

"Mate. I get that you're trying to be cute and all. But

you are taking me to the very limits of what I consider professional courtesy."

"Fair enough. I apologize. You and Terra have operated most of the technology of this era for me, and I do appreciate it."

"That right? Because when Terra took your cell phone away because you were spending hundreds of dollars online shopping and getting the snacks shipped to the wrong address, you threw quite the fit."

It was true. Leif had been rather upset when his quest to eat a snack from every country on Earth within a single hour had been thwarted. He would have fought back harder when they took the phone from him, but it had been a small miracle he'd found where to purchase the snacks in the first place. He knew he would not be able to replicate his results.

Also, they had been right. The snacks never arrived, or if they had, they'd gone to a previous address. The most difficult thing about the modern world was when it came up against the ancient world of magic that had reawakened when Terra found Freya's first artifact.

"I think the phone was too much for me. I can accept that. This suit seems useful. I'll try to master the controls. How do I connect the helmet to the air supply?"

Mads showed him and offered a quick rundown of how the various vents and valves were supposed to work together to give a mortal more time underwater than they usually had. It was all fascinating, the ways these mortals solved their problems. They came up with an idea. For example, bring air underwater. Then they built and built, refining methods and adding devices until it seemed like it had always worked that way.

Leif wondered what his time in this realm would be like if Freya had sent him here even a single century later. Surely, the technology would continue to evolve at blistering speed. What this society would accomplish, assuming they survived, was truly something to wonder about.

However, Leif would not trade it for his time with Terra. Or with Mads, for that matter. He had grown lonely in the library of Asgard, and now that he was here, he found he liked the company far more than expected.

"Were you listening?" Mads shouted at him through the mask. It was vaguely hard to hear, and Mads' face was going fuzzy around the edges. Leif's legs weakened, and he was overcome with a desire to sit, then lay down.

Before he could fully recline, Mads ripped the mask from his face, and Leif felt himself wake up with a breath of fresh air.

"You were running out of air, you idiot," Mads told him.

"I'm not…an idiot," Leif wheezed, though he could admit that, at this moment, maybe he was. Not that he would ever say it aloud. "If I ran out of air, why weren't my lungs burning?"

"You weren't *out of* air, only low. Your lungs will make do as long as they can. I would have thought you'd notice, but maybe there's something to do with your brain not functioning properly."

"I resent that! Far more likely, the *seidr* was augmenting as best as it could. I'll have to talk to Terra about ways we can best use our magic with this equipment."

"Better to wait until morning, though, eh? She seemed exhausted. Not that I blame her. Fighting a snake in the middle of the night sounds like a nightmare I never want to experience. Better to let her have a good night's sleep than wake her up and deal with her being all grumpy."

"On that, we can agree," Leif replied.

They went back to working with the equipment, but Leif made no more major breakthroughs before they heard a commotion above deck.

"You think the crew can handle that?" Mads asked. It sounded like they were running around and yelling at each other. Never good signs.

"We might as well check to make sure," Leif suggested.

"Couldn't agree more," Mads stated.

How he shucked off his equipment as fast as he did mystified Leif.

One moment, the professional thief was dressed in full SCUBA gear, from underwater helmet to flippers and everything in between. The next, the tank was hung up, the flippers were off, and he was heading up the stairs.

Leif stepped onto the deck to find the calm colors of the sunset replaced with the black of night and the ship's bright white lights. They illuminated the deck in harsh light and harsher shadows, but it was not the activity on the deck that had everyone moving so frantically.

There were things in the water.

"I need a positive ID on these organisms and a path out," Captain Joana called over radios clipped to the crew members.

"If everything all right up here?" Leif asked Alfred.

"Nothing to worry about, sir. Only a school of...err,

squid. We think. They sometimes come to the surface at night.

"They don't look like squid to me," Romero rumbled. He was standing against the exterior wall of the above-deck cabin, mostly in shadow, though his eyes caught the light.

"Looks like there are fewer to port, captain," Alfred announced, and the ship changed direction slightly.

Leif approached the side and looked over the edge. The first thing he noticed was how fast they were moving. It was hard to tell in the glare of the lights with the dark all around them, but when he saw the lights catch the water splashing and foaming around the prow of the boat, he realized they were moving at a rapid pace.

And the creatures in the water were moving with them.

Leif did not need a good look at them to know what they were.

Snakes. They propelled themselves along, matching the speed of the vessel, surfacing and vanishing beneath the choppy water so Leif could never get a decent count of how many there were.

Dozens seemed a fair guess.

"Are we getting clear?" the captain asked through Alfred's radio.

"They seem to be adjusting course to match, Captain. Maybe they're attracted to the lights?"

"We can't sail blind at this speed. There shouldn't be anything out here, but we can't take that risk." It was the pilot's voice, Leif assumed, though he had yet to meet her formally.

"Cut our speed. Let's see if they're being drawn to the noise or something."

Leif nearly stumbled but managed to grab the railing and catch himself from falling forward when the boat abruptly slowed.

"Isn't this like the ocean equivalent of going upstairs when the killer is in the house when we should obviously be going into the yard?" Romero asked.

"I don't know, mate. I was thinking more about bait fish. I don't want these things to spook us so much that we end up crashing into something," Mads replied.

When they slowed, the snakes kept going, or so it appeared. Then, Leif noticed they were not racing along with the boat anymore, moving in one direction. They now slithered and swam back and forth, breaching the surface, then diving below. They were all the same shiny, silvery color as the scale Terra had, though most were smaller than the scale had been when Terra first showed it to Leif.

"I'm going to go out on a limb here and guess those things have a touch of magic to them?" Mads asked.

Leif fumbled for his spectacles, which were around his neck instead of on his face, after trying to fiddle with the SCUBA equipment. He put them to his eyes and watched the writhing white creatures churn around the boat. It was faint, but the signature of magical energy was present.

"Only a tiny bit for each one," Leif announced. "Hardly enough to be concerned over. If anything, I would say this gives us a good indication we're on the right track."

"Loving the optimism," Mads replied, though Leif recognized his cold sarcasm.

"I'm cutting the lights. Maybe they're attracted to them.

All crew, stand by with handheld flashlights," Captain Joana stated.

"Anyone want to take a bet whether this is going to work?" Romero took out a cigarette and lit it while the lights were still on. "Two to one says it doesn't."

"Hundred euro on that bet," Mads replied. "I'd gladly pay to get rid of those things."

"Hundred it is. Look a lot like the white snakes in the forests of Spain," Romero rumbled. "Which doesn't make a goddamn lick of sense unless there's parts of this story I haven't been told."

"Mate, if these things swim off, let's have a drink and a chat. You'll buy, though, since you'll have my cash."

The lights shut off, and for a moment, Leif could see nothing. The white glare on the water had been so bright that his eyes needed to adjust to the abrupt darkness. The first thing he saw were the stars overhead. So many. Thousands. Millions. More than any other part of Midgard he had been to, more than some parts of Asgard.

Then, as his eyes continued to compensate, he saw movement in the water. It had not slowed or abated. If anything, there was more of it.

"Spot check," the captain ordered.

Alfred switched on a flashlight and cast it across the water's surface. He revealed a nightmarish scene. There were now hundreds of snakes. Some were as small as Leif's pinky fingers, while most were closer to the size of his forearm. A precious few were closer to the size of his leg.

"Mate, I'm thinking we should be a bit worried about now," Mads pointed out.

Leif peered through his spectacles, trying to focus especially on the larger specimens. He saw nothing a dart of his energy should not be able to dispatch. These were young, and like the young of many creatures, even Jotun, they were not nearly as fearsome as they would be when fully grown.

"I don't think we need to be alarmed," Leif began cautiously. "The smallest ones present a negligible threat, and even the larger ones don't seem to have much magic."

"Goddamn it," Romero muttered, then took a long drag of his cigarette. "I knew I should have stayed in Spain. Even with those bastards trying to carjack us."

"He said there's nothing to worry about!" Mads insisted.

"He looked through a pair of reading glasses at a dark sea crawling with the freakiest-looking snakes I've ever seen, then said there's not much *magic*. If you expect me to think any of this is normal, you are in for a disappointment."

"But we don't need to be worried. Right, Leif?"

"I would advise against falling into the water at this moment, but I don't think these are particularly formidable foes. In fact, I would say they appear quite frail. Nothing to worry about."

Leif did not believe in luck. His great-grandmother was the master of *seidr*. She saw how the past and present conspired together to create the futures mortals both craved and feared. Luck was only another way of talking about the threads Freya could see plain as day.

However, he could not help but think saying "nothing to worry about" had invited quite a bit of bad luck.

No sooner did he utter those words than a massive tail shot from the water like a pale pillar. It rose higher than the deck, then the cabin in the middle of the boat, then the crane arm near the back.

The scariest part of it extending so high was how much of the creature was still hidden beneath the surface.

"What in the hell is that?" Romero shouted.

All the crew were saying pretty much the same thing, albeit in Swedish.

The tail ignored them. It briefly hung in the air, then crashed onto the sea in front of the boat, splashing water onto the deck in a display that must have meant "go no further."

"Perhaps there is *some* small cause for alarm," Leif amended.

"I was really hoping to lose that bet," Mads grumbled.

Leif nodded. "I had thought it prudent to let Terra sleep, but perhaps we should awaken her and hope she takes out any grumpiness on whatever the hell that tail belongs to."

CHAPTER ELEVEN

<u>Below the deck of the *Skidbladnir*, east of Umeå, Sweden, Saturday night</u>

Terra had done it. She'd proven that, although violent, the Vikings had been instrumental in keeping a global culture alive during what some historians called "the Dark Ages." It was inarguable that the Vikings had conducted raids in which they had stolen crops, valuables, and even people. However, thanks to her research, this was proven an outlier to the regular pattern of their behavior.

Digs from across Northern Europe, Southern Europe, Northern Africa, and the Middle East showed the same things. Vikings introduced people to foreign concepts, art, and craftsmanship techniques that would have remained isolated had they never set out in their longboats. Thanks to their movements, the food and culture of the Western world grew and changed at a faster rate than it would have without someone serving as ideological couriers.

Now, she would present her findings to the

International Organization for Archeologists Who Are So Smart and Look Cool, Too.

Despite never having heard of it before, Terra was extremely excited to be the keynote speaker. She was next, ready to share her slides of the artifacts she found that proved her theories of cultural exchange.

The only problem was that she could not find her clothes. She wasn't naked, thank the Norse gods, but she only had on her old, ratty shirt with the comic book Thor. The one with holes in it and stains from never wanting to throw it in the washer. She thought she'd lost the shirt in a move when she was thirteen years old, so she was both thankful to have it back and concerned that it was the only thing she had to wear, and it barely covered her rear.

"You need to get up there," her fellow researcher insisted. Though he had an odd obsession with trying snacks anywhere they went, she was thankful Leif Freyason was working with her on the project. However, it was odd that he always carried around a hammer and wore an eyepatch.

"I don't want to," Terra moaned.

"You need to get dressed," Leif ordered. Which was funny because now he was shirtless and covered in kelp tattoos.

"We're under attack, and we need your help."

He grabbed her shoulders and shook her.

Terra woke up.

Leif stood above her, wearing a black wetsuit with reflective piping, of all things.

Terra groaned. The only thing worse than being woken

when you desperately needed sleep was being woken from a somewhat decent dream into an even weirder one. Why on Earth was the Asgardian dressed like he was about to go into a shark tank?

"Terra, we're under attack. There's more of those snakes."

"They'll go away. I have a presentation to get back to." She shut her eyes and tried to roll back over and make herself comfortable. The beds were pretty good.

"Not anymore. We're under attack. The snakes found us. There's a big one. We need the Chosen of Freya."

Terra forced her eyes open and turned back to see the apparition of Leif. He was still wearing a wetsuit, standing above her bed in a room beneath the deck of the *Skidbladnir*. Which made sense. They had chartered this boat to investigate a site that might hold the last piece of Freya. The magical artifacts had already attracted beings from other realms and likely had again.

Which meant this wasn't a dream.

"Crap, crap, crap." Terra popped out of bed. She was wearing sweatpants and a blue sweatshirt that said "SWEDEN" in gold across the front. Leif had to be wearing a wetsuit because they were on this boat so they could get somewhere to dive. Everything about the situation made sense. Well, everything besides her being the representation of a goddess on Midgard, and the threat of a giant serpent, but those were aspects of Terra's life she had come to accept.

"The boat is all right? We're not sinking?"

"Not yet," Leif replied. "But there are hundreds of

snakes out there and the tail of a rather large specimen. Seeing as how you defeated the last in battle, we were hoping you might do something along those lines again."

"Right. Of course," Terra agreed. Seemed like there wasn't much point in holding back now. She had refrained from wearing her magical armaments thus far because they still had not yet decided how to share the existence of Norse magic with the world. Still, such secrecy was not nearly as important as ensuring that Freya's artifacts were not taken by a magical snake or lost to the bottom of the ocean.

She took Brísingamen from its case and put it around her neck. When she clasped it, she felt its energy flow through her and the ship's architecture open up. She had been paying close attention to how much higher the deck was than the rooms below it.

She wasn't confident she could teleport while the boat was moving, but it was currently stationary. Perhaps not the best tactical move, but it would make Terra far more maneuverable. Assuming she could use her ability to teleport at all.

She would have to presume this snake had the same ability to nullify magic abilities. Maybe she would be able to get one strike in before it knew to block her? It was not as if the snake she'd killed could have communicated with this one.

Next, she grabbed the bracers and clicked them onto her wrists. After they closed, any indication of hinges or clasps vanished. More than any of the artifacts, the bracers felt like part of Terra. She had possessed them the longest and practiced using the strength they granted her, as well as the other abilities they allowed.

Fireballs. Darts of blinding energy. Concussive blasts. And perhaps most importantly, given her current situation, the ability to create a bubble of protection around herself so she could breathe and survive the icy cold water.

She grabbed the feathered cloak as well, but rather than putting it on, she gave it to Leif.

"You're sure?" he asked, but he did not hesitate to throw the cloak around his shoulders.

"If I can teleport, I don't need the ability to change into a bird. If I can't teleport, I'll need you to save my butt. And don't forget, plenty of birds can swim as well as fly."

"I was thinking the form of a great cormorant might be particularly useful."

"Not a puffin?"

"I'm hoping it won't come to that, but if these snakes refuse to retreat, I may take the form of that formidable creature." His eyes twinkled, and Terra knew he was ready. He was no longer the confused, out-of-time librarian he had been when he first came to Midgard. Leif had spent as much time training as she had and was skilled with the techniques Bygul's Eye afforded him. Terra hoped Freya's feathered cloak would make him a true asset in battle.

With her bracers on and Brísingamen around her neck, Terra grabbed Freya's ax.

Immediately. she felt its power flow through her. The ax was built to master *seidr*. It would grant her the fate she desired. Which, at the moment, meant keeping her friends alive and sending these snakes back to whichever realm they came from.

A shout of "incoming" from above, and Terra bounded from her room, shoes be damned. She had a feeling she would not stay dry for this battle, anyway, and the shoes would be a hindrance in the water.

The sound of gunfire greeted her when she stepped onto the deck.

"What in the hell is that thing?" Alfred shouted. He had been the one to fire the gun, a small, snub-nosed revolver he held in both hands like he worried the kickback might knock him off the deck.

Terra was pleased that at least Joana's crew had *some* weapons.

"What do we have?" Terra asked Mads.

He was armed with a much more formidable assault-style rifle. Romero had a shotgun. The duffle between them still looked heavy with weapons and plenty of ammunition.

"Oh, not too much. Just *that*." Mads pointed to a pair of massive eyes rising from the sea. They broke the water first, and the huge head of a viper followed. It had pits on the front of its face and a long, forked tongue that flicked back and forth as its massive coils propelled its head higher. Five feet. Ten feet. Soon, it towered over the boat. It was the same pale, silvery color as the snake she had battled.

"I take it the one you fought was about this big," Leif stated.

"Actually, this one looks much bigger," Terra replied. Then, she addressed the serpent.

"What do you want?" she demanded.

"For starters? Your life," the snake replied. It pumped its tail, rose further, and proceeded to belly flop onto the ship.

Or it tried to.

Another member of the crew fired a few noisy shots from a handgun, and Mads opened fire, plugging more than a dozen rounds into its pale belly.

The snake recoiled from the gunfire. Instead of crashing onto the boat, it splashed alongside it, back into the water.

"Was it talking? Please don't tell me it was talking."

"Oh, it's going to do far worse than talk," Mads warned.

"Why did we stop?" Terra asked.

"To see if they were attracted to the sound of the engine," Alfred replied.

"I don't think the noise pollution was what was bothering them," Mads suggested.

Terra banged the flat of her hand against the window to the cockpit. "Let's go! I don't care where, but get the hell out of here!"

"Make it so!" Joana shouted at Anna, and the pilot threw the ship into motion.

They surged ahead, leaving the huge snake behind for about a minute before it gave chase.

"Please tell me you have more than handguns for defense," Terra stated to Alfred.

"We only have these to scare off pirates! We didn't think there would be a sea serpent!"

"Those aren't going to work. What else do you have?" Terra doubted they would be able to flee the snake for long.

"We have explosives. Some people use them to scare off whales and sharks. We bought some because your boss—"

"Show me."

Alfred hurried to the back of the boat and opened a crate. Inside were a dozen or so neatly packed explosives. Terra grabbed one, looked at how to set the charge, and tossed it into the water behind the boat.

They raced away. A moment later, a great geyser of water and snakes blasted into the air and splashed back down.

Yet there was no blood. No giant chunks to indicate they had defeated the massive serpent.

"It's still coming!" a crewman shouted. "It is Jörmungandr himself! We are doomed!"

"Not yet, we're not," Terra announced. The snake was swimming through the wake of the explosive. Had they scared it? Did that mean they could use the bombs to hurt it? It was worth a shot. Barrow had placed the order for the explosives, after all. Best not to waste resources!

One of the explosives went off, then another, another. It felt like the entire ocean was exploding in their wake. Even though they were racing away from the blasts, water rained down on them.

Water and snakes.

"Should we be worried about these, boss?" Mads asked, kicking one of the smaller snakes off the boat with his boot.

"Their venom is magic. I can see it with my lenses," Leif announced. "So yes, let's not assume a bite from them won't harm anybody."

Terra ignored the smaller snakes as Romero, Mads,

Leif, and the crew shot at them and kicked them off the boat. One of the crewmen grabbed a shovel that was normally used for scooping bloody chunks of chum into the ocean, judging by the stains on the handle. That seemed more effective than the guns.

Good.

They had to be able to handle the small ones while Terra took out the big one.

If it was still alive.

There was a chance the explosives had taken it out.

However, Terra saw a large shape in the water. She did not think it likely that a whale had heard the explosives and decided to investigate.

A moment later, the snake exploded from the water on the starboard side of the boat. Its head rose, then a sinuous body that kept coming as if it would never end. It was matching the boat's speed and able to jump from the water even at that pace. Which was to say, it was both fast and strong.

Not important at the moment, though. All that mattered was the snake had opened its jaws and was trying to gore one of the crew at the front of the boat, trying to knock away the smaller specimens.

Terra was not about to let that happen.

She teleported forward, putting herself where she needed to be. Or she would have if the boat wasn't moving. The effect of what was essentially the ground moving beneath her feet was tricky to compensate for, but Terra was still close enough to run forward and get between the snake and the crew member.

She swung up with her ax and sent a blast of concussive

force. It crashed into the snake, and although it did not rip the creature in half like Terra would have liked, it did force its giant jaw shut before it splashed into the sea.

"It's here!" Terra shouted.

Mads appeared, peppering the massive serpent with bullets. It dove to get away from the onslaught, but Terra did not see any blood in the water.

"Did I get it?" Mads asked.

"I think you hit it."

"Considering you don't sound happy, I'm going to take that to mean it's not dead."

"Magic snakes with Kevlar scales? I think I could have used more disclosure!" Romero called.

"You and me both, mate. Bulletproof snake is a new one to me."

Terra glanced at the deck of the *Skidbladnir*. Her team had either killed all the smaller snakes or kicked them back into the ocean. The only ones still on board were dead. Mads, Romero, and the man with the shovel must have killed some of them, but there were too many to ascribe them all to those three. Which meant some had died in the blast. A good sign!

Terra was already formulating a strategy for defeating the giant serpent if the only way to hurt it was to use its own venom against it like she had before.

The giant snake emerged from the water a moment later, striking at the boat itself. Joana's assessment held, and its fangs did not puncture the hull. The snake did not seem happy about this development. It struck Terra instead, but she sliced at its tooth with her ax. The snake withdrew and ducked its head underwater.

It wasn't a retreat, of course. That would be too easy. Instead, the snake's tail shot from the water on the other side of the boat. It thrashed toward Alfred and surely would have taken him out if Leif hadn't thought quickly and created a barrier. The snake's tail grabbed that instead and crushed it.

Rather than wasting his magic trying to resist the monstrous snake, Leif let the barrier break, then fired a few darts of energy at the snake. They hit its scales and bounced off. If this snake could stop magic like the other had been able to, it did not seem to think the darts of magic were a big enough threat to bother with.

Terra was more than willing to push its boundaries.

She teleported to the other side of the boat and sliced at the tail with her ax. She struck it and was rewarded with a scale flying free and a spurt of blood. The tail thrashed and vanished over the side of the deck into the dark ocean.

"Maybe we should get the crew inside?" Mads suggested.

"Hell, considering our bullets aren't doing a damn thing, maybe we should head inside too," Romero added.

"That's fine," Terra agreed. "Get everyone in and keep them safe. Leif and I can handle this."

She looked back to the water. The snake was already there, racing alongside the boat and lifting its head. It lunged at her, and Terra stepped back, but that was fine with the huge serpent. It landed its massive girth on the boat and flicked its tongue at Terra.

The snake was so massive that the boat tilted toward it, and the pitch of the engine changed as it lifted from the water.

"Kill the engine before it burns out!" Joana ordered, and Ana obeyed.

Suddenly, the roar of the engine vanished, and the sound of the splashing waves fell silent. Terra heard the snake's huge scales rasp against the deck.

"What do you want from me?" Terra demanded of the serpent.

"I crave nothing of you," the snake replied, then lunged at her, which was both rude and expected. Terra teleported out of the way. Not having to worry about the boat moving anymore, she reappeared a few feet away, exactly where she needed to be. Freya's ax was already in motion, coming down on the snake's head.

It saw its fate unfold, but it did not surrender to the path Terra had tried to make *seidr* put it on. It jerked its head back, displaying speed a creature of that size simply should not have possessed. Still, it was not fast enough to escape Terra's blow.

Freya's ax sliced through its massive slit eyes.

The snake hissed in dismay and flung itself backward, off the boat, and into the sea.

Finally, Terra saw the blood she had been waiting for since the battle began. Not enough, though.

The snake dove under, gained speed, then burst back from the water, more focused on Terra than ever. Great for the crew. For Terra? Not so much.

It rose over the top of the boat, then came down with such force that Terra popped into the air from the moving deck. She let her arms cartwheel as she clutched the ax. Let the snake think it had unbalanced the little human.

The snake lurched toward her, and Terra understood where it was moving to. At the height of being knocked into the air, she teleported into place.

Or she tried to.

When she attempted to activate the magical power, she felt a pressure where the flow of *seidr* should have been. Instead of disappearing and reappearing to the side of the snake's path, she fell through the air.

The snake struck. Terra got a bracer up, and its fang hit the metal, making it ring like a gong.

The blow knocked Terra back. She hit the deck and slid, crashing into the railing with the small of her back. She got back to her feet, but as soon as she tried to run forward, she found the huge serpent had snagged one of her ankles. She smashed to the deck, and massive coils of snake piled on top of her, trying to crush her.

She swung the ax as much as she could and heard the dull *slap* of metal on flesh. Hot blood sprayed her face, but she only managed one blow before the snake tightened its coils. It squeezed, and she could move no longer. Her muscles protested, then her bones, as the snake squeezed tighter.

"Terra!" Leif yelled distantly. Gunshots sounded, then something struck the snake. The shovel?

The snake's grip loosened, and she glimpsed the night sky again. Blotting out some of the stars was a mighty eagle. It dove for the snake's face, talons extended. The snake could have killed the bird with a single snap of its jaws, but it was protecting its single eye. Terra had already blinded half its face. It could not risk the other half.

Mads understood this as well as Leif did. However, instead of taking the form of a bird of prey, Mads fired slugs of metal at the snake's face.

It hissed at him, then released Terra to whip Mads with its long tail.

Terra got up and swung her ax into a section of its tail.

It hissed and jerked toward her. Then, it opened its jaws and sprayed venom from the back of its throat.

Terra reacted instinctively. She swung Freya's ax, creating both a fireball and a shield of energy. The two forms of magic, previously uncombined, joined together into a shield of flame that burned the venom droplets away. Only a few got through, landing on Terra's skin and burning worse than any fire.

Terra sent *seidr* to the places where the venom touched, and it fizzled into nothing.

She did not think she was capable of pulling off the same move to save her friends if the snake turned its venom on them. Unfortunately, it was in the process of doing exactly that.

Terra flipped her ax around, then leaped into the air. At the apex of her jump, she blasted out a wall of shielding fire. It reached her friends moments before the venom did, flaring brighter when the deadly poison landed.

"Get inside!" Terra yelled at Mads and Romero. "You can't let the venom touch you!"

Mads cursed, but he ducked inside the cabin. Romero followed him.

"Just the two of us," the snake hissed, but then Leif interrupted its little moment by dropping from the sky and clawing its face.

The snake flinched back from the bird, barely dodging before whipping its tail overheard and trying to knock him from the sky.

Terra was not going to let that happen. She stepped forward and grabbed the snake by its tail where it thickened, well away from the thrashing tip.

The snake did not so much turn its attention to her as try to kill her.

Its coils seemed to come from everywhere at once. One moment, Terra was grabbing it. The next, she was trapped inside its heavy bands of muscle.

"Feed, my brothers and sisters. Feed on the rest of them!" the snake hissed, then pulled Terra overboard.

She splashed into the water, using the shock as a catalyst to create a bubble of protective energy around herself. It could protect her from the cold of the ocean and allow her to breathe, even underwater, but it was not the sort of spell that would stop her ribs from being cracked.

However, Terra had no concern for herself.

The snake siblings had taken the word of their larger brother as an order and were crawling up the sides of the boat. The explosives had killed more than a hundred of them, and Leif, Mads, and Romero had killed dozens more, but there were still at least twenty.

And Terra couldn't do a damn thing to stop them.

Leif swooped overhead, still in the form of an eagle, and she told him to save her friends the only way she could think of.

"Tell Joana to move! Get away from here! I'll find you if I can!"

The snake yanked Terra under the surface and into the ocean's depths.

At times, it was hard to have faith. Being a believer could be the easiest thing in the world when things were going well, and perhaps it was even easier when good things were on the horizon. Faith could be harder to hold when bad things happened. It could feel nearly impossible to cling to that which we chose to believe when it seemed such faith was the very reason we suffered.

This was one of those moments for Leif.

He saw the Chosen of Freya and all her shining armaments pulled beneath the sea by a snake that could have sank their ship if it cared enough to bother.

Yet he *had* faith. He believed in the powers of his great-grandmother more than anything else. He believed in Freya more than he believed in the knowledge held in the library of Asgard. He believed in Freya more than he believed in the strength of Thor. Freya had put *her* faith in Terra, and Terra had put her faith in herself and in Leif.

That meant as much as Leif would have liked to dive under the sea, transform into a cormorant, and spear the snake's other eye with his beak, he would not.

Terra had told him to get the rest of the crew clear, and with good reason. Snakes were crawling from the sea, any one of which possessed the venom necessary to kill someone. Terra had put her faith in Leif to keep the others safe, presumably so that when she emerged triumphant from the ocean, they could continue with their mission.

So, as much as Leif hated abandoning Terra, he pushed the idea from his mind and returned to the ship. He was not abandoning her. He was keeping the faith. She would prevail in the depths, and when she did, she would need a warm towel and some of those garlic bagel crisps Leif had found in the cabin.

What she would not need was a ship full of snakes.

Leif pumped his wings and swooped down from the sky, talons extended. The second his foot touched a slippery, eel-like water snake, the talons snapped shut around it. It took no effort to hold the snake. The talons were made for plucking fish from the sea. By comparison, a snake was practically all grip. Leif bent his hooked beak and ripped the snake's throat out, then dropped its body into the water.

He swooped back toward the deck and found Mads and Romero at the cabin door. Mads had commandeered the shovel and used it to decapitate any snake that tried to come across the threshold. He had already killed a handful, and a puddle of blood and venom was pooling at his feet. It popped and sizzled like hot oil and water.

Leif landed on the cabin roof and took the form of a human.

"Don't touch that venom. It could be near-lethal, even from skin contact."

"Gee, ya think, mate? I could never have imagined venom from a pack of *goddamn magical water snakes* might be worth avoiding!"

"Fair point. I'll get back to it," Leif replied.

"I'd appreciate that!" Mads snapped.

"I'm going to do what I can to finish them off. Tell the captain to get out of here."

"But Terra—"

"Terra is the one who said to keep going. She'll be fine, but she can't fight to her fullest if she's worried about the rest of us."

Mads cursed mightily, but he nodded. "Let's get out of here!"

Joana had no questions of faith or loyalty to contend with. Her client had told her to drive away from the mass of poisonous snakes inexplicably crawling onto her boat with murder in their hearts. She did not hesitate to give the order, nor did Anna hesitate to fire up the engine.

Leif, still outside, transformed back into an eagle. He dove and swooped across the deck as it picked up speed. With a little finesse, he could use his talons to gore the snakes instead of grasping them. He became an angel of death, swooping down, slicing, and eviscerating serpent after serpent. Many died on the deck, but some were snagged by the hooked talons and careened into the sea.

The boat was soon almost free of the creeping reptiles.

"Leif, mate, help Terra! There's only a few of these squiggly bastards left. We can handle them!"

Leif had faith in Terra. However, his time on Earth meant he had a little faith in Mads, too. The snakes were nearly gone. Mads and Romero had a better chance than she did.

"I'll see you soon!" he called as he flew away.

"But if they survive, how are they going to catch up to us?" Leif heard Romero ask.

"If they survive, we're going to sit down and have a stiff drink and a long chat," Mads replied.

Then Leif could hear them no longer as he was flying back toward Terra. She was his grandmother's chosen. She had great strength and even greater spirit. If anyone could persevere against the serpent, it was her.

Leif flew as fast as he possibly could, all the same.

CHAPTER TWELVE

Underwater, the Gulf of Bothnia, Saturday night

Terra felt the pressure both from the sea and the snake's crushing coils. The only reason she was still alive was because she had both pressures to contend with. The snake seemed convinced it could pop her head like a grape simply by pulling her deeper into the water instead of using its coils to properly squeeze the life out of her.

Yet Terra still had her bubble, and she used it to protect her from the power of the sea.

Finally, when she was so deep that the starlight was gone, the snake released her.

She floated as the snake came around, then unhinged its jaw as it swam at her. She knew it was a huge creature, but she had not realized it could swallow her in a single bite. Now, she understood.

She swung her ax at its open mouth, and it jerked backward, surprised its prey was still alive. Terra tried to take advantage of that surprise and teleport away, but the snake was not shocked enough at her still being alive to let her get away so easily.

That was fine. Terra could breathe down here as long as she had her bubble. She could cut through the scales with her ax. She could win this, though it did not look like it would be easy.

The snake moved toward her. Terra swung her ax, but it was already somewhere else, attacking from a different angle. It was shockingly agile in the water, and Terra was doing her best to simply keep her ax between herself and the serpent's jaws. Surely, such a large creature should not be able to move at such speeds, but the snake clearly had magic in its blood. Therefore, the rules did not affect it.

Terra, on the other hand, was not particularly adept at fighting underwater. She found her strikes were slower, though she could put more power into them as if she was able to push off against every square inch of water. It might have given her an advantage over a regular foe, but the snake was already comfortable in the water and more powerful than it was nimble. All her added strength truly did was let her keep up.

The snake knew it, too. It kept darting toward her but pulling its strike at the last second, forcing Terra to expend energy dodging and preparing to block. The snake, on the other hand, was so large that it hardly had to move to get a different position to attack. She felt like she was being toyed with, and she did not like it.

So when she felt the snake's tail try to wrap around her ankle *again,* she let it. The great beast thought it could try the same trick? Let it think that. One coil wrapped around her ankle, then another. Before the snake could pull her into the much larger rolls of its body, Terra swung downwards with all her might and chopped into the tail. At the tip, the scales were not so hardy. The ax went through them, then the skin, the flesh, and all the way to the bone.

The snake tried to yank its tail away, but it lacked control. Instead of releasing Terra and pulling away, it simply dragged her through the water. That was fine with Terra. She had been water skiing before.

She straightened her body out, and before the snake whipped her in a different direction, she swung down and sliced. The tip of its tail came clean off, and blood clouded the water.

Leif was too slow. Despite flying back as fast as he could and spotting Terra beneath the surface, he was unable to reach her in time.

And he had been so close. He had transformed into a cormorant, dove into the churning sea, and pumped his wings to swim after her. Yet before he could get close enough to make any difference, more of the smaller white snakes surrounded him.

They were much more difficult to dispatch with a cormorant's beak than the hooked talons of an eagle, and Leif was only able to escape a few of them before he had to change back into his human form.

He had been in Asgard long enough to watch the importance of sea travel rise on Earth. Part of his training had been how to survive at sea, so almost by instinct, he made a bubble around himself.

It was not enough to protect him from the snakes.

They came fast and all at once. None of that human hesitation, none of the instinct to wait and see if another warrior could do the dirty work before you had to. The snakes surged at Leif as if each wanted to personally be the first to rip a chunk of flesh from him.

He lit up his knuckles with white-hot fire and cracked one in the skull. Its scales blistered on contact, and it faded away.

Leif had chosen correctly.

He made the heat spread from his knuckles across his hands and slapped around his body. He was using magic faster than he ever had in his life. It was the sort of expenditure that, if he'd read about it in the libraries of Asgard, he would have checked the author's sources. Water boiled as his fingers passed, and snake after snake tasted the heat of his energy and burned away, their blood unable to handle the rapid temperature change.

Still, some got through.

Leif felt pain in his calf so intense that he nearly dropped his protective bubble of air simply to feel the cold of the sea against the wound.

Fangs pierced his shoulder. He grabbed a tiny snake, no larger than a pen, that nonetheless had caused a considerable amount of damage.

The pain crept through him, and Leif knew the venom was at work. It would be heading for his heart, or his brain, or his soul, given the nature of the snakes.

Leif would not allow it.

He took the burning heat from his hands and pulled it back inside. The veins in his fingers stood out, crackling and popping as if made of electricity. They glowed white and threw sparks as the energy moved through the back of his hands to his wrists, forearms, and biceps. The energy reached his core and found the venom attempting to get past. Leif flared the energy, and the venom burned away. His entire body was glowing now, but still, the snakes did not retreat.

They were foolish and practically suicidal. They showed none of the battle awareness their larger sibling had. Were these recently hatched and yet to learn about the consequences of their actions? Or were they some sort of magical spawn? If they were babies, why had so many hatched at once?

Leif wanted the answers to these questions but would not get them. The snakes continued snapping at him, so Leif kept his hands moving. He chopped, grabbed, and punched, imparting bursts of heat to every one of the slithering reptiles that dared get close to him. Still, there were too many, and he only had two hands.

Between keeping his fingers pulsing with heat and his veins coursing with the same energy to burn away the venom, he was going to run out of *seidr* and drown.

So he extinguished his hands and brought the energy from his veins into his core. When a half-dozen of the snakes had sunk their fangs into him, he unleashed a wave of lightning that shot out from him in all directions.

One moment, snakes were mobbing him. The next, he was in the middle of a sphere of snakes trying to escape as they fried to death. Leif kicked away from the carnage toward the giant, swirling cloud of blood that had consumed Terra and the largest snake of them all.

Before he made any progress, the snake emerged from the cloud, fury in its remaining eye.

It knew what Leif had done to its fellow snakes, and it was going to make him pay.

It looked like Terra already had.

In the haze of blood, Terra thought she would have the advantage. She thought she could move in the cloudy water and avoid the snake's detection.

She was wrong.

While Terra primarily used her vision to fight, the snake used its sense of smell and vibrations.

Every time she moved in the water, she sent tiny ripples out the giant snake could feel with every inch of its body. She swam a few feet through the murk, and the snake's head appeared, tongue flicking. It opened wide and tried to swallow her.

She kicked into a backflip and managed to put her feet on the snake's upper lip and kick off. By the time she got her ax around to swing, it was too late. The snake had vanished into the cloud of its own blood.

Terra thought she could tell which direction it went and swam that way, only to find the water cloudy, not with blood but venom. Droplets passed through her magical barrier, and her skin burned.

A flash of *seidr* took care of the burning, but the snake could sense the *seidr* even more easily than her movements.

As soon as she flared the magic, the snake was there, ready to gore her with a fang. She barely dodged and clobbered the side of the snake's neck with her ax. Despite plenty of strength behind the blow, it did not break the scales. They were incredibly durable, and only her most well-aimed shots could cut through them.

Not a great situation to be in when she couldn't see a damn thing.

Something moved against her, and she struck out, but the snake was already on the other side, tightening its coils around her. She was trapped again. Trapped in a cloud of blood that she thought might be a harbinger of the battle to come. It had been, she supposed. Only it had portended the wrong outcome.

The snake coiled more tightly, and Terra felt a rib pop out of place. She tried to flex, to break free, to dig the ax into a weak spot, but it held her too tightly. It was over.

The snake wanted to make sure of that.

Its great head rose from the murk. It glared at her with its one good eye, drew back, and lanced her through the shoulder with a giant fang.

Pain exploded in the wound and radiated outward, an internal firework of agony.

Then, the snake released her. Forgotten.

It pumped its long tail back and forth, clearing the water enough for Terra to see Leif. He was higher up, near the surface of the water, being bitten by more snakes than Terra could count.

They were all wriggling and trying to escape. Leif was frying them with a pulse of electricity.

"My siblings!" the giant snake hissed, coming to the aid of its tiny kin. It was too late. Leif had killed all the snakes.

Already, debris from their rapidly dissolving bodies clouded the water around him.

It was an awesome show of power, more impressive because when Leif first came to Midgard, there was no way he could have accomplished anything close to it.

Terra might have taken the time for pride if Leif hadn't looked exhausted from the effort.

He turned to face the giant serpent pumping its body toward him through the water and grimaced. His movements looked sluggish. He had to be exhausted, but he still created a shield around himself before the snake snapped its huge jaws.

Terra had to help. She tried to swim toward the snake, but the pain was so severe that she could hardly move. She was not going to die like this. She would not be poisoned to death while she watched her friend being eaten. Her fate would not end here. This was not why she was chosen by Freya.

She felt the power of Freya's ax in her hand, the master of all magic. It was a more formidable weapon than the venom of some snake. She called upon it to let her keep fighting, to let her end this battle in victory before she succumbed to the cold of the ocean or the venom in her veins.

Then, the pain lessened. *Seidr* had felt the same fate she had foreseen for herself, and the power of the ax took away some of the venom to help her achieve that fate.

Time to make it happen.

She swam toward the snake, but she was too slow. The snake was crushing Leif. It had stopped trying to bite him and was wrapping him in its heavy coils. He still had a shield up, but it was only a matter of time before the snake popped it like the bubble it was.

Leif had given up on overpowering the snake and was trying to reason with it, bless his heart.

"Just tell us what you want of Midgard, and we can help! Did Jörmungandr put you up to this? We know his siblings! We can work with you!" She could hear him thanks to the bubble he wore. Amazing that he could make the power work despite being in the jaws of the angry monster.

The snake hissed at the mention of the legendary world serpent.

"I hunger," it hissed. "I hunger, and your flesh has what I crave."

So, that was creepy.

Terra felt the truth of it, though. The snake was hurt and wanted magic, food, or both, presumably to restore itself. It thought Leif would be the equivalent of a protein shake. Terra could not let that happen. She would rather die in battle than watch her friend eaten by this horrendous serpent. If that was the effect of a Viking goddess of battle on her psyche, so be it.

With the snake's energy focused on Leif, and perhaps because she had wounded it, it was no longer suppressing her ability to teleport. Maybe it thought it had beaten her badly enough that she was no longer a threat. Maybe it didn't have the energy. It almost surely did not expect another magical morsel to appear before its open jaws.

However, when Terra teleported next to Leif, the snake knew it. It opened its jaws wider, and as its fangs neared them, tiny streams of dark poison flowed from the hollow tips, leaving cloudy streams in the water.

"Drop the barrier. Mind the fangs," Terra told Leif.

He was accustomed to her teleporting and appearing next to him. Less so to her telling him to drop the only bit of magic protecting him from certain death.

"I think it would be easier to mind the fangs with the barrier intact," Leif stated, but then he obeyed Terra's command and let it drop away.

The giant snake was much too close for them to dodge. Much too powerful for them to have any chance of escaping. Terra grabbed Leif and held him close as the unhinged jaws of the serpent snapped down on both of them.

Teeth were all around them, and despite the huge fangs being the only ones capable of injecting its prey with venom, a mix of water and the deadly fluid filled its mouth. It stung Terra's eyes and her skin, especially where she had been gored.

Still, what was a little pain to the Chosen of Freya?

Terra had not allowed herself to be eaten by accident. She had done battle with the snake and found it a formidable foe. She was barely able to cut through its plate-like scales. After she had, though, its flesh proved far less protected.

Now, she had gotten past all those scales.

Ax in hand, Terra plunged into the snake's throat. She turned backward and saw Leif, barely visible in the gloom of the snake's mouth. Little more than a pair of glinting lights that were his magical spectacles.

More light poured into the snake when she sliced her ax through its throat. She tore its flesh, its veins, its muscles. Blood and gore sprayed her, then the magic of the snake was disrupted, and her ax ripped through its scales to the outside.

Terra willed herself to cut against the snake and pushed down until she burst from the giant gash in its body, perhaps ten feet lower than where she'd started.

The snake was dead.

It had been swimming for the surface. No longer.

It was still drifting upward, but barely.

Leif swam from the hole in its neck.

"That was awful," he complained.

Terra said nothing. She kept her eyes on the snake. It had to be dead. She had cut through the muscles and veins in its throat. Nothing could survive that. She hoped.

Fortunately, the snake did not seem prone to resurrection. It stopped drifting upward and sank into the abyss.

As it fell, the scales nearest the lethal wound Terra had inflicted flaked away, then crumbled into powder. After the scales were gone, the flesh underneath dissolved into blood, then its bones disintegrated as it fell deeper into the dark of the sea.

Fish came, as fish did, and nibbled at the rapidly disintegrating corpse. They seemed frustrated with the meal, as it kept breaking down faster than they could eat.

In less than a minute, all that remained of the legless leviathan was a single scale. It drifted back and forth. The fish followed it, nibbling at its edges.

Leif gestured with his fingers, and a mote of energy blasted out and turned the scale into ash that swirled into the water. The fish scattered from the energy blast. When they returned, they found nothing to satiate their appetite.

"Better safe than sorry," Leif stated. "I'm not quite certain what the life cycle of giant talking snakes is, but considering we saw so many of them, I don't think it's a lengthy process. And, of course, some foods can change the eater into nightmares of every sort."

"No complaints here," Terra replied. "I tried to keep a souvenir from the last one, and it broke anyway."

They swam for the surface, broke through, and dropped the bubbles around themselves. The air felt colder than the ocean, but seeing the moon above was a relief.

"Any idea which way they went?" Leif asked.

Terra scanned the horizon and spotted a pair of blinking lights. At this distance, she could not be sure it was the *Skidbladnir*, but they had not seen any other ships out here in the cold sea at night, so it seemed likely. Frankly, Terra was tired, and her shoulder hurt like hell. If it was a fishing boat, they'd almost certainly have coffee, which was good enough for her.

"Take my hand," Terra invited. Leif did, and Terra teleported them in the general direction of the ship. It took a few tries to cross the sea's surface. Not the most pleasant way to travel. Terra did not think she could teleport them directly into the water, so she had to make them appear a foot or so above the surface each time. Which meant each teleportation was followed by an icy plunge.

After a few of these, they got close enough to the ship to see it was the *Skidbladnir*. It was moving along slowly, and the crew aboard was shuffling across the deck with water hoses and mops, so the threat had passed.

Terra teleported her and Leif onto the deck of the ship.

"Terra!" Mads shouted and ran toward them.

"Nice to see you, too," Leif muttered while Mads wrapped Terra in a huge hug. It hurt when he squeezed her. It hurt quite badly.

"I knew you'd make it," Mads told Leif. "You're too stubborn to die."

"I am not," Leif replied stubbornly.

Mads grinned and threw an arm around his shoulder. "Good to have you back, mate. You don't look so bad, especially compared to her." Mads nodded at Terra's shoulder, and she glanced down.

A hole remained between her breast and shoulder. Purple gunk dripped from it, and veins of angry red and purple marks radiated outward. She hadn't completely cleared the poison, then.

"Same nasty crap that's on the deck," Mads pointed out. Indeed, the crew was mostly spraying the residue of snakes away, which included quite a bit of noxious venom. One of the crew's push brooms was smoking.

"So much for a low profile," Terra muttered.

She went through a series of movements Leif had taught her to center herself and invigorate her body. It was an exercise Leif used to warm up for battle and to test himself after an injury. Terra associated it with being healthy and hale. When it came to magic, intention was the most important factor.

As she performed the movements, she focused on Freya's ax in her hand and used its power to purify not only herself but the entire crew and the deck itself.

A minute later, she finished the movements and felt a gentle warmth radiate from the ax. It washed over her, and she loosened up as the venom was expunged from the wound in her shoulder, and the hole closed up.

After her body was fully healed, she released a wave of energy so sparkling and effervescent that any cartoon princess worth their beloved prince would have been impressed. The sparkling shockwave spread across the deck, then dropped and pushed all the venom into the sea. The world's most magical squeegee.

"You're better!" Mads exclaimed.

"Not a bad trick, that," Leif added.

"Do you need anything?" Romero asked when he approached. He held a large, shiny knife. It must have been dripping with snake ichor moments ago until Terra's magic cleaned it.

Terra looked toward the east and saw the first hint of dawn illuminating the night sky.

"Seeing as I'm not going to be getting any sleep, I could really go for a cup of coffee."

CHAPTER THIRTEEN

The cabin of the *Skidbladnir*, the Gulf of Bothnia, Sunday morning

The *Skidbladnir* crew accepted the events of the previous night with a surprising amount of grace. Terra had expected the captain to scream at them, to curse them for dragging her into the nightmare the previous night had been, but she did not. When she heard that Terra wanted coffee, she ordered a fresh pot brewed, then placed an order for breakfast as well.

"About last night," Terra tried to start the conversation.

Joana held up a hand to silence her, and Terra was more than happy to stop speaking.

"Your employer paid us a good deal more than we usually charge, and we are not a cheap vessel. I had not expected magical snakes...but we're all right, so I guess that might be enough. Can we expect more things like this to happen?"

Terra wanted to say no. She wanted to say they had

beaten the worst of them, and it should be a relative cakewalk from here on out. But she couldn't lie to the captain.

"We should expect more of the snakes, at least. We might be lucky, and they'll wait until dusk. I haven't seen one during the day yet. If we can complete our mission before then, it might change how things go."

"We will do our best to be prepared," Captain Joana replied, then politely excused herself. Terra knew the feeling. It was not easy to discover that not only did magic exist, but its existence imperiled those who knew about it.

She sat at a table in the main cabin. A moment later, she was served a steaming cup of hot coffee. She sipped it appreciably, savoring the bitterness.

"Do you have any cream?" Leif asked one of the crew.

"You barely survive a battle with a sea serpent, and you still need cream in your coffee?" Mads scoffed.

"It's *because* I barely survived that I *want* cream. What's the point of all this struggle and strife if there are no perks?"

"That's actually a pretty good way to live your life," Romero put in.

Terra had given up on keeping anything from Romero. He was on this mission for additional security, which meant he had to be ready to fight off hordes of magical snakes with deadly venom. They could not afford to keep him in the dark any longer.

Everyone looked like they had a million questions to ask, but before they could, Alfred brought out a platter heaped with pancakes, scrambled eggs, sausages, pickled fish, and a pitcher of fruit juice. They dug in, and for a moment, it almost felt like a snippet of a regular life.

Maybe they were tourists out here in the north to see a rare bird or a whale and had gone through the misfortune of a stormy night that left everyone sleepless and out of sorts. How could one eat a pancake and deem it needing more syrup in a world where giant talking snakes tried to swallow one whole? It hardly seemed like the two situations could exist at once, and Terra thought that might be because they were not supposed to.

Midgard and the world of the giants were not merely different planets but different *realms.* These snakes might have looked like reptiles from Earth, but appearance was the only thing they shared. They had spent their night battling with otherworldly beings. That they could do that, then eat pancakes for breakfast, was nothing short of miraculous.

They would have to do their best to ensure they enjoyed another breakfast the next morning.

"So, this artifact. Seems like the snakes are after it. Is there a museum they want to put it in or something?" Romero asked.

Terra snorted a laugh. "We moved on from battling archeologists a while back."

"That's not true," Mads pointed out. "We just dealt with half-dead Goodwin."

"But he wasn't really an archeologist anymore, was he? More of an undead avatar for Hel."

"He was still an archeologist," Terra insisted. "That's one of the main reasons she picked him. She knew he would be able to find the pieces of Freya for her. He only had those skills *because* he was an archeologist. And a good one, too, even if he did try to kill me multiple times with that necro touch of his."

Romero's mouth hung wide open with half-chewed pancake inside. "And by *she*, you mean—"

"Hel. Beautiful, mate, let me tell you. Until she turns her face." Mads picked up his napkin and blocked his face from Romero. He dropped it a moment later to reveal a ghoulish expression.

Romero remembered to chew his pancake. He swallowed, then sipped his coffee as he tried to work up the gall to ask what he needed to ask. Terra didn't blame him. If anything, she felt bad that they had not fully informed him of the situation sooner. He obviously knew they were dealing with more than knives and guns, but it was apparent Mads had not told him everything there was to know about their little operation.

"So this is all some Viking shit?" was the best he could manage.

"Norse, technically," Leif countered.

"Which means?"

"We're on the hunt for artifacts left on Midgard by Freya, the goddess of beauty and battle."

"The…goddess."

"That's how these two think of it, mate, but I'm not so certain," Mads offered. "I was raised a good Christian, right? I can't be out here gallivanting around, dealing with the Norse gods."

Romero waited for the but.

"But the fact is these artifacts are something special." Mads winked. "Terra nearly has the entire set, and each one grants her a different ability."

"And they were made by a goddess?"

"Almost certainly not," Leif insisted.

Romero looked visibly relieved.

"They were mostly made by dwarfs," Leif explained. "Freya has an appreciation for things of beauty, but she is no craftsman. These objects are sacred to her, though."

"And there's no denying they make Terra something fantastic in a fight," Mads added.

"And you're looking for the last one?" Romero asked.

Terra nodded.

"But you don't know what it is?"

"Not exactly."

"What about what it does?"

"Uncertain."

Romero nodded, taking this in. He had worked in security for a long time, so he was accustomed to known unknowns.

"What do these other things do?" he asked.

"Most of my power comes from the bracers. They give me enhanced strength and agility."

"As well as the ability to breathe underwater, make fireballs and darts of light, amplify sound, and a hundred other uses you should really practice more often," Leif expounded.

"Jesus," Romero blurted.

"Not at play, technically," Mads corrected.

"This piece of metal around my neck is called Brísingamen. It allows me to teleport from one place to another instantaneously."

"So *that's* why no one was worried when you were left behind the boat."

"I was worried, mate, don't get me wrong. But if the choice was to sit there and bite my nails while I whimpered about it or stomp those snakes' skulls into pixie dust, I'm going to pick the more active role."

"Sure. Fair," Romero agreed. "The feathered cloak is one of them too, right? I know the eagle helping us was actually Leif."

"Very perceptive," Leif told him.

"You still had your glasses on while you were hunting snakes, mate. Wasn't exactly hard to piece together that the eagle wearing glasses was the same as the big, tall bloke who literally vanished before the eagle appeared."

"Plus, you didn't wear the cloak until then," Romero added. Terra could see the gears turning behind his eyes. He was coming to terms with this or trying to. Romero knew he needed to understand the situation, at least somewhat, if he was going to survive it.

"We normally leave the artifacts in Terra's possession, but I have studied with some of them and learned to use them since I came here."

"To Earth."

"We call it Midgard where we're from," Leif explained.

Romero nodded and blinked, nodded and blinked, trying to internalize the impossible information. "And then there's the ax. Is that it?"

"Technically, Terra used the golden tears when she died. They are no longer in her possession, but they have passed through her, and she gave them to her…benefactor, so I believe those still count."

"You died." Romero actually sounded *less* shocked. People coming back from the dead was a thing in many religions and folktales, and even regular people sometimes claimed to witness it. Compared to magically empowered jewelry, it wasn't much of a stretch.

"No, I didn't," Terra stated.

Leif and Mads said nothing. They looked at her, then at each other, then away.

"It was a close thing, and yes, I was healed in an unusual way. The ax is my most powerful artifact, though. It can cut through other magic and was created to master *seidr*. Sometimes, it takes time to figure out how to best use it, but it has not failed me yet."

"I don't know," Leif retorted. "Would you really call being eaten by a snake a success?"

"You what?" Mads nearly spit out his coffee.

"We did not *get eaten*. We tricked it into letting us get past its scales," Terra countered.

"I guess you didn't want to tell me that because the taste of my urine in the water was more convincing to the snake that I was genuinely scared?" Leif asked.

"I was going to say you need a new wetsuit, but now you definitely do," Terra remarked.

Everyone laughed, even Romero. So he was adjusting to this new reality, or trying to, anyway.

"So these snakes are old-time baddies? You've tangled with them before?"

"Not really, no," Terra returned. "You were there when it was Beatrice and Forseti. After that, we dealt with—well, let's call him someone with superhuman strength, then a woman leading a cult of people who worshipped death."

"If that's the version of the story you think I can handle,

we can leave it at that," Romero decided. "But the snakes are new?"

"They are indeed a new development," Leif affirmed.

"Terra messed with one already."

"But I didn't think they would be out here," Terra stated. "Maybe by the actual site, but not in the middle of nowhere."

"I was surprised they attacked a ship like this one. Modern, sleek, you'd think they would know it was a real challenge," Romero observed.

"Not all that smart," Leif suggested. "I don't think they understand much of the modern world, nor do they wish to. They were driven by hunger, one that isn't sated by fish and kelp. I think they really are attracted to magic."

"But I thought creatures that needed magic could not exist on Midgard?" Mads questioned.

"Oh, so there's rules to all this crazy shit now?" Romero asked.

"How they got here is anyone's guess," Leif stated. "There seems to be something to them being drawn to magic, though. I think they emerged somewhere in the water and are now coming for what magic they can sense.

"As they grow, they seem to become somewhat more intelligent, and they likely need more magic to sustain them. Though considering how large that one was and the limits of its vocabulary, I shudder to consider the size of one that could truly hold a decent conversation."

"Wait, the snakes talk?"

"Oh, yes. Although they aren't great at holding a conversation, it seems," Leif replied to Romero.

"Uh, yeah. I got that vibe."

"And we still don't know where they're from?" Mads asked.

"Well, I tried to speak with the largest of them. When I asked about Jörmungandr, I was answered with a particularly vicious hiss. It seemed like perhaps they were angry with the world serpent. That and their appearance makes me think they are his offspring in some way."

"So magic snakes with daddy issues. Great," Mads muttered.

"Did it give you any idea how many there were?" Terra asked.

"It did not share with me anything about its brood size, no," Leif replied.

"Well, there were some in Spain," Mads pointed out. "So I think there's quite a lot."

"We just faced *quite a lot*," Romero countered.

"Indeed. Because of their great number, I hesitate to think we can hunt them all down. I wonder if it would be better to let them grow to the size where the magic cannot sustain them. They might disintegrate from the lack of power if they get large enough."

"That might be how they do things in Asgard, but we're not doing that here. How long would it even take? A week would be too long."

"I imagine it would be a bit longer than that, yes. And you are correct, of course. Without a stone wall to protect it like Asgard has, Midgard would be overrun with the snakes."

"What about if we get to the source?" Terra asked. "They came over here somehow. Can we figure that out and force them back the same way?"

"Perhaps." Leif shoved a bite of egg into his mouth. "At the least, we might be able to shut off their access to magic and starve them out. I don't think they would last long in this realm without magic, considering how they all break apart when they die."

"But how would we do that?" Terra asked. "We can't go to Jörmungandr's front door and ask him to make his kids leave us alone."

"Actually, that's not a terrible idea." Leif shoved a huge piece of pancake in his mouth, forcing them to wait for him to elaborate as they watched him chew.

"Pretty sure this boat doesn't go to the edge of the world or wherever he lives, mate," Mads suggested.

"No, of course not. When I first came here, the idea of going to another realm would have been laughable, but you're more powerful than you were then. It would be possible to make a portal spell, I would think."

"I thought it was difficult to travel between the realms," Terra pointed out. "Hel was obsessed with being able to do it. She wanted the pieces of Freya to do exactly that. Oh, duh."

"Precisely! If we can find the final piece of Freya, you can open a portal there. Currently, I lack the power and the esteem, but I think it could work for you. I have the spell for it, at least. We could try."

"If Freya's pieces will allow us to travel there, can't we ask her?" Terra wondered.

"She will respond in dire moments, as she did when you nearly died, I might point out. I hardly think this qualifies. You cleaned the venom from the deck easily enough."

"Oh, wow. She'll help you out, but only when it's that

bad?" Romero asked. "Sounds like an American insurance company."

"I do not want it to come that," Leif insisted. "But we are close! I can feel it!"

"I've heard this before," Mads remarked.

"It's true," Leif claimed. "I don't have my map on me, but I checked, and it confirms what I already felt. We are closer than we have been and on the right track. Terra, can you sense it yet?"

Terra had been contemplating that question. In answer, she found her bracers were glowing. She moved them around, and they seemed to glow most brightly when pointing directly ahead. "That's new," she mused.

"So we find this last piece of Freya, then what, head out to meet a galactic-sized snake?" Mads asked.

Romero shook his head. "I think I preferred it when it was people trying to kill me with bullets. Simpler than all this."

CHAPTER FOURTEEN

The deck of the *Skidbladnir*, the Gulf of Bothnia, Monday afternoon

No more snakes, demigods, or Jotun attacked for the remainder of their voyage. Neither did any pirates nor the ghosts of Vikings.

Terra was no longer certain which of these things were genuine threats and which were not. She could not help but think the snakes had stayed away for a reason. Had they defeated the largest one? Or was there a bigger brother or sister out there plotting vengeance?

Despite her misgivings, she was eventually able to fall asleep and nap through the late afternoon and night. So when she woke late the next morning, she felt well-rested and ready for more of whatever the nine realms threw at her.

As they neared their destination, the sea changed. They knew they were getting close because Leif's map bore a golden mark that he assured them he had not put there. They were nearing the final piece of Freya. Terra would take up the mantle of the goddess of battle. If she could survive the journey there.

She had never spent much time on the ocean, but she could tell something was odd about where they were. It was the middle of nowhere. The horizon was as empty as it had been for the entire day, yet the water seemed different.

The waves crested more here as if they could feel an island hidden beneath the surface. Terra kept thinking she saw shadows in the water, the outlines of ancient buildings or drowned trees, but the surveillance hardware and mapping software detected nothing.

When she told Leif about what she sensed, he did not discount it.

"Sometimes, things leave ripples through the threads of *seidr*. My grandmother would not have chosen this place without reason. There was power here then, and power still remains. You are probably sensing some of that."

"Does that mean the snakes might be here?" Terra asked. "If they are attracted to magic, do you think they're drawn to this place?"

"We should assume they are, yes," Leif confirmed. "Though considering they have been spotted all around the world, perhaps we won't have to contend with so many of them."

Terra gave him a long look, and his resolute optimism faded like footprints on the beach at high tide.

"You really think we're going to get this one easily?" Terra pressed.

"No, not at all." Leif chuckled.

"Pardon me, but we've got something." Captain Joana approached the pair of them with obvious deference. After the battle with the serpents, the captain's demeanor had changed. She had always been respectful, but now she treated her passengers as something more than human. It should not have been so odd to Terra since she'd battled a giant snake underwater for more than ten minutes, but it kept making her wonder about her humanity.

Was she even still human? She *felt* human and wanted to belong with the people of Earth, but was that delusional? Sometimes, the Norse gods came to Earth and walked among the people here. Was Terra's continued presence here no more than that? She was certainly different than Captain Joana and her crew. More powerful. More aware. With responsibilities no mortal should have.

It was a lot to think about. Keeping it all in her head made Terra feel aloof, which only heightened the distance between her and the captain. Would more of these moments come if the world learned about the magic in her control? Only time would tell. For now, she was lucky enough to have an extremely capable and seemingly unflappable captain in control of the ship they needed for their mission.

"What have you got?" Terra asked.

"Might be easier to show you, but I think we found your lost city."

Terra followed Joana into the main cabin and to the cockpit. A few screens showed different readouts of the data they were drawing in. The SONAR came back with an interesting mix of ninety-degree angles, but the 3D model stole the show.

The computer was compiling all it could to show what remained of a village. Most of it was nothing but lumpy piles, but they were regularly spaced and ran in more or less straight lines. Terra understood them to be homes or maybe storage buildings. Maybe twenty of these piles in different shapes and sizes appeared. Some were relatively well preserved, revealing the regular geometry of their floor plans, while the currents and tides had scattered others.

"They built on top of this hill. They must have seen the sea rise higher and higher before it took everything. Well, nearly everything."

Joana scrolled through the 3D model to reveal not everything had been destroyed. Past the piles of rubble, there appeared to be a fully intact building, sitting there at the bottom of the sea.

"I'm going to go out on a limb here and assume that's your target."

"Absolutely," Terra replied. She had no doubt the artifact, and likely another beautifully carved and impossibly well-preserved statue of Freya, waited inside.

"How close can you get us?"

"Not close. The land rises even higher behind that temple. It almost looks like they built into a hill or something. There's a few more elevated features like that around here. I'm sure you noticed the water looks different? That's because it's not as deep."

"It's too shallow for you to get close?"

"Not exactly," Joana revealed. "A few dead tree trunks are still sticking up here and there, but quite frankly, it's the threat of the snakes. I can't take this boat into an area with less maneuverability if there's any chance those things will come back. I can't risk my crew. That is unless you can guarantee there won't be any more?"

"If I could promise you that, I would have already," Terra countered. "Unfortunately, it's probably wise to expect more of them. I'm glad none attacked while we traveled this way, but they are attracted to the…energy in the area."

"I saw you do impossible things. I understand the snakes are also impossible, but that means I need to stay back while you go in."

"I understand. Thank you for everything. I know it can be a lot."

Joana shrugged. "Sometimes it gets old looking at seabirds and whales. Now, though, I find it's all I want to do for the rest of my career."

Terra chuckled. "I know what you mean. The prospect of finding a bunch of coins guarded by nothing but layers of debris sounds a lot better after last night than it did a month ago."

"I guess we can't ever go back, huh?"

"Better to move forward," Terra agreed. "Now, if you'll excuse me, I'm going to suit up."

"Oh, yeah? You're going to actually wear a wet suit this time instead of pajamas and jewelry?"

"Figure I should look the part," Terra quipped and excused herself.

She found Leif and Mads below deck, already suiting up.

"How did you know we found it?" Terra asked.

"Leif showed me his map, but I was already down here,"

Mads replied. "It's not like we stopped so we could go shopping."

"Fair point, but I thought you were going to take the sub," Terra suggested.

"It was damaged in the snake attack," Mads told her. "Their venom messed up some of the components. Alfred says it should be fine, but I'd rather not go into a nest of snakes in a tin can that's not functioning to the best of its abilities.

"Romero still going to stay up top?" Terra asked.

"That's the plan. If anything goes wrong, and we can be sure something is absolutely going to go *quite* wrong, we'll need someone to bail us out. Or at least to recover our bodies and tell the boss man what happened."

"Cheery as ever!" Leif announced.

"You bringing all your magic weapons, I assume?" Mads asked.

"I was planning on it. I have the cloak in a waterproof pouch and the ax in a case. I'm not planning on using the SCUBA gear, but if something goes wrong with my magic, I don't want to learn that I accidentally sliced through an air hose."

"Hopefully, we'll be able to find the piece quickly. If snakes were here, they would have already attacked," Mads suggested.

"Unless they're waiting for us to get off the boat."

"Or if they can't get the piece and want us to figure out how."

"They might be nocturnal. It's still daylight, after all."

"You two are not the best at pep talks, you know?"

"Truthfully, I agree finding the piece will be the simple

part." Leif was fully suited up and poking through a leather-bound tome that Terra knew possessed all sorts of magical spells. He traced symbols in the air while looking at the book. "I wish I could bring this down with me, but the water makes that impossible."

"You don't normally use a magic book for your spells," Mads observed. "Why now?"

"I brought this with me from Asgard and have been using it to guide our training. Normally, the things we do are simple, but this spell is another thing entirely. Technically, I'll be casting it on the behest of our Chosen here, which complicates things. But as long as I get the symbols right, I think we can manage the intention without much trouble."

"Are they especially fancy symbols?" Terra asked.

"Not particularly, no. They are the same runes Odin came to understand after trading his eye for the wisdom at Mimir's Well. That is the wisdom of runes and the letters that followed, which you all know. Complex concepts can be spun into being with a few simple sounds and ideas."

"But you know all those. You've worked in a library for your entire life," Mads pointed out.

"Of course, the runes themselves are not special. It is the proper position and the correct order that matters. I will be drawing them in the air with no paper for reference, so I have to get them all correct without being able to see what I'm doing."

"So, if you get it wrong, what? You have to try again?"

"Well, if I abort the sequence early enough, yes. However, if I form too much of the spell and do it incorrectly, I may accidentally send us to Muspelheim. Not all the realms are as well protected as Midgard. It's the middle realm and thus held in balance. Most of the rules on the lower realms keep things from getting *out,* not getting in."

"And by Muspelheim, you mean…"

"The burning world of fire giants," Terra supplied.

Mads' expression made it clear he did not need her to elaborate.

The stakes were high, and Terra could not help but lean over and take a peek at Leif's book. "Make sure those are crosses and not X's."

Leif smirked. "As restless as you were all winter, I'm surprised you didn't want to go to Muspelheim simply to have a bit of a brawl."

"Let's get the last piece of Freya first and make sure there's no more snakes before we start talking about battle royales with giants," Terra insisted.

"Well, we absolutely *must* get the last piece of Freya before we attempt any of this. If I were to try this spell now, the best we could hope for would be to end up on a branch of Yggdrasil. And even if we could see the realm surrounding Midgard, where Jörmungandr's domain is, getting there across the twisting paths of the world tree is no simple task. Why, even if we find Ratatoskr, he lies as much as he tells the truth."

"So, assuming we find the piece and open the portal, what happens then?" Terra asked.

"Well, the spell I am working on won't technically take us there. I cannot make such a portal. What I can do is create a sort of portal request. When I do that, you step in front of it, and it should open up."

"It *should?*" Mads asked.

"Well, I've never done anything like this before, and I'm sort of winging it!" Leif exclaimed.

"Winging it? Mate, you can't wing us to the wrong realm!"

"That won't happen. Assuming I get the runes correct, we will send a request to Jörmungandr's domain, and he should allow us to enter."

"What if he says no?"

"That's what I'm not sure of. It's possible Terra can simply force her way in. Terra and Odin have that ability, and despite claiming the contrary, we all think Loki can do it as well. If that's the case, you'll simply step through, and my portal request will become a proper portal. If not, we should stay put and form another plan."

"Like hiring a few dozen magical snake hunters to make the oceans safe from this scourge," Mads suggested.

"Not the most efficient plan, I think, but I will admit those are the same broad strokes I was thinking," Leif replied.

Leif practiced his spell a few more times, and the three of them checked their gear to make sure it was secure. Then, nothing else could be done except the mission itself.

They ascended the stairs, then let Romero help them attach their air tanks and flippers.

Mads was ready first. He sat on the edge of the deck, winked at them through his mask, then tumbled backward off the boat and into the water.

"Come on in! The water's fine," Mads announced over the radio installed in their masks.

Terra went next. She had used gear like this for swimming in the Great Lakes, but doing so in the frigid waters of the North was another thing entirely. She splashed in and checked to make sure her artifacts were where she had left them.

Leif entered last, nearly losing his mask in the process. Truly, he should have drowned, but he had put a bubble around himself, so he was able to calmly put his mask back on while everyone aboard the boat screamed about the loss of contact and whether he was all right.

"You mind doing one of those for me, too, mate?" Mads asked.

"Oh, does our resident mortal want a taste of magic?" Leif asked.

"Not if you're going to tease about it, but yeah. I mean, I'd rather use the mask because we can communicate more easily, but I don't want to drown. Even if it means asking you for help."

"The bubbles let us communicate, too," Terra pointed out.

"Well, magic's solved about everything except how to find the last piece of magic, huh?" Mads suggested.

They practiced moving around in the water, diving down and coming back up until they were reasonably confident with their abilities.

Then, they began their descent.

Terra quickly found that her enhanced strength meant when she kicked her flippers, she moved through the water as effortlessly as an aquatic mammal. Leif and Mads did not fail to notice.

"You mind going at mortal speed?" Mads asked.

"I'll do you one better. Grab my shoulder harness, and I'll tow you down there."

"I could use a ride, too," Leif joined in. "These flippers are terribly awkward, are they not? I feel like my feet are slower than they should be."

"It's not about the speed of your kicks," Terra explained as they both grabbed a shoulder. "It's about the power." She scissor-kicked, and down they went, into the cold dark of the northern ocean.

If all went well, they would find the final piece of a goddess and prove Terra's worth to not only the world but to all the realms. Then, if they actually survived, which was no guarantee, they would attempt to teleport directly to the realm of a demigod said to be so powerful that he encircled all the Earth. As if that were not enough, they were going to try to convince him to stop his children from ravaging the Earth despite him being the obvious reason they were here.

To say they felt the pressure was a bit of an understatement.

CHAPTER FIFTEEN

Underwater, the Gulf of Bothnia, Monday afternoon

They made it about ten meters down before Terra understood the captain's unwillingness to go farther. The seafloor was still a good way beneath them, but already, the branches of a few trees reached for the light coming from the surface.

"Call me crazy, but should those even exist like that? Shouldn't they have been rotted away by ocean termites or something?" Mads wondered.

"Maybe the magic has been spilling out here longer than the other places. Perhaps to protect the artifact from the powers of the sea," Leif posited.

"If you look through the gloom, you can see we're already above what must have been a hill," Terra pointed out. "I wonder if we've already entered the settlement.

Besides the errant tree preserved in the ocean, there was nothing to indicate this area had once been above land, let alone a Viking village with a sacred temple. They descended lower as the seafloor continued to rise. Layers of silt hid much of it, but Terra made out trenches running down the hill. Could streams have formed those long ago? Huge boulders were strewn about as well. Perhaps landmarks for the people who once lived here?

The water was murky near the seafloor. Now and then, something swam away beneath them and kicked up the silt from the bottom, making little plumes.

"Oh, look, a fish!" Leif pointed out.

"That's not a fish, mate. The big ones are sharks."

Mads was not wrong. The shark was a few meters ahead of them, but it did not seem perturbed by their presence. It moved its tail so slowly that it hardly seemed to be swimming.

"He's a gentle boy, isn't he?" Leif suggested.

"Unless he smells blood," Mads muttered.

However, the shark was not interested in them. When they swam closer, it noticed and vanished into the depths.

They continued forward, passing over a group of rays buried in the silt. Leif gleefully pointed them out with a floating ball of light he sent a bit too close to them. One popped from the silt, then another, until it seemed the entire seafloor consisted of rays. Their undulating bodies clouded the water with silt, and Terra, Mads, and Leif lost sight of them as much as everything else.

It was a good thing they were holding onto Terra. Otherwise, they might have difficulty finding each other in the low visibility. Terra was not precisely sure where they were supposed to go, but she continued forward, using her momentum to guide her.

Then, they passed through a magical barrier, and the silt vanished. It was like a filter that let anything larger than a fish through, but none of their debris. Terra saw the school of rays vanishing into the distance, not that she cared about the odd, flat creatures any longer.

They had reached the temple and the buildings Joana had identified from the surface. Down here, the piles of rubble were more clearly the remains of structures. A few rocks were still stacked up at the base of the walls.

Those bits of surviving architecture alone represented a major find in archeology. Would the building methods match those of the Vikings who lived in mainland Scandinavia? If they could find tool marks on any of the stones, they could use those and the general wall patterning to possibly identify what era they were erected in. That wasn't even considering the objects potentially hidden among the ruins. Or pieces of objects, anyway.

However, it was hard to think about that when the temple waited past the rubble, its wooden walls still standing, its pitched roof clean of silty debris.

"I'm not an archeologist, but that's not supposed to look like that, is it?" Mads asked.

"Are you kidding?" Leif had forgotten to press the button on the radio, so Terra heard his voice in her bubble. "That's *exactly* what a Norse temple should look like!"

Terra could not argue with that. The temple looked like a miniature version of Valhalla. Its wooden walls featured wide beams broken up at regular intervals by huge tree trunks carved into elaborately stylized creatures. A serpent. A whale. A boar. A pair of cats. From the intimidatingly high walls rose the pitched roof. Beams of wood accented the corners and made the structure look like it had horns. Even the wooden shingles were visible.

Terra did not doubt magic was at work here. No sea life clung to the temple. No barnacles covering the carvings, no kelp sprouting from cracks in the walls. A few feet away, several clams nestled in the rubble, but the temple itself was free of any life.

"I can't believe it's in such good shape. This find could change everything. If we shared even photos of this temple with the world, every archeologist on the continent will want to come here. It's so well preserved that it might force them all to consider the existence of magic, or at least other forces than they are used to dealing with."

"Not so sure they'd want to come," Mads pointed out.

"It might not look like much, but down here, this is all basically impossible," Terra clarified.

"I'm not saying they wouldn't like it. I'm saying they might not want to swim past *those*."

Terra had not noticed anything besides the temple, but she followed Mads' headlight down the hill, away from the temple to the corpse of a massive shark. It had bite marks along its gut and two huge punctures in its throat.

"Oh, dear," Leif exclaimed. "We should let go of Terra in case whatever did *that* appears."

Terra did not argue. She slowed her pace as Leif and Mads released her, then got their bearings, kicking along to keep up. Now that Mads had brought her attention to the dead shark, she realized the sea floor was riddled with the bodies of huge sea creatures.

Something that looked like an eel lay nearby, though its head was missing above the gills. An impossibly large octopus was missing tentacles and a chunk of its central mantle. The skeleton of a whale lay on the bottom, home to nothing but a few starfish and crabs picking through the remains.

"Should these sea creatures even be here?" Mads asked. "I didn't exactly think this part of the world was known for octopuses."

"Animals have always been more sensitive to magic than humans," Leif explained. "Humans can sense it as well as animals, but for so long, your kind has tried to push any inkling of magic you feel away. You pretend your logic is so much better."

"You think these animals sensed the magic here and were drawn to it?" Terra asked.

"How is that a good use of intuition?" Mads demanded before Leif could answer. "These fish should have sensed the magic and stayed *away*."

"I don't think this place has been dangerous for long. Your people are quite good at catching as much of the world as possible on camera, and they have captured some of these snakes. They must have done this."

"But they've been here long enough to strip a whale to the bone?" Mads asked.

"There were *a lot* of little snakes," Terra pointed out.

"I am liking everything about this less and less," Mads stated. "Romero, everything still all right up top?"

"We're sitting fine up here," Romero replied. "Getting weird down there, huh?"

"You don't know the half of it."

"And that's fine with me."

"Let's enter the temple and see what we can find," Terra suggested.

"Roger that. Keep us posted on how it's going down there," Romero returned.

Terra pointed her headlight toward the temple. It was so beautiful it nearly took her breath away. She *knew* the reason it looked this way was because of magic, yet she kept thinking it was a miracle that it could be so well-preserved. She supposed that was what some people would call magic. Before she could get too deep into the philosophical implications, she approached the temple door.

She rested her flippers on the seafloor and touched the huge door handle. It resisted at first, but with the slightest pulse of magic from the bracers, the door swiveled on its hinges. Terra could *feel* the hinges rubbing against each other through the vibration of the water.

Of all the things they had found down there, those metal bits should have been the first to corrode. Yet they seemed as well-oiled as they must have been when this place was built.

Terra pulled the door open and peered into the gloom of the temple's interior. A few small windows were cut into the tops of the walls. The eaves outside hid them, but in here, they were practically the only thing Terra could see. They let in faint beams of light that shone in the darkness.

She'd thought it was dark outside, but she had been able to see far more than she could now. The only things visible were inky darkness, the shafts of light, and perhaps the faint outline of a door on the far side of the room.

She swept the room with her headlights and discovered stylized human figures leering back at her. It was hard to tell, but perhaps a dozen of them filled the place, six on each side and another at the far end of the room.

She swam to the closest one, moving slowly, waiting for a snake that never emerged. The figure appeared to be a huge log carved into a rough human shape. It was relatively crude, more the indication of a person than a realistic rendering, but that was not to say it lacked beauty or significance.

It was clearly the face of an old woman in distress. Her eyes were wide open, and some indication of wrinkles were carved to indicate her age and emotional state.

Terra looked at the rest of her body, trying to find some clue who this was supposed to represent. One of the Norns, perhaps? She wore a garment draped over her shoulders. The only part of her that stuck out was a hand formed either into a gesture of cautious greeting or an ominous warning. Could the fabric shawl mean she was weaving the tapestry of *seidr*? Terra touched the statue, trying to get a sense of any magic it possessed, but she felt nothing. Whatever had preserved this temple did not come from this statue.

She glanced back at Leif and Mads, who were still near the doorway.

"I'm going to look at the next one, see if any of these have any relation to Freya," Terra told them.

"You do that, luv. I don't like the feeling of this place one bit," Mads replied.

"Oh, look, a statue of Bygul!" Leif ignored Mads' fear and swam toward a statue on the opposite side of the room.

"Do you sense any magic from it?" Terra asked. Mads, she noted, had followed close to Leif.

"Not particularly, but Bygul is with Freya. I don't think any of its magic would be here."

Terra swam to the next statue and discovered the face of a man. The artist had spent time trying to get the features right, and where the old woman had been wrinkled and craggy, this man's face was smooth and handsome. More than handsome, really. Almost beautiful like Freya.

"Is this Freyr?" Terra mused. Freya's brother was a central figure in the goddess' life. Was that what this temple was? A place to worship the life of Freya and the forces around her?

Terra swam to the next statue. It was a dwarf. The one who'd made some of the artifacts Terra now wore, perhaps? She felt like she'd found a pattern, and she swam on faster. Every temple to Freya they had discovered featured a giant, perfectly carved marble statue of the goddess. Surely, she was at the end of the room, surrounded by the altar Terra had glimpsed the outline of in the gloom.

She knew she should check each statue, but she felt drawn to the end of the room. She swam past statues, hardly looking at the well-carved hog sitting on its haunches like a loyal dog. Freya's war pig. She kept going past another dwarf, a child, a younger woman.

She had to reach the altar!

When she finally got close enough to illuminate it, she found only a pedestal and a bit of silver that framed nothing at all. Bits of broken marble were strewn across the floor.

The statue of Freya had been destroyed.

Mads never held archeologists in particularly high esteem when it came to their nerves. These people spent their careers investigating murders that had happened hundreds of years ago. The only thing that would jump out and bite them was a new hypothesis. Their biggest fear was dripping water in the wrong place.

Yet, in this underwater temple, it was Terra who was unshakable. While Mads' headlight darted left and right, trying to look everywhere at once but not seeing anything, hers stayed steady on the rows of statues along the sides.

"Place gives me the creeps," Mads told Leif. He regretted it almost as soon as he said it. He had a working relationship with the Asgardian, but he relished taking the bony librarian down every chance he could. The way he saw it, if he made fun of Leif for liking cheese-flavored crisps, Leif certainly had the right to insult him for being scared of an empty temple.

"I don't like anything about this," Leif agreed, surprising him.

"Glad it's not just me," Mads replied.

"The sooner we find the artifact and get out of here, the better. The idea of spending a week coming down here every day is not a prospect I wish to consider."

Mads had to remember to keep breathing through his mouth and not mess up his SCUBA equipment. He had sort of assumed Terra and Leif would find what they were looking for, and they would be on their way, likely to battle more snakes. The idea of being down here all week, searching and finding nothing, sounded like a nightmare.

"What can I do to help?" Mads proposed.

"Let's check these statues," Leif suggested, and Mads followed him to the opposite wall of the temple. It was so dark inside that even when he neared a statue, he could not see the wall behind it, only blackness. His headlight found the face of a poorly carved figure. Picasso might have liked it, but to Mads, the nose was too big and too hooked, the eyes too sunken. The mouth twisted into an expression of pain and fury so intense that surely no human could have made it.

"Looks like Odr, Freya's husband," Mads postulated as he swam toward the next statue.

This one wasn't so bad. It depicted a young girl whom the artist endeavored to make pretty. What she was doing down here, in the gloom at the bottom of the sea in a temple surrounded by sea monster corpses, was something Mads didn't want to dwell on.

"That's one of her daughters, I'd bet," Leif announced.

"Thanks for the art history lesson." Mads couldn't care less who these statues were supposed to be. He had an eye for valuables and doubted these poorly carved pieces of wood would fetch much. Maybe they'd be worth something in the right circles, but at an auction house, something so big and heavy would likely get passed over. Besides, they weren't looking to decorate someone's back garden. They were looking for an artifact of Freya.

So while Leif swam past the statues, checking each one in turn and telling Mads about their mythological connection to his great, great, however many removed grandmother, Mads checked the statues' hands for trinkets.

Maybe one of them was wearing a ring or a belt. He

doubted there'd be another necklace, considering Terra already had one that could make her teleport, but you never knew. The double necklace thing had come in and out of fashion in Mads' lifetime. It could certainly have been a thing back in Viking times.

"I found the statue of Freya," Terra announced over the radio. Mads did not like the way she said it. She should have been excited, or better yet, swimming out of the temple with a box in hand. Instead, she sounded disappointed. "It's been destroyed."

"Oh, dear," Leif replied less than helpfully.

"That sucks," Mads stated, which he immediately recognized was hardly better.

"There's an inscription on the pedestal, though. I think it's the clue. I'm going to see if I can decipher it. Keep looking around. Maybe the statue wasn't holding it. Maybe it's stashed somewhere else."

"We'll keep our eyes open for magic boxes," Mads assured her.

They continued looking at the statues. Leif kept muttering about who they were, though less enthusiastically. Mads checked the bases and the floor around them, looking for some hint of hidden compartments. He thought he'd found one behind a statue and was heading to investigate when the radio crackled, and Leif's panicked voice sounded in his ear.

"Did you see that?" Leif asked, whipping his headlight back and forth.

"I didn't see anything, mate, and you probably didn't either. You need to calm down and keep your head on a swivel, not swivel it around."

"It was right behind the statues, in the gap between them and the wall. It was large."

Mads watched Leif's headlight move up the wall.

"I don't see anything," Mads said to calm Leif, but even as he did, he took out his needle gun. Technically, it was an APS underwater rifle. It had a 5.6mm cartridge loaded with twenty-six steel bolts specially designed for firing underwater.

Regular bullets were notoriously inaccurate underwater. The engineers who'd made the APS underwater rifle had done so with this challenge in mind. Instead of slugs, it had bolts or "needles" created with hydrodynamic forces in mind. It was inaccurate above water, but below the surface, the needles flew fast and far. They had more impact and range than a spear gun, and they could punch through wet suits and even the plastic domes of less-than-substantial submarines.

It was slightly bigger than a pistol, with a longer barrel and a large clip that made it tricky to move around underwater. The best way was to move the gun sideways so the clip didn't create drag. Using it tended to make the wielder look like a gangster who had decided to go diving.

Mads had not used one in a long time and was pleased when he found one in Sweden. He had paid handsomely for it, then paid even more to make sure it couldn't be traced back to him. Now, in this dark temple where he could see next to nothing, he wished he didn't feel like he needed it.

Leif's headlight found nothing in the high rafters of the temple, but Mads no longer doubted Leif had seen something moving.

A light shone from the end of the temple, and Mads glanced that way to see Terra had formed it with magic and was holding it inches from the statue's pedestal. Maybe she was getting close to figuring out where the artifact was? Or not, because she snuffed the light out after only a few seconds.

Something was wrong. Mads looked around in the darkness, trying to figure out what it was. Then, he saw it.

One of the shafts of light coming through a window appeared to be moving. It was because something had swum through the water and disrupted the medium through which the beam propagated. Considering Mads had not seen a single living thing since they had entered the temple, he did not think something moving above them unseen was good. It did not make him think it was simply a fish up there sneaking around.

"Terra, I think there's something in here with us."

Despite the statue being broken, Terra would not give up hope. Leif had felt magic coming from this place, and she had seen the marks on his map. *Something* was preserving this temple. No way it was in this condition without the help of magic. The most logical answer was that Freya's artifact was still hidden here somewhere.

Maybe someone had thought it was in the statue and destroyed it. Or maybe they had been unable to find it and destroyed the statue in frustration. Or maybe they did it out of spite.

It didn't matter. The important thing was Terra could

not give up. She had to figure out where the piece was hidden.

She turned back. Leif and Mads were examining the statues on the opposite side of the temple from where Terra had explored. If they found something obvious, they would tell her. It wouldn't be something obvious, though. Otherwise, whoever or whatever broke the statue would have taken it, and this place would have fallen to the forces of the sea.

But what to do? Terra was sorely tempted to take her ax to the statues. Maybe one of the cryptic, carved effigies held an ornate box inlaid with rose gold inside. Maybe whoever destroyed the statue had simply destroyed the wrong one. Maybe they had followed a clue to the wrong place...

That was it! There had been clues with each of the previous artifacts. There had to be one here. Terra turned back to the pedestal where the statue of Freya had stood.

She fanned the water at the pedestal's base, and a thin layer of marble dust floated away. It had settled into words carved into the base.

"I think I have something!" Terra announced, but she was so intrigued that she didn't bother activating her radio or the *seidr* needed to make her bubble carry her words to her friends.

She gently rubbed her hands over the stone pedestal, and more of the marble dust came away. Some of the stone crumbled under her fingers, and she cursed. It seemed whatever force had broken the statue also lifted the magical preservation from the pedestal. Unlike the perfectly preserved temple, these markings were eroded with age and dirty with dust from the statue they had once supported.

Still, Terra was an archeologist and more. She controlled *seidr*. She understood much of her power came from her ability to understand runes and the power they gave her over the material world. Runes took the raw magic of the universe and put it in terms the gods could understand and use. Similar to how written language helped humans, but a step closer to the magic source.

She studied the runes, looking for some indication of what they meant or even where to start. She thought she recognized the rune for "boar" but also the runes for "noise," "help," and "truth." She tried moving her head to get different angles of light, but it hardly helped.

She tried a ball of light next. That helped more, but not enough. The light only revealed how eroded the etchings were. Although some of the runes, especially those near the top of the inscription, seemed to be glowing. Was her magic restoring them? She snuffed out her light.

She moved a hand closer to the pedestal and let some of her *seidr* flow from her fingertips into the stone. She saw something, a glimmer of change, but she lost it when she heard Mads over her radio.

"Terra, I think there's something in here with us."

"Just a minute," Terra replied, which Mads did not like.

He raked his headlight across the room, looking for something, anything. Before he found any indication of whatever was in here, Leif produced a sphere of light.

"Mate." Mads brought his needle gun up and prepared to use it. The light was too bright and made it harder to see while Mads' eyes adjusted. He could only see the ball itself and Leif nearby, his features thrown into high relief.

There was nothing around him, though. No sea beasties. No ghosts of dead Vikings. Nothing but the old temple.

Until the sinuous undulation of a snake entered the light.

It was large for a snake, nearly fifteen feet long, and fast in the water. Its eyes were locked on the ball of light as it whipped its body back and forth, getting closer to the glowing orb.

Mads could see nothing past it. Not the statues, the wall behind them, or the ceiling. He could only see the snake coming toward Leif.

And he wouldn't let Leif get bitten.

Mads took careful aim. The needle gun was accurate if he took his time, lined up his shot, made sure he wasn't drifting.

The snake was nearly upon the orb of light, but that was fine with Mads. Knowing where it was headed gave him a clear shot.

He waited, watching the serpent's undulating movements until he could tell exactly where each coil of the snake would be next.

Only then did he fire his weapon.

The needle made the faintest sound as it shot from the end of the barrel toward the snake. His aim was true, and the needle found its mark. It punched a hole in the snake, about a foot down from its head, and flew clean out the other side.

Blood spilled from the snake and clouded the water red. As soon as it did, the light in the room changed to a muted red, and Mads could see deeper into the shadows.

But there was no time to sightsee. Despite being shot through the neck, the snake was still swimming toward Leif, pumping more frantically, baring its fangs.

It struck, and Mads was too far away to help. However, Leif managed to catch it by the throat, directly above where Mads had shot it. The snake pushed forward, struggling to break free as it gagged on Leif's hand. Its tongue and fangs stuck out, casting shadows through the red light that fell on Terra, who worked faster than ever on the pedestal.

Then the snake remembered what it was. Instead of trying to bite Leif, it twisted its body around his hand, wrapping his arm in its coils.

Leif was stuck. He couldn't let go of the snake's head, or it would bite him in the throat. However, one free arm was not enough to keep it from wrapping him. He struggled, trying to keep the fangs and the bulk of the snake at bay but only succeeding at one. As he fought with the snake, his ball of light flickered, then faded and went out completely.

So it was Mads to the rescue. He swam toward his friend and the snake. They were thrashing around far too much for him to get a clean shot with the needle gun. He needed to be close so he could get a proper angle.

Or stab the damn thing if it came to that.

He drew closer, swam above Leif as the Asgardian tumbled and wrestled with the snake.

Then, he saw his shot.

Leif's hand was still strangling the snake, shoving its biting mouth away. About a foot of its neck was stretched from beneath its jaw to where Leif clutched it.

Mads got where he needed to be, aimed as best as he could, considering the amount of time he had, and pulled the trigger.

The needle leaped from the gun and punched through the snake's throat. At this range, it had enough force to go through and come out the back. The water clouded with blood as Leif and the snake continued to struggle, but after a moment or two, the struggle stopped. Leif released the snake's head.

It floated limply as he shucked its long body off him.

"I appreciate that," Leif gushed.

"Not a problem, mate. Not a problem at all. Shooting it was easier than trying to see a damn thing with your ball of light like a spotlight in this place."

"You don't mean that. It was better with the light on." Leif reignited the floating orb a few feet in front of him.

It wasn't nearly as harsh anymore since it remained a dull red from the blood in the water. Not exactly an encouraging thought, but considering it was not *Mads'* blood, he supposed it was good news.

"I must say." Mads waved his hands through the blood to make it dissipate faster. "That wasn't too bad. After the great big one on the surface, I was expecting something a bit more intimidating down here."

As he cleared the blood, the orb's light spread farther until it reached the floor, the statues, the walls, and finally, the ceiling.

Faint beams of light streamed through the tiny

windows placed high on the walls, the only source of illumination not tinted red with the dead serpent's blood.

Until each of those windows went dark.

Mads had not bothered to count them, but he did so now. Six windows had been forming six shafts of light until this moment. Now, each was black, and from the red light of Leif's magic, Mads saw the outlines of six mighty serpents pushing their way into the temple.

Their milky white, silvery scales caught the red light and made them look like raw flesh. They looked furious with Leif and Mads for intruding on this space and killing one of their own.

"Uh, mate? Not to be the bearer of bad news, but you might want to take a look up there."

Leif slowly raised his eyes to the nest of massive serpents shoving into the temple.

"Ah. Yes, the stuff of nightmares. If we make it through this, I might not want to sleep ever again."

"Let's hope you get the chance." Mads grunted, then took aim with his needle gun.

CHAPTER SIXTEEN

Temple of Freya, the Gulf of Bothnia, Monday evening

Leif had no fear of snakes. They did not exist in Asgard, so to him, they were creatures of imagination. A specter more than a threat. He understood these were bigger and more powerful than the regular snakes of Midgard, but he had become a formidable warrior! He had already battled one much larger than these and had come out the victor. He would prevail again!

Or so he thought until he fired a dart of glowing energy at the closest snake, and it opened its mouth and swallowed the energy like a pickled sardine.

"That's going to be a problem," Leif stated.

"Not the time for problems, mate. It's time for solutions." Mads fired his clunky firearm underwater. The nail-like projectile it fired shot through the water and struck one of the snakes. It did not stop crawling through the window, though. When it fully emerged, and light could once more stream into the room, red blood clouded the beam.

The snake didn't seem to care. It kept coming for Mads.

That made it the exception. The other snakes seemed focused on Leif. It was not because he had attacked them. If that were the case, surely Mads would be the greater threat. That they were coming for Leif had to mean they found him a better target. It was likely because they wished to eat his magic.

Not a pleasant thought.

Surely, they could not be immune to all of it, though.

Leif created a ball of fire. It was a self-contained thing, its edges hissing and bubbling as the interior stayed pure flame. He sent it through the water, and it struck a snake but hardly discolored the scales.

"Fire underwater, mate? Seriously? You can do better than that!" Mads had plugged the snake coming at him with multiple shots. It was still coming, though its movements were slowed. He was doing better than Leif, though.

Of the six snakes, four of them were after the Asgardian.

Options for how to best use his *seidr* popped through his head, but none seemed the right choice. He was strangled with indecision, floating in the water, not moving, not attacking. Then, a snake plunged its fangs through his chest.

Yet it wasn't Leif the snake had struck, but an illusion he had created using the power of Bygul's Eye. It dissipated into wisps of *seidr*, but the snake was pleased rather than frustrated. It slurped up the power before it could return to Leif.

Another snake came at him, and Leif created another illusion as he flitted away. This wouldn't work for long, but it might work for long enough. Terra only needed to solve the puzzle, then she could join the fight and show these snakes what she was made of.

In the meantime, Leif needed to stay alive. He created another mirage of himself only to watch another snake's fangs slice through it.

Mads had managed to kill the snake coming after him, and now he turned his attention to Leif's many pursuers.

"You got nothing, mate?"

"They keep eating my magic!" Leif protested.

"Well, lure them around, and I'll try to plug them!"

Leif tried to do exactly that. He created illusions of sharks to send at the snakes, forms of Vikings with ethereal weapons that chopped and slashed at the milky scales and did nothing but buy a few seconds before the snakes swallowed them whole.

Mads fired his needles, hitting more often than he missed, but the snakes were huge, and the muscular tubes of their formless anatomy hid their hearts. Mads was not landing killing shots as much as he was pissing off the snakes. The water grew more turbid as the snakes thrashed and charged the mammals they wished to eat. The water clouded with their blood.

Leif looked at Terra, still stooped over the clues, desperately trying to solve the puzzle and claim the last piece of Freya to turn the tide of this battle at the bottom of the sea.

Terra's attention was split between the fight escalating in the temple and the puzzle before her. Her friends were outnumbered and overpowered, but neither had been hurt yet. She had a sinking suspicion the sea held far more than these six snakes. If she could not solve this puzzle now and claim the last piece of Freya, they might never be able to return here. Her mission would fail, and the realm of Midgard would fall to the whims of the gods and Jotun, who wished to claim it for their own.

She had to solve this puzzle.

The frustrating part was that it seemed simple enough. It was a short phrase, something about calling for help? Terra felt like she would have solved it already if she could make out the whole inscription, but she could not. Unlike the rest of the miraculously preserved temple, the inscription was worn and crumbling. Perhaps it was victim to decay because something had struck the statue of Freya. Perhaps it was part of the puzzle.

Was it as simple as calling for help?

Terra turned and raised her voice. "Give aid to the Chosen of Freya!"

And it was a good thing she did.

A snake had been sneaking up behind her. It had been on the cusp of striking when Terra had the good fortune to turn. It stared her down with malevolent intent as it opened its gaping maw to strike.

However, Terra was not frightened of this legless wonder. She had fought and killed a snake longer than this, clothed in nothing but her pajamas and armed only with her own skills. She had destroyed one of its brothers that dwarfed this one.

It would not intimidate her, and for the arrogance of thinking it could, it would die.

Terra swung Freya's ax at the snake's skull between the eyes.

Now, instead of the front of its face opening horizontally along the seam of its mouth, it opened vertically through the slit Terra had sliced between its eyes, through its skull, and out the bottom of its jaw.

It died instantly, but because it had been swimming toward her, its body kept coming in the collision course it had created for its prey.

Terra let it pass and checked on the battle raging inside the temple. Leif and Mads were waging simultaneous wars of deception and attrition. Leif created illusions that the snakes chased after and consumed. Meanwhile, Mads shot them with his needle gun. No doubt they would hear about his heroics if they all made it through this.

Though maybe they would not. Or not without Terra's help anyway. Leif was not attacking, only using his illusions. That had to mean his magic was not working against the snakes. Mads' weapon had wounded every snake, but it looked like he'd only killed one of them. They needed Terra to turn the tide. She felt certain more snakes were coming to join the battle, so she would have to set the puzzle aside while she helped her friends.

She glanced back to see the snake's dead body had pushed against the pedestal and snagged there, unable to drift away.

Unwilling to bear the sight of such desecration, she grabbed its tail and pulled it away. She was too late. Its blood had already painted the altar, a dark stain that she hoped the water would wash away.

A dark stain that sank into the runes that Terra had been struggling to read.

A dark stain rife with magic that was restoring the eroded characters.

Terra grabbed the snake's corpse and pushed it back against the pedestal. Its blood soaked further into the runes, and their edges sharpened.

"Declare the companion of and stalwart companion of Freya and be carried from your troubles to victory!" Terra read, plain as day. "Leif, who is the stalwart companion of Freya?"

"She's got quite a few!" Leif hollered back through their bubble-to-bubble connection as he swam around the room, dodging snakes. "Is that really relevant right now?"

"It's the answer to the puzzle to find the last piece!" Terra replied.

She teleported away from the pedestal and grabbed a snake's tail. She yanked it away, but before she could do anything further, the water's force nearly crushed the air from her lungs. She released the snake as she tried to catch her breath.

She had forgotten underwater teleportation was a tricky thing. She was only alive because the bubble around her displaced the water, allowing it to slap against her rather than appear within her. She couldn't turn the tide by zipping around and dispatching the snakes.

It might have been different if the snakes wanted to eat her, but they were going after Leif, leaving her behind. The way to win this was with the last piece of Freya. She felt that clearly. *Seidr* was speaking to her, giving her the outcome of the battle. If she could only grab hold of her fate and twist it into the form she could already sense.

So, she swam back to the pedestal. "Names of her companions, Leif. Go!"

"Well, there's her brother Freyr, of course. Her father Njordr, and her husband Odr, though few would call him stalwart. Oh, no, you don't, you slippery eel of a lizard!" Leif darted away from a snake and sent a magic eel to distract it, which the snake promptly consumed.

They were all people featured in the temple statues, Terra realized. She called on each in turn, then Freya's daughters, but nothing happened. There was no response to any of her declarations.

Did it mean the cats who pulled her chariot? They were stalwart and carried her around.

Then, Terra remembered the rune for "boar" she'd seen, and suddenly, the answer was so clear she could almost hit herself with its obviousness.

"Hildisvíni, come to me!" Terra declared.

A circle of magic radiated out from the pedestal. It washed over the battle in the temple, but it changed nothing. The snakes continued to attack Leif and Mads. The temple revealed no hidden compartments, no secret passageways. Nothing changed.

Well, almost nothing.

The mouth of the boar statue opened and revealed something inside, glinting in a shaft of light made red with the snakes' blood.

Terra swam toward it, but it was too far.

Above her, the snakes had pushed Leif and Mads back-to-back and were circling tighter. Leif threw up mirage after mirage, but the snakes ignored them. They had eaten enough magical appetizers and hungered for the main course.

Leif created a spherical shield around himself and Mads, and the snakes struck at it. Their fangs punctured the dome of magic easily enough, but no other part of them got through. At first, anyway.

One snake removed its fangs and recoiled for another strike. Leif closed the holes in the dome, but another snake was already striking. Cracks and fissures ran from one hole to the next, and soon, the dome around them was cracking, held together by a dwindling supply of magic and Leif's willpower.

One of the four remaining snakes turned toward Terra, flicking its tongue and slowly approaching, keeping well out of range of her ax. Terra kept swimming until she reached the boar statue.

She reached inside its open mouth to find a small, carved figurine of the boar. She picked it up and turned toward the snake. It did nothing. It stayed in her hand, inert, a piece of stone made into the rather adorable image of a boar sitting on its haunches.

"Hildisvíni, I know we haven't met, but I could really use your help about now!" Terra shouted to the little figurine.

Then, the stone began to grow.

CHAPTER SEVENTEEN

Temple of Freya, the Gulf of Bothnia, Monday evening

First, it was only a change in weight. The battle boar figurine seemed to grow heavier, but then Terra felt it move in her hand. It flexed its little haunches, and a thin layer of stone cracked away, revealing bristly fur and muscles that no sculptor could have reproduced, no matter how accomplished.

Free of its stone shell, the boar grew and grew and *grew.* It thrashed in the water as it went from the size of a tennis ball to a soccer ball to a watermelon. It kicked its leg, turning as it enlarged, each kick making more ribbons of muscle stand out on its legs.

In a moment, it was as large as Terra, then larger. It finally stopped thrashing and kicking when it reached the size of a small horse.

It turned and looked at Terra with huge eyes framed by a pair of giant tusks sticking from the end of its snout. It did not seem dismayed to be underwater. It snorted, and Terra felt its deep rumble of sound through the water.

"Those snakes are trying to hurt my friends, Hildisvíni. Can you help?"

The huge boar snorted again and turned toward the battle. He kicked off the temple floor and rose. He moved quite easily through the water, though it did not look like he was actually swimming. More like running along a road no one else could see.

Hildisvíni charged through the temple toward the closest of the four snakes, the one that had been coming for Terra. He threw his massive snout into the snake's belly, and his tusks punched the silvery scales like they were paper.

The snake tried to pull back, to escape, to make this wound into something it could survive, but Hildisvíni was not feeling merciful. He snapped at the snake and threw it under his hooves. They were hard as stone, and their edges ripped through the snake, tearing it to pieces as it tried to escape.

The three remaining snakes abandoned their prey behind the crumbling bubble of shielding energy and turned toward the battle boar.

The first of them barely had a chance before Hildisvíni was upon it. He gored it with his tusks, took a bite from its middle, and the snake was no more. It dissolved into bits of scale and blood as the boar moved on to the next snake.

This one was almost ready for the assault. It dodged Hildisvíni's tusks and bit the boat in the back of the neck. But its fangs could not pierce the tough hide. One broke on the first attempt, and the snake changed tactics, trying to envelop the boar in its rolls instead.

It was hard to make out the details in the gloom and the

low lights, but it almost looked like Hildisvíni was made of gold. Like the figurine had not transformed into a creature of flesh but a facsimile made of metal. He certainly showed no animalistic fear. He hardly seemed to notice the snake squeezing him as he lumbered toward the final snake.

This one sprayed venom from its mouth into the battle boar's eyes, which finally did something to stop Hildisvíni's mad attack. The boar squealed and threw his head around, trying to knock the blinding poison from his eyes.

Leif was more than happy to assist the boar. He dropped the shield and created a twisting tendril of force that pushed water from his hands and across the boar's face to carry away the poison.

That was all the help Hildisvíni needed. The boar charged toward the snake that had sprayed him. He opened his jaws wide and crushed the snake's head. Then, he slurped up the snake's body like it was a particularly large and delicious noodle.

The last snake still coiled around the battle boar tried to tighten and constrict the mighty beast, but it couldn't do a thing to the massive girth. Hildisvíni dropped to the floor of the temple. There, he rolled onto his back and wriggled, smashing the snake beneath the massive ridges of his shoulders. The snake might have escaped, but it had been trying to constrict Hildisvíni and couldn't untangle itself.

Hildisvíni continued wriggling until the snake's body tore in half.

Nothing remained of the snakes except bits of scales and blood, already rapidly disintegrating, becoming nothing now that the magic allowing them to exist in this world had been freed from the containment of their bodies.

The top half of the last remaining snake hissed, then dissolved. The battle was done.

Hildisvíni got up and snorted around the temple floor. He looked like he was sniffing for buried food despite being in an underwater temple.

Leif and Mads swam down.

"Glad to see you're all right," Mads told Terra.

"Same to you."

Leif ignored them both and swam to the huge boar.

"Is that Hildisvíni?" he asked, stooping like the huge boar was an energetic golden retriever. "Is that Freya's favorite battle boar? Is it? Is that my old buddy? Who's a good boy? Huh? Is it Hildisvíni? Is Hildisvíni a very good boy?"

Hildisvíni apparently thought he was the *best* of boys and was quite pleased to be recognized as such. He lunged forward and hunched his shoulders, sticking out his front hooves and lowering his massive head so he was closer to the ground. Terra had seen dogs behave like that a thousand times.

"You're the best battle boar, aren't you? But Hildisvíni, do you have...*the zoomies?*"

Hildisvíni squealed in delight and tore past Leif. His mighty hooves cut chunks from the floor of the temple before he rose into a water column, running along an invisible path that took him in loops across the temple walls. He corkscrewed, did flips, and squealed and grunted in delight the whole time.

"Come, you big, fat piggy! Come back down here!" Leif

shouted at Hildisvíni.

The huge boar loped back to the floor, then daintily alighted beside Leif. Despite being underwater, he lolled his tongue out, then collapsed on his side, breathing heavily from the excitement. Even on his side, Hildisvíni was nearly as tall as Terra.

"Mads, Terra, this is Hildisvíni. He truly is Freya's most stalwart companion. He is a tireless warrior and has never once failed to come when she called him to battle."

"Tireless? He looks pretty exhausted to me," Mads remarked.

The huge hog snorted and climbed back to his hooves. He stared down his snout at Mads.

"I didn't mean nothing by it, mate. Honest. I'm only saying that after defeating four of those snakes, I could use a breather myself. No shame in needing to catch your breath. We're all getting older, and my cardio's not what it used to be. And I'm barely in my thirties."

"Thirties?" Terra echoed.

Mads shrugged and winked.

Hildisvíni was mollified, though.

"Hildisvíni, may I present to you Freya's chosen of this age. This is Terra Freyasdatter, still known as Freya Olsen in some places."

Hildisvíni took two steps toward Terra, then closed his eyes and lowered his huge snout until it rested on the temple floor. He bent one knee daintily and prostrated himself in front of Terra.

It was an honor Terra hardly felt she deserved and one of the silliest things she had ever seen. The figurine she had pulled from the mouth of a statue had come to life, or an approximation of life anyway, saved her and her friends' lives four times over and was now bowing before her.

"Hildisvíni will be loyal to you because your power over *seidr* is one and the same as his true master, Freya. But he does respond well to praise," Leif whispered.

"Right." Terra stepped forward and scratched the huge boar behind the ears. His bristly hair was so strong and stiff that it felt like metal. Like a steel brush one might use to scrub rust from a car part or clean a particularly dirty grill. Underneath was not a metal plate but skin that felt as thick and tough as leather.

"Thank you so much for saving us, Hildisvíni. You're a big, strong boar, aren't you? A big, strong boar who's not afraid of snakes. Can you help us some more, big guy?"

Hildisvíni raised his head and gave an affirmative snort.

"Wonderful," Terra replied. "You really were amazing in battle. To put it succinctly, that'll do, pig."

"I've got to say I'm a bit surprised the last piece of Freya turned out to be a pet," Mads commented.

"That only shows your ignorance of the Aesir and Vanir," Leif was quick to state. "Nearly all of them had a treasured companion. Odin had his ravens and wolves, of course."

"Wolves?" Mads asked.

Leif snorted so hard in derision that Terra worried his magic might fail him and he would drown, but his bubble persisted. "Geri and Freki? An amazing pair of beasts. Perhaps more formidable in battle than Odin himself. They had an appetite for the corpses of the slain, but of course, never those who would go to Valhalla. Yet another reason to die bravely, fighting your enemy instead of running the other way."

"Charming," Mads intoned.

"Even Thor has his goats," Leif continued, warming to his subject. "They pull his chariot, of course, but he can also slay them and eat their flesh as long as he gathers their bones in their hides. Amazing creatures, those two. I would say Thor does not deserve them, but he has proven loyalty to those goats time and time again. In fact, there was this one time—"

"Maybe later, mate. As it stands, I think I get it. Hildisvíni the battle boar is a good pig."

Hildisvíni snorted in appreciation and nuzzled Mads. Being mortal, he had none of the super strength available to Terra and Leif, so he was nearly shoved aside by the friendly swine's bulk.

"What's the plan? I'm thinking we head back up, breathe some actual air instead of this recycled fart bubble and canned gas that magic and science are granting us, and regroup?"

"We can play it that way," Leif agreed. "Though I worry about Terra teleporting the three of us up there. It's quite a distance, and it takes more *seidr* to teleport multiple people. We're going to need some power to open the portal. Still, if that's what Terra thinks is best, we can do that."

"What I think is best? Is there another option?" Terra asked.

"I came prepared to open the portal down here. I thought we would find the piece and head straight to meet Jörmungandr."

Terra chewed her lip, wondering how essential speed was. "Mads, check in on Romero. See how they're doing up there. Hildisvíni, don't let anyone get into the temple, all right? If you see any snakes, don't chase them. Just squeal really loud and give 'em hell if they try to get in."

The boar quirked his head at Terra in confusion.

"She means if the snakes try to get in, stop them by any means necessary," Leif explained to the huge hog, who snorted in understanding before ambling toward the temple entrance. "You have to understand that 'give 'em Hel' means something quite different to the ancient Norse," Leif explained.

"Yeah, sorry. I figured since the magic and possibly robotic pig could understand English, he would understand that," Terra replied.

Leif chuckled. "Don't be ridiculous!"

"I'll try not to, but with you on my side, it's always a temptation. Now, come on. Let's swim up, take a look through one of those windows, and see if anything else is coming our way."

They kicked their flippers and ascended to the temple ceiling, then looked outside.

They did not like what they saw.

Dozens of snakes were heading their way, though it could have been hundreds, given the low light and how the water made it difficult to see things in the distance. Even worse, the snakes came in all sizes. From the size of a pencil to the massive, ship-crushing bruiser they had dealt with before.

"They must have sensed the battle and come to the call

of their dead brothers' and sisters' death rattles," Leif suggested.

"Not great," Terra replied.

"Not at all," Leif agreed. "What do you want to do about it?"

Terra didn't have long to decide. Maybe a minute before the vanguard of the huge swarm arrived. "Mads, what have you got?" she asked.

"News. I'll leave it up to you if it's good or bad. He says there's a bunch of snakes up there. Little ones. Big ones. All of them coming our way."

"Not attacking the boat?" Terra asked.

"Why would they?" Mads retorted. "They have explosives and guns up there, but no magic. The snakes are coming this way because you two have what they want."

"If there is another battle with the snakes, I'm not sure how much help I will be. The last ones adapted to my abilities and ate my illusions as snacks. I suppose I could use the ax to battle, and you could punch through them, but I find that option fraught with risk."

"Then we go to meet Jörmungandr sooner rather than later. Leif, open the portal."

"I'll get started," Leif agreed.

"Wait. Get started? How long will it take? You make it sound like you're starting the stock for a soup from scratch," Mads stated.

"Certainly not more than ten minutes," Leif replied.

"Ten minutes! We don't have ten minutes," Terra exclaimed. "Mads and I cannot possibly defend this room for that long. There's too many openings."

Hildisvíni turned his head and snorted at them.

"What's that, boy?" Leif asked.

Hildisvíni snorted and pointed his snout toward the back of the room.

"There's a secret room back there?"

Hildisvíni snorted and stomped his hooves.

"It's hidden beneath the pedestal? Well, why didn't you say so sooner? Come on!"

Leif swam to the pedestal and ran his fingers across the markings. Despite the snake blood being washed away, its effects were still clear on the inscriptions. Leif ran his finger over the markings on one side of the pedestal, then the other. He shoved against it, and the entire thing slid to the side, revealing a rough staircase leading under the sea floor.

"Hildisvíni, thank you! Can you guard the top of the stairs while we get down there?"

The hog snorted, left the temple entrance, and came to the stairs. Already, snakes appeared in the distance, coming toward the temple door. There were so many that Terra could not even guess their number. Which was obviously a terrible amount.

Hildisvíni barreled toward the stairs, moving faster than the rest.

"Grab hold of the hairy hog!" Leif cried, and they all tried to snag the hog's thick bristles.

Terra sank her hands into the hair on the back of the hog's neck and was pleased to find her grip was quite good. The golden, bristly hairs seemed to *extend* and wrap around her hand as she grabbed them, holding her as much as she held them.

"It's like a hairy handshake," Mads remarked as Hildisvíni pulled them down the stairs.

The passageway was quite large. Considering this temple had been either selected or built to hold this mighty hog, Terra would not have been surprised to discover the stairway was specifically designed to accommodate his massive girth.

The hog ran down the stairs without touching the steps, using the same invisible road it had been employing since it sprung up from the figurine. Terra gripped the bristly fur more firmly, then swung herself up and around to land on the hog's back, behind his shoulders and the ridge in the middle. She actually fit well. For a huge, hulking pig, Hildisvíni's back was narrow enough to accommodate her legs. It was his mighty belly she would not be able to wrap around.

Hildisvíni continued down the stairway until they emerged into a large natural cavern. Immediately, Terra thought of all the other caverns where statues of Freya had been found. Each had been in a natural cave.

Now, this temple hidden at the bottom of the sea made more sense. Surely, whoever built this place found the cave first and erected the temple on top of it. It made Terra wonder about the history of this place. Had the temple above always been an austere structure, home to nothing but statues, or was there a time when it served some other purpose?

Valhalla featured so prominently in the lore of the Vikings that most scholars assumed dining halls were an important part of their society. The temple above could have been a place of feasting. The pride of an island that had long since sunk under the sea. It could have hidden this secret room beneath it until the sea began to rise and this chamber flooded.

Maybe they'd brought the statue of Freya up the steps to the temple when that happened. Maybe the statue had fallen because it was never intended to live out the centuries up there. Or maybe it had served as a magical sacrifice. The Norse belief system prized sacrifice highly. Maybe the destruction of the statue had preserved the temple, even as the sea took it.

These would be the sorts of questions archeologists would have to grapple with if magic was exposed to the world.

Currently, the only archeologist who knew about magic and its effect on the world was in this chamber, figuring out how to best defend it from hundreds of snakes that wanted nothing more than to drain her of that power.

So it was a problem for another day, to say the least.

"We got things squiggling!" Mads shouted from the bottom of the stairs. "I would say a terrifying amount of squiggling."

"Leif, get started on the portal," Terra ordered. "Hildisvíni, let's take the door. Mads, shoot anything that makes it past us."

Hildisvíni didn't turn and face the stairs, though. Instead, the huge hog tromped to a massive boulder a few meters from the entryway. The boulder was bigger than the hog, and Terra understood why Hildisvíni was interested in it almost immediately.

"You want to use that to block the door?" Terra asked.

In response, the battle boar threw its shoulder into the

massive stone. It hardly budged. So Terra joined him. Together, they shoved their *seidr*-enhanced strength into the boulder and managed to move it a few centimeters.

"We're running out of time we didn't have in the first place!" Mads fired his needle gun up the stairway.

"You hit one?" Terra grunted before throwing every bit of strength the bracers afforded her into the boulder.

"There's so many that *not* hitting one would be the real challenge," Mads retorted.

Terra gave up on banter as she focused on moving the boulder. Hildisvíni provided a massive amount of brute strength, but fulcrums and leverage might have been beyond the hog's rather formidable intellect.

Terra shoved her ax beneath the boulder, wedged it in, and lifted as the mighty hog pushed. Freya's ax appeared made of wood, but it was reinforced with the magic of a goddess. It bent but did not break, and with their strength combined, the boulder tumbled on its side.

Terra and Hildisvíni raced after it, not letting it lose momentum and settle into place. They smashed their shoulders into it before it could come to rest, and it tumbled a second time. It was so big that two tumbles were enough to place it in front of the entrance.

Mads was swimming above it, having barely dodged being squished flat.

The boulder settled into place, blocking ninety percent of the cavern opening. Only two small holes remained on the upper left and right of the boulder. They were just large enough that Terra imagined she could wriggle through if she was not wearing SCUBA gear.

Still, a hole that allowed a human to pass through could

admit quite a large snake.

The first of the serpents saw this. No sooner had they put the boulder in place than a massive head poked through. Before it could squeeze any more of its girth into the cave, Mads was above the snake. He placed his needle gun at the base of the skull, where it attached to its spine, and fired.

A hole blew out from the back of the snake's head to the front of its throat. If it had any death rattles, they took place on the other side of the boulder, in the passageway where Terra could not see them.

Mads showed some serious initiative by taking the macabre step of holding the head of the snake he'd killed so it could not slip from the hole and allow more snakes through. At least not until its body flaked away and broke down. Hopefully, that would be enough time for Leif to open his portal.

Hildisvíni certainly seemed to be handling the other person-sized hole on the opposite side of the boulder. The hog floated above the cavern floor. It almost looked like he was standing on an invisible platform instead of swimming. Still, every now and then, his huge legs moved back and forth a bit, indicating the hog was doing something like treading water.

No giant snake had come through Hildisvíni's hole yet, which Terra would qualify as a tactical mistake. Instead, smaller snakes tried to pour through. Each time one emerged, Hildisvíni snapped his jaws and gobbled them up like spaghetti.

"Holler if you need me. I'm going to check on our escape route," Terra told Mads.

"You mean our escape route to a plane of existence with a snake so massive it's going to make all these seem like worms?"

"More like microbes, if I'm properly wrapping my mind around the sheer scale of Jörmungandr, but yeah. That's the only ticket out of here unless we want to fight all these snakes from Joana's boat."

"I'll do what I can," Mads replied.

Terra left him and Hildisvíni as she swam deeper into the cavern. Leif stood roughly in the middle, speaking loudly as he recited a litany of runes. Each time he spoke the name of a different rune, a glowing form of it appeared from his chest and floated in front of him. When he spoke four or five of them, they would combine into a string of runes and float off to join a spiral of runes that grew larger with each one he spoke.

Already, the string of runes had formed a circle a few feet in diameter. Terra had no idea how many runes that had taken because although they were about a foot across when they emerged from Leif's chest, they were less than an inch each by the time they joined the swirling circle. He could have spoken hundreds of them at this point.

Leif gave no indication he had noticed Terra. He continued his litany and made the portal grow larger and larger.

At first, it was only a circle of glowing runes. Then, Leif reached some sort of tipping point, and the circle started to spin. The water in its center grew opaque, almost like it had frozen over. Leif kept the runes coming from his chest and pouring into the spell, and the opaque disc rippled. At its center, it grew translucent once more, like a window wiped clear of fog. Yet it was not the other side of the cavern Terra saw through the hole but another realm entirely.

Terra could not see much at first. Only a mist rolling through a landscape far brighter than the pitch-black cavern they currently occupied. Leif kept chanting, and the portal opened wider as it added more runes to its edge.

A vivid green mist rolled over a pond. Leif kept chanting, and the portal opened wider. Terra could not see much past the mist, but there were mountains in the distance, perhaps. However, she could not tell if they were mountains or banks of clouds stacked upon each other, higher and higher, until they rose past the boundaries of the disc.

It was wider now, wide enough for Terra to crawl through, but Leif showed no signs of stopping. He continued to chant, wishing the portal larger.

Terra stole a glance behind her and saw that while Hildisvíni still dominated every snake that came through the hole the same way a toddler might dominate a bowl of macaroni and cheese, Mads was having more trouble. The snake he had shot through the skull was nearly gone. Mads hauled at its spine and some of its ribs, trying to keep them lodged in place while snakes tried to pull them out of the hole.

Mads had to know it was a delay tactic because the bones he was using to block the opening were falling to nothing in his hand. A smaller snake tried to push through, and Mads released the crumbling bones and used his needle gun to punch a hole through the snake's head. Still, more were coming.

"How long, Leif?" Terra asked.

Leif didn't answer. He kept chanting, growing the portal wider and taller with every syllable that left his mouth.

Terra left him to it and went to help Mads.

He pulled back and reloaded his cartridge while Terra took position over the hole with Freya's ax. A snake poked its head through, and Terra decapitated it. Two smaller snakes tried to come in, and Terra separated their heads from their necks. It was like the world's highest-stakes version of whack-a-mole.

She didn't know how many snakes she killed before they stopped coming, but she knew that she had not won. When the snakes stopped poking through, the boulder started to move. At first, Terra thought perhaps Hildisvíni was moving it, but the huge hog looked as perplexed as she was at the lack of more snakes. They shared a look, and the boulder rumbled and scooted an inch away from the tunnel.

"Brace it!" Terra shouted at Hildisvíni, and the boar obeyed. He came down to the ground, planted his hooves on the cave floor, and pressed a huge shoulder against the rock. Just in time, too, as the boulder was already scooting forward.

Terra should not have been surprised by a snake using a single, extended push to move the boulder instead of repeatedly ramming it. That was what snakes did, after all. They constricted by slowly adding more pressure, taking advantage of any flinch or misstep their prey made, like the mistake of exhaling.

The snake on the other side of the boulder must be

doing the same thing. Terra could almost see it, thanks to the power of *seidr*.

It would have its body pushed against every edge of the tunnel, corkscrewing its way down for maximum force to shove against the boulder. It only needed to push the stone a foot or two forward to let dozens of snakes into the chamber.

If that happened, Terra was not so sure they would win this fight in the dark. They had headlights and orbs of light, but the snakes did not seem to need sight to sense their surroundings. They would be able to outmaneuver and overwhelm the four of them, even if one of the four was a giant magic battle pig.

Then, Leif was there. "The portal is stable!"

"And it's going to the right place?" Terra asked, peering through a circular window into another dimension filled with placid green water and tendrils of mist.

"Pretty sure! Not the land of fire giants, at least."

"Then why didn't you go through and call for us to come?" Terra asked, her shoulders still pressing against the boulder.

"I told you I can open the portal, but I cannot *use* it. I lack the proper qualifications. You are the Chosen of Freya. You must ask for permission to enter, and hopefully, it will work.

"Hold my boulder," Terra told him and approached the portal.

The moment she stepped away, the boulder inched forward, and snakes poured into the room. Mads and Hildisvíni were ready. They shot and ate snakes, respectively, while Terra went to the portal.

Something moved in the mist. Something large and slithering. "Who is trying to enter my realm?" a low voice boomed.

Terra wanted to wait for the speaker to reveal himself so she could properly greet him and show due respect, but there was no time.

"I am Terra Freyasdatter of Midgard. I have been Chosen by Freya, and I possess her artifacts. I have her golden bracers that grant me her strength and ability to use *seidr* as I see fit. I have Brísingamen, which grants me the ability to move faster than any mortal. I have Freya's feathered cloak, which allows me to take the form of any bird and travel about in that form. I have her ax, which I use to slay those who oppose me and defend everyone else. I also am now friends with Hildisvíni, her mighty battle swine."

"And her tears? Everyone knows of Freya's tears."

Terra thought it a bit preposterous that this serpent would take her at her word for all the other artifacts and not be able to sense the tears that had gone through her, but perhaps this was all part of a respectful greeting. A sort of salutation.

"I battled the minions of Hel, the daughter of Loki. Hel sent a man back to Earth as an avatar of her power, but he was strong enough to face me. He killed me in battle, but before my soul could be claimed and taken to Folkvangr, I used the tears to come back to life. I no longer have them on my person because I gave them to Freya herself, who thanked me for their safe return."

"Mmm..." the voice rumbled. "And what do you wish of the mighty Jörmungandr, whose might is such that if he rolls over, all of the lands of your Earth will be swallowed in water?"

"An audience. Nothing more. His children run wild on this world, and I wish to understand why he would let such chaos come here instead of using his own power, which of course must be far more formidable."

Okay, so maybe the last bit was not exactly the entire truth, but Terra had learned honesty was not something the Norse gods held in high esteem. Deception was part of their very being, and while she did not think she could deceive this snake in its own realm, she did think a bit of rose-tinted flattery might grant her the chance to try.

It seemed she had miscalculated, though. The voice said nothing, and the fog did not part but grew thicker and more concealing.

"Terra, luv, not to rush you, but I can't hold this anymore!" Mads had abandoned his post and was swimming toward Terra at full speed. "If my choices are being eaten by a snake at the bottom of the ocean or being eaten by one in a place where I can take off my gear, I'll take the latter."

Terra didn't know what to say, but then she didn't have to. The portal glowed brighter, illuminating the room, and the fog on the other side cleared. Terra felt the portal had opened.

"Come on, he's letting us in! Let's go!"

Leif and Hildisvíni did not need to be told twice.

Hildisvíni kicked off from the boulder and swam toward Terra. Leif understood that boar's power better than anyone, and he did not let it go to waste. He grabbed the bristly hide and was dragged away from the boulder.

Without the pair of them to hold back the stone, a massive snake pushed it out of the way as if it were nothing but a pebble.

It hissed as it entered the chamber but then retreated.

Not to run away, of course, but to grant enough space for tons of smaller snakes to enter. Smaller being a relative term, as many were thirty feet long.

"Come on!" Terra grabbed Mads' hand as Hildisvíni ran past. He snagged the boar, and they were all dragged through the portal into another realm.

Leif turned and managed to shut the portal behind them before the snakes reached it. The last thing they saw of Midgard was lost to the serpents.

CHAPTER EIGHTEEN

The realm of Jörmungandr

Terra stepped into ankle-deep green water. It stretched in all directions to the horizon. There was nothing but the water, shallow, in slightly different shades, and with a layer of mist clinging to the surface.

"The air is good to breathe," Leif announced, removing his SCUBA mask.

"Bloody good to hear that, mate. I was getting sick of all this." Mads shucked his mask and tank off.

Hildisvíni snorted and stomped one hoof. A ripple spread out from where he touched, traveling farther until it was lost in the mist.

"I guess I should take this off, too." Terra removed her mask and tank, as well as her flippers. It was odd to stand here in this infinite expanse of green water, but there could have been worse things to wear than a wetsuit. Terra only wished they had packed shoes. As it was, they would be walking through murky water for who knew how long without being able to see where their bare feet stepped down.

"Hello?" Terra asked the vast expanse.

"Please, come in," a voice boomed all around them. Terra thought she saw something massive moving in the green water ahead, but then the fog banks closed in, and it was gone. Whatever it was, it did not make ripples big enough to reach Terra and her friends.

"Any ideas?" Leif questioned.

"I thought you had the plan, mate. Coming to this land of pea-green soup was your idea."

"Forgive me for being at a bit of a loss when first stepping into the realm of a demigod."

Hildisvíni snorted and gestured ahead.

Terra looked. The fog had parted directly in front of them, and in the distance, mountains rose from the green water into the sky. The clouds behind those mountains parted, and more mountains appeared, then more behind them, until Terra was not sure if they were standing on the outside of a planet or the interior of one. As her gaze followed the mountains farther into the distance, there seemed to be some hanging upside down in the sky.

"Okay, so this place is not some far corner of Earth, then," Mads surmised.

"Were you really in doubt?" Leif asked. He alone seemed undisturbed by the horizon that was not a horizon.

"I don't know, mate. Ankle-deep swamp isn't exactly the most majestic of places."

A wind picked up, blowing in their faces and parting the fog in front of them, making the surface of the water ripple. It was not one horizon that confronted them but multiple. Terra could not truly wrap her head around what she was seeing.

The mountains rose and seemed to flip. Beside them, there appeared to be another planet in the sky, also covered in mountains nearly buried in mist. Everything except the tops of the mountains was thick with vegetation as if the green of the water was some sort of algae that crawled across everything it could, even if it had to jump through the sky to do so.

"I didn't mean anything by it," Mads told the sky before squeezing his eyes shut. Terra understood. She was also getting a sense of vertigo. She was seeing a landscape her mind had never conceived of witnessing. Her brain was trying to make sense of it and mostly failing.

Her only advantage over Mads was that she used the flow of *seidr* to accomplish the impossible all the time. She could not make sense of what her eyes were telling her, but part of her had become accustomed to not making sense of things.

The ability to teleport or turn into a bird had that effect on people.

The realm seemed to respond to Mads, and the fog moved back, blocking most of the mountains. Or maybe that was Terra's brain trying to make sense of things when there was none to be made.

Without the long views, they could at least proceed. Not that Terra was sure they were even doing that. They walked along the path through the fog in front of them, but with nothing but endless green water and distant mountains not bound by the rules of geography, it was hard to judge their progress.

"I don't understand where we're going, but maybe we can move faster?" Mads asked. "Last time I checked with Romero, the snakes were not attacking them. But if they were all coming for magic, and that magic's gone, they might turn on the boat."

"I think that would be prudent," Leif agreed. "This place… It's not what I thought it would be."

Terra wanted to know what the Asgardian had been imagining when he opened the portal here, but Mads' suggestion seemed the more pressing one.

"Hildisvíni, would you mind if we all got a ride?" she asked the mighty boar.

Hildisvíni grunted, then bowed his huge head. The boar was massive, but Terra did not think he was large enough for three riders. Still, she wouldn't decline, especially after she had asked for the ride. Terra clambered onto his back, grabbing fistfuls of thick, wiry hair to help pull herself up. She settled into place and found that Hildisvíni seemed wider and bigger than he had been.

"A neat trick, noble pig," Leif remarked. "But of course, a simple enough thing for someone as special as you."

Hildisvíni squealed in delight as Leif leaned against him, then made his hands into a foothold for the vertically challenged Mads. Mads did not protest. He simply climbed up onto the back of the pig, then scooted close to Terra and held onto her waist. If he felt awkward about the proximity, he did not show it.

Leif scrambled up next, showing no hesitation in grabbing the pig's hair in his fists.

"Do you have any idea how Hildisvíni came to be in

that temple instead of with Freya?" Terra asked when Leif settled in place.

"I cannot even guess. It had been quite some time since I last saw Hildisvíni, but that is the nature of things in Asgard. Sometimes, gods wander for decades. Odin is especially prone to going about his business and letting Asgard function without him."

"But surely Hildisvíni was not wandering around by himself," Terra suggested. "He's a good, loyal pig, isn't he? He wouldn't leave Freya in a lurch."

"Of course he wouldn't." Leif patted the big hog's flank. "Freya surely sent him there, likely in anticipation of this moment. She can be as inscrutable as the rest of them, but her eyes are always to the future and the fates she can sense unfolding."

"So she sent the big golden pig so we could survive the snakes and ride him through this interdimensional swamp?" Mads asked.

"Perhaps. Or perhaps Hildisvíni's true purpose is still ahead of us. I would not venture a guess. I can hardly sense a single strand of *seidr*, while her holiness Freya can see entire tapestries. What about you, Terra? Can you sense where we are supposed to go now?"

"The only part of this place that makes any sense to me is the path in the fog." Terra gestured in front of them.

Hildisvíni grunted in agreement and started forward.

On the back of the boar, they moved more quickly through the landscape. Or perhaps it was fair to say the landscape moved more quickly around them. Hildisvíni plodded forward, his huge legs carrying them across the green water. As they moved, the fog parted now and then to reveal mountains to their right and left or sometimes above them in the sky.

They passed a floating mountain with a thick stream trickling from it into the green water below. They saw a planet in the sky that seemed to possess an eye as vivid as Jupiter's before it was lost to the fog. They saw boulders rise from the green gunk. Terra kept her hand on her ax, ready to strike the snakes she expected to be waiting for them through the fog, but no attack ever came.

"Are we sure we're going in the right direction?" Mads asked when they had passed the umpteenth floating boulder. "I expected us to reach those mountains by now."

It was odd. Mountains seemed to come and go on either side of them, but the formation they were moving toward seemed as distant as it had when they started their walk.

Then, Hildisvíni's hoof clacked on stone, and the boar stepped from the pond onto a wide piece of rock. No soil or grass grew on the surface, but plenty of pools formed in the low places, choked with rotten vegetation. Hildisvíni minded them carefully and did not put his hooves inside any of the puddles.

"It's so disorienting," Terra remarked. "I guess that makes sense, though. It's a place made to hold a snake that can crush the entire Earth. It has to be bigger than a planet but also not bound by rules like gravity."

"Jörmungandr is bigger than that," Leif pointed out. "Big enough to crush *Midgard*, which is much more than Earth."

"So this place makes sense to you?" Mads snorted.

Obviously, he did not trust that Leif could comprehend it any better than him."

"Not exactly, no," Leif admitted. "I had always heard this realm was a place of wonders. I heard of the floating mountains and the skies filled with planets, but I seem to recall hearing of waterfalls that fell from one to the other, making rivers through the sky."

"We saw a waterfall," Mads replied.

"True, but it looked no fresher than that." Leif pointed to one of the thick puddles of slime trying to grow in the cracks of the rock. "My great uncle Freyr came here once and said he had never seen so many stars. He said it was a place that made him truly marvel at the branches of the world tree. This…well, it looks like it's seen better times.

"It has been long since my realm has held such splendor." Again, the voice boomed from all around them. The words were in old Norse, inscrutable and unknown to Terra despite her knowing how to read runes, yet she found her brain had no difficulty changing them into sounds and meanings she knew.

She glanced back and saw Leif had heard the words. Mads, too, seeing as how he was turning back and forth, looking for the source.

"Your realm? Then we must have the honor of speaking to the mighty Jörmungandr, whose presence we of Midgard both fear and hold in awe," Terra replied.

She could not see the world snake, but surely that did not mean the same was true of her. Jörmungandr could surely see her. For all she knew, she was standing on his back, or he was looking at them from some hidden pool in the green water they had left behind them.

So, she did not stay on her mount. Instead, she lowered herself with as much grace as she could muster, then bowed deeply. She would have curtsied, but she thought the skin-tight wetsuit lent itself to more of a bow. She did not want to rip the crotch out in front of a tridimensional demigod of destruction.

The sky seemed to chuckle at her words and the seriousness with which she took her formality. "Well reasoned, little mortal. It is indeed Jörmungandr to whom you speak. I have not had a visitor to my realm for centuries, and perhaps the place could use a good cleaning."

Leif climbed off the pig next, though with none of Terra's smooth grace. She wondered how he would look riding a horse. Probably not great. Mads, on the other hand, slid off the back of the hog as easily as melted butter. Terra did not believe there was a scenario on Earth in which Mads would not be able to glibly navigate, and it seemed his sleek confidence extended to the realms beyond Midgard.

"My esteemed holiness, for I know not what else to call you," Leif began. "This realm is as you like it and, therefore, more than suitable for us. It is nearly too much for our minds to comprehend. I was simply stating the power of this place is such that even the minds of the gods cannot adequately describe it." Leif was following Terra's lead and laying on the compliments.

"You may call me by my name. It is a good name, after all. Yet your flattery goes too far, Asgardian," Jörmungandr boomed. "Your gods trapped me in this place. They know what it contains and what it's capable of better than any other."

"You like the green slime because you can hide in it, then?" Mads asked.

Jörmungandr chuckled, and the ground shook. "I like this mortal. He is...spunky." It was a phrase in old Norse, but her brain made it into a single word. Mads at least looked embarrassed to have been called spunky by the giant hidden snake.

"I do not hide, little man made of meat and bone. Revealing my true form would shatter your minds. You can hardly fathom the scale of your own planet, and I am far larger than that. I would not break the fragile brains of my first visitors. Besides, were I to take my true form, I cannot be sure this realm could contain me. The last time I tried was during the previous Ragnarök.

"Is that why you have come, mortal who has been chosen by a god? Do you wish to do battle with one as mighty as I? It has been long since a human has had the arrogance to try to slay me. I have slain Thor with my strength. You understand this? My venom made his heart stop, and his muscles grow so weak, he dropped his little hammer."

Terra did not think it a prudent moment to point out that in the same fight, Thor had killed Jörmungandr as well.

"I did not come to battle you, Jörmungandr the powerful."

"Are you certain? I am not like my father. I have no love of deceptions. I will not be tricked and captured like my brother and sister. I am in this place because I bide my time until Ragnarök comes once more. Do not tempt me into bringing it about with lies and trickery.

"If you wish to fight, we can fight. You have the pieces of Freya. That is why I let you into this realm in the first place. If you wish to see how they fare against me, raise your ax now, and let us see how many worlds we can destroy in our battle."

"I do not wish to destroy a world," Terra replied. "I want to save one, and I need your help. We came to your realm for aid, not to battle."

"It amuses me that you would come so far merely to talk, but so be it. It is long since I have had a visitor. I can spare a few moments of my eternity for company as amusing as this."

Terra drew a deep breath and tried to formulate her thoughts. How did one go about appeasing a giant snake who was the son of a god? How did one convince a monster to call back the plague he had released upon the Earth?

Before she had so much as a moment to put her thoughts to words, the stone beneath her feet rumbled, then broke free from the rest. The three of them stumbled, and they grabbed the unshakable mound that was Hildisvíni. The boar did not bother trying to stay on his feet. Already, he lay on his huge belly, as immovable as a boulder.

Terra would never be able to properly describe the sensation she felt as the world changed around her. It almost felt like riding an elevator upward, but the force beneath her feet was more substantial, like standing on top of a mountain. However, a mountain did not feel like its roots might turn to jelly as it grew higher, pushing through cloud banks.

Terra had time to see the ground around them had not been left behind but was rising with them, turning the piece of stone they stood on into the peak of a mountain. Then the tip entered a thunderhead, and she could see nothing past her friends and thick clouds. Lightning cracked in the distance, and Terra felt the static charge all over. The droplets of cloud around them grew bigger, and rain splattered them.

Onward they rose, through cloud and rain and wind, then through a great mass of leaves, as if their mountain had thrust itself up through every rainforest on Earth. The leaves vanished as quickly as they had appeared, and they were passing through waterfalls that fell from planets across the path of their mountain. The waterfalls were lost in the cloud, or perhaps they had *caused* the clouds because a moment later, they emerged into clear space.

Below, their mountain vanished into a huge bank of thunderheads that stretched across the rounded curve of a globe. Beyond them was green water and more mountains, but none as tall as the one that still took them ever higher.

The air temperature dropped, and Terra's wetsuit became miserably cold. Frost covered Hildisvíni's golden bristles, but the pig was not perturbed. He shook like a dog, hardly moving his bulk yet nearly knocking Terra, Leif, and Mads from the top of the mountain. The ice crystals flew clear and instantly sublimated, turning into a puff of a cloud already far below them.

Terra found the moisture in her own suit sublimating as well. Mist streamed from her and her friends, then they were dry and comfortable despite an unfathomable cold she could sense more than feel beyond where they could all reach.

She shivered, aware of the lurking danger of this cold. Leif stood on wobbly legs, one hand on the huge hog. With the other, he produced the pack with the feathered cloak and gave it to Terra.

She took it, opened the pack, and threw the cloak around her shoulders. It nestled around her, warming her upper body. She felt a thrill of pleasure as the feathers extended down her back, growing to the full size.

She reached for the edges of the cloak and pulled it around herself. As soon as she did, she felt a chill, and her wetsuit shattered to pieces and disappeared, leaving a different sort of cloud behind them as the mountain grew.

She was naked for only a moment, though, and only beneath the soft feathered down of the cloak because it changed. It formed itself into a sleeveless white gown with gold feathers across the shoulders and sticking up around her neck. The cloak was all golden now, making the white dress even brighter. Terra herself looked like the glowing center of a star as it whipped around in the wind of their ascension.

"Wish I could do that." Mads tugged at his wetsuit.

The mountain ascended higher until it was not only the roundness of a single globe beneath them but other planets they were rising above. Past one of them, moving out of the shadow of a planetary eclipse, a glowing sun appeared. It hardly warmed them, it was so distant. They passed through another cloud, though this one was made of bits of stone and frozen water. A nebula of space dust larger than Terra could fathom.

Finally, the mountain stopped growing, and Terra looked out at a vista of stars, planets, and cosmic dust vaster than any ocean, vaster than her human brain could fathom.

In this cosmic constellation of glowing stars and clouds of dust, something shifted and moved. A few stars winked out in places, while others appeared where none had been before. Then, it was the titanic head of a snake looking down on them, with distant galaxies for eyes and stars for the points of its teeth.

Jörmungandr gazed at Terra in her white dress and gold feathers, with her golden bracers and torc, ax in hand, with a golden battle pig at her back.

"Very well, Chosen. What is it you wish to speak of?"

CHAPTER NINETEEN

The realm of Jörmungandr

Terra struggled to make eye contact with the pair of galaxies that seemed to stare from the inkiness of space and into her soul. She did not let herself flinch or look away. She was here representing Freya, a goddess older and wiser than the world serpent. Confidence and posturing were perhaps even more important to the gods than anyone else, and she could not let Jörmungandr see her sweat. Even if he was looking at her with eyes made of countless stars.

Instead, she threw her feathered cloak over her shoulders, planted her feet squarely, and let herself exude confidence. She had the physique of the goddess, the knowledge earned from hunting her artifacts across the northern hemisphere, and the confidence to use those artifacts to deadly effect. She did not know how she would battle a serpent made of stars, but she knew Thor had somehow defeated the mighty snake by wielding his hammer. Surely, her ax and bracers could accomplish a similar victory.

She let Jörmungandr see her confidence, but she did not threaten him. For while she would do battle if she needed to, she was not about to pick a fight with a serpent so powerful that even it wriggling in the depths would be enough to send tidal waves to destroy the lands of Midgard. Given Jörmungandr's current size, she wondered if those waves would be more akin to the energy and gravity that might come from a collapsing black hole.

"Your children have come to Midgard and put many innocent people in peril. I have seen hundreds already, and we know they are spreading through the seas of the Earth in great numbers. I wish to understand why you sent your children to attack our realm. We heard no warning of your displeasure with us. If we had, we would have endeavored to make it right. You are Jörmungandr. Far more powerful, feared, and respected than either of your siblings."

The stars above shifted and moved in the heavens as if the huge snake was slithering about, thinking of a response. Terra's brain could barely understand what she was seeing, but a part of her was terrified. It was not only the snake's head made of stars but its entire body comprised of the vastness of space. If he decided to turn against her, she wouldn't even know where to throw the first punch.

"Why do you mention my siblings? They have nothing to do with my offspring. Neither of them has come to visit me in my realm. They do not know my children. They are both churlish and wrathful. Do not speak of them here without reason." As Jörmungandr spoke, stars exploded into supernovas and became no more.

"I apologize, Jörmungandr." Terra bowed deeply to

show her sincerity. "I only mentioned them because they have both transgressed upon Midgard. Fenrir came trying to gather the pieces of Freya so he could make a home there, while Hel tried to use the artifacts to grant her the power to travel between the realms. I can see now how ignorant I was to think you would have even considered sending your children to my realm to pester me."

"We only thought that because they were trying to kill us," Mads pointed out.

Terra expected a meteorite to blast from the heavens and incinerate her thieving friend, but Jörmungandr did not smite him into nothing.

"It was only your magic, I expect," Jörmungandr stated after a moment. "I can sense your power. It rivals many of the Vanir. My progeny must be unable to resist it. I did not send them to Midgard. I do not care what they do. It is not my will that they destroy your realm, and I do not care for these trinkets you wear."

"Pardon my ignorance, powerful one, but if you did not will them to destroy the realm of Midgard, how is it they were allowed to leave your realm at all? Surely, they have not dared rebel against you," Terra suggested. "Some are quite large by the standards of humans, but compared to this form you show us, they are still tiny things."

Leif seemed about as incapable of speech as the battle boar. Maybe that was a good thing. He could certainly put his foot in his mouth back on Earth, and he seemed practically star-struck with the world snake.

"I do not follow all their movements," Jörmungandr replied dismissively. "They are many, and they make demands on my attention that I have no interest in filling."

The stars slithered through the sky as if the snake was making a barrier around himself like a lousy dad crossing his arms at a parent-teacher conference when he received news about his kid that he did not want to hear.

"Pardon my impertinence, but is it possible their mother could have put them up to this?" Leif asked. A bold move, asking about a deadbeat dad's wife, but Jörmungandr did not mind, thank goodness.

Instead, the cosmic snake laughed at Leif's words. The mountain they were standing on shook with mirth, causing a few rockslides down below.

"There is no mother to my children. I am the world snake. I am the brother of Fenrir and Hel, yes, but that does not mean the male form is my only identity. All things are within my coils. Male and female. Water and fire. My venom can gouge rivers from the earth as surely as I can flood them.

"I need no woman to make children. I grow with the very conception of the universe. As the gods and mortals expand their understanding of Yggdrasil and its many branches, I too expand. When I last fought Thor, it was not in the form of space and the stars you see before you because you mortals did not understand any of it."

"You grow more powerful as we acquire more knowledge," Terra mused. It was a potent thought.

The stars above seemed to shrug. "I grow weaker when your kind falls into ignorance as well. It was a dark time when you humans forgot how to travel your tiny Earth. There are times I feel it happening again. When your little wars grow too intense, for example. But with luck, I will not lose this size again."

"Where do your children come from, mate?" Mads asked. "You're growing with human knowledge, and I mean no offense by this, but your children did not seem quite as sharp."

"When I grow, I shed my skin and take on new forms. Every time I do, some of my scales fall away and manifest into minute versions of myself. Some have gone on to girdle planets of their own, but a great many stayed in this realm. It was made to be big enough to contain all aspects of me, and they are but another aspect."

"So it is you who sent them for us?" Mads asked. It was so close to an accusation that Terra felt her breath catch. She did not want to battle this mighty serpent. Not if it could be helped.

Yet again, Jörmungandr showed a soft spot for the thief.

He chuckled, and a field of shooting stars flew across the sky as he did. "They are aspects of me, but not me. I do not control their minds any more than the mortals of Earth control the minds of their own children. However, the last time I shed a skin was in the aftermath of Ragnarök. To say I was disappointed in how that turned out is an understatement. They are likely filled with my rage and ire. Not that I blame them. We should have vengeance for what was done to us. It is unconscionable."

"And despite this, you did not send them to Midgard?" Terra pressed.

"If I had sent them, I would not lie about it. I am not like my father. I am a being of vast power. I have no need for deception. I was mad for what you would call centuries, but since then, I have lost interest in such feelings.

"I spent a time watching planets being sucked into suns,

and I must say, compared to that drama, the skirmishes of gods and mortals are not worth my efforts. More interesting to watch a planet lose all life than to observe for a while before everyone becomes frightened and stops their tiny little wars."

"But if you did not send them, how could they have come to Midgard? It is not easy to move between the realms," Leif pointed out.

"That is true, but my children are many, and my realm is vast. There are roots of Yggdrasil that drink from my pools, branches that shade lakes. My children could have found a root and explored it."

"The branches of Yggdrasil are supposed to be a confusing tangle. How could your children have navigated it without your help?" Terra asked.

"They are many, and they are fearless. They might have found ten paths that ended in their deaths for everyone who made it through. Over time, they must have found a route, and probably without the help of that worthless Ratatoskr. Now that they know the path, I would imagine more will come to Midgard than the scouts." Jörmungandr seemed amused at the idea.

Terra could not find the humor in the idea. "You're saying it took your children centuries to find a path here, but now that they have, they can follow each other along it as they wish? Does that mean more are coming? How many children do you have?"

The world serpent shrugged, and a branch of a nebula shifted in the sky, agitated by his movements. "I do not keep count, but over the years, there have been many.

Probably not a million, but something like that. I tried counting once but grew tired."

"A *million*? You're saying the hundreds we saw are not even a small part?"

"Of course not," Jörmungandr purred. "I always have some children who are less patient than others. They must have been the ones who found the path there. I do not think the others will want to stay behind, though. They find this world boring and dull. They have not the imagination I do. They cannot conceive of what they cannot see. Now that there is a path, they will seize upon it. Perhaps I will finally have some tranquility here."

Terra glanced at Leif and Mads, who looked as freaked out as she was. There were potentially *a million* snakes coming to Earth? Nothing could stop them! They had the ability to block magic. It would take a full-on war to end the threat, and Terra doubted the Earth could survive *that*.

"Jörmungandr, my lord. If your children come to Earth, it will cause great chaos."

"Yes. The idea amuses me."

"But the gods will not be so pleased," Leif insisted.

"It's true," Terra added. "They have come to like the way life on Earth is progressing. They will not like it when these snakes try to gobble everyone up. They might come here and wage war on your realm."

The snake did not seem bothered by that idea.

Terra tried a different tact. "Or if your children are successful, will your own realm not shrink because of the lack of understanding? Could your children cause this place to shrink?"

"It is too big anyway," Jörmungandr replied petulantly.

"I once kept it in better shape than this, but that takes too much effort, considering the size. No, I would be glad to see my children devouring the people of Midgard.

"And as for a war, I welcome the gods in combat. I bested Thor last time. I stopped his heart with my venom, but I showed restraint. I will not do that again. This time, I will poison every bit of him so his heart will never restart. It will be a proper battle, and I will have victory. Then, perhaps my father will come and see me in this place to celebrate my success."

"Man," Mads muttered. "All of Loki's kids really have daddy issues, huh?"

"Daddy what?" Jörmungandr asked.

"Nothing, oh powerful one," Terra was quick to say. "It is only that we wonder if Loki could have done something with your children. Is it possible he showed them the way to Midgard for a chance to take the artifacts he desired?" Terra asked.

The sky rumbled at that. Terra wondered if entire planets had been destroyed or if it only looked that way.

"My father does not share his plans with me. If he had been to my realm, I would know it. He is a worthless being and hardly worth the power he gave me. If my children are working with him, they know him better than I do."

It was the first time they had seen the snake angry. Terra wondered if they could use that. His indifference was not helping them, but could his fury be turned into a tool? It was the sort of thinking a Viking would be proud of.

"We think your father must be involved," Terra announced, which nearly gave Leif a heart attack. "After all, your brother and sister both had aims on Earth. They would not have done that without someone pulling their strings."

"You underestimate them," Jörmungandr growled, and the mountain beneath their feet shook. "We are not his shadows but forces in our own right. He feared us because, like Odin, he knew his children would be more powerful than he was. We do not act because he tells us to. We do as we wish. We are forces more dangerous and powerful than his shallow deceits."

The stars moved around them, and the snake appeared to grow more distant.

"I did not mean to imply you were his pawns. We came here to speak to you about your children, not your father. I apologize." Terra bowed, looking down the steep sides of the mountain at the planet far below them. A storm raged in the distance. She wondered if that was some part of the world serpent, if everything in this realm was part of him.

"You need not apologize to me, Chosen. There is truth in your thinking, even if it is not true of me. Often, children do all they can because of their parents or in spite of them. It is different for me, I would like to think, but I am not so sure it is different for my children. Their anger is my own. They are in Midgard because I allowed them to go. I have neglected them. I do not think they will listen to me now, though."

"Surely, you can try!" Terra exclaimed.

"A waste of time," Jörmungandr responded. "They will not listen to me. There is no point in pretending they will."

"You won't even give it a shot, mate? Isn't that why they ran off in the first place?" Mads asked.

The stars shifted, and the huge illusion of the snake

appeared to grow closer. So close that its cosmic jaws felt like they were right in front of them, ready to open up and swallow the planet on which they stood.

"You are bold, little human, to speak to me in this way. You must understand what I can do to you and your world, yet you still speak so freely. It amuses me."

"Well, jolly good. We made it all the way to this world, only to give the father of the snakes attacking Earth a good chuckle. Heroes, we are," Mads intoned.

Jörmungandr actually smiled at that. "You have indeed traveled a great distance to be here, and it has been a long time since I have had visitors. I admire the spunk of your kind. The way you think your pathetic little lives carry weight far greater than they do. You are concerned about my offspring? Fair enough. If you wish to deal with the many that have already reached Midgard and the many, many more that are surely on their way, I have a solution."

"We are honored, Jörmungandr! Thank you!" Terra replied. "What is it we can do?"

"Simple. Kill me."

CHAPTER TWENTY

The realm of Jörmungandr

"We want you to help us save Earth from your children. How would killing you help with that?" Terra asked.

"Plus, how exactly are we supposed to do that?" Mads added. "I can't imagine it's that easy to stab a snake in the heart when his heart is a distant planet."

"There is a way," Jörmungandr revealed. "This form I am currently in is spread across this entire realm, but I can consolidate myself into something you might more readily recognize. I can make a body your ax could bite, your bracers could affect."

The mountain they were on seemed to rise higher. The world beneath them fell away as the mountain punched through another cloud bank, and they rose above the endless green water they had found when they first entered this realm. It was as if they had looped back around to where they entered. Despite the cosmic nature of this realm, there did seem to be limits, and Jörmungandr had thrown them through one.

Yet everything was not the same as it had been. The green water was no longer still, and it did not seem so shallow anymore. Beneath the surface, something huge and twisting moved, disturbing the placid surface and hinting at a great leviathan.

Then, something rose from the water. Or perhaps rose *with* the water was a better description, for it looked like some mighty force emerged, and the green water became its scaly hide. Water poured and dripped from it, never fully running away, never fully revealing the massive serpent before them, as tall as the mountain.

This body of Jörmungandr was still more nebulous than his children had been, but now Terra could see where to strike it with her ax. She saw how she might attack the serpent's face, blind it, then slit its throat and spill an ocean of blood into this realm. But to what purpose?

"Why should I kill you?" Terra asked. She felt the pieces of Freya, each ready to aid her in this fight, though she was far from certain she could win if the serpent decided to fight back.

"My children are part of me. They are my scales grown into serpents, thanks to the magic in my blood. If I die, they will cease to be. They will lose the magic that is them."

"And you will be reborn? Is that your wish?" Leif demanded.

The snake made of the green sea shrugged. Great waves of water rolled from it and splashed back into the expanse below. "Perhaps I will be reborn as I was after the last Ragnarök. Perhaps not. I do not think it matters."

"How can the end of your own existence not matter?"

Terra asked. "If you do not wish for reincarnation, what do you wish for?"

"I wish for nothing. I have no purpose anymore. No purpose I can see."

"That's living, mate," Mads told him.

"Ah, you see? I miss the moral clarity of mortals."

"You miss that which you never had?" Terra asked.

"I am immortal. That is true. I will continue to live as long as the nine realms exist, but that was not how it was supposed to be. Even when the Aesir and Vanir dumped me in the oceans of Midgard so long ago, I knew I would return for the final battle.

"My siblings and I were foretold to rise up and end existence. We were the forces of Ragnarök. We *were* Ragnarök. The end of the world would come at our fangs, and finally, the world tree would have its end. That is how things work in Midgard, is it not? All things come to an end. We were to play our part in making this truth an eternal truth."

"But then Ragnarök happened, and the world didn't end," Terra concluded.

"They lied to us," Jörmungandr hissed. "From the moment they brought us to Asgard, bound like animals, they told everyone that we must be feared, for we would be the death of them and the world itself. And we were. We killed them, just as they feared. But then they came back."

"Not so easy to kill a god," Mads offered.

Leif said nothing. He seemed terrified of this entire chain of reasoning.

Terra would not strike at the world serpent until she had some sense of what Leif was thinking and whether he believed this was all a feint to trick Terra into lowering her guard. However, she did not feel it was. Jörmungandr had seemed distant and confused when they first arrived in this place. His siblings had been angry about Ragnarök, too. Yet he had a different solution to the problem than they did.

"It's impossible, and they knew it. Their Allfather saw it all, thanks to the eye he took out and traded for knowledge he should not have had. Your patron probably played a role as well. She had a way of making others do as she wished. They knew what Ragnarök was. They knew even if we won, we would lose."

"But isn't it better that way? Isn't it better if the world gets to keep existing?" Terra pleaded.

"How is that preferable? The world will go on forever, and my siblings and I will never be free from our cages? Death is far preferable to that. You mortals know your time is limited. It causes you to do all sorts of wonderful and horrid things. You make art and build things to leave as your legacy. You wage wars to take what you can while you are still living. You struggle and fight and scream into the dark because you know there is an end to it all.

"But for me, there is no end. Not even the promise of Ragnarök. There is only this prison they made for me from which I can never escape. I have no purpose. No reason to exist. I had thought I would bring about the end of things, but that was a lie."

"So you told this to your children, and they unleashed themselves upon Earth?" Mads demanded.

"I do not know what they have heard. I do not summon them or make demands of them. Sometimes, I speak my thoughts aloud so I can at least hear something in this place besides the sounds of my own imprisonment. Sometimes they listen. Perhaps too much.

"It does not matter. if they are a plague on your earth, I will help you end it because you can help me end the plague of boredom and meaningless existence I suffered until you came here. You are all interesting, and for that, I will do as you wish and let you put an ax through my heart."

"I...I'm not sure I can," Terra stammered.

"I know how you mortals think about death. You obsess over it, even as it terrorizes you. I understand. If you need some time to discuss this, it is nothing to me. A few more minutes of this existence is preferable to another thousand years."

Jörmungandr bowed, water cascading off his concealed form as he sank back into the green water. He did not disappear but became a shadow beneath the surface.

"Well...do we have thoughts on this?" Terra asked.

"You think we can speak candidly?" Mads asked, looking at the sea below them and the mighty serpent it now concealed, or had perhaps always concealed.

"He was pretty clear about not liking tricks. I think we can," Terra replied.

"I think he is being genuine and really does wish for Terra to end his life. But I implore you not to do it," Leif stated.

"One vote for no, then. You mind explaining why, mate? Seems like he's leaving the net wide open, and we got a striker ready to make a goal," Mads remarked.

"The world serpent has a place in existence. He may not currently like it, but he has a place. I can imagine it doing damage to any number of the realms. It could leave them all unguarded to things worse than an apathetic serpent."

"Unguarded? You really think Jörmungandr is protecting Midgard?" Terra asked.

"He encircles the realm. That is his nature. I am not arguing that he wishes to keep it safe, only that he is a presence any force that wishes to move against Midgard must consider. If he is gone, it may be that the Jotun see a way in and take advantage. It would not be beyond them to move as soon as they see a chance."

"But there are already monstrous snakes on Earth," Terra pointed out. "Waiting to see if more come instead of the ones we have seemed like a nebulous threat versus a very real one."

"I suppose," Leif allowed. "And perhaps you are right. Perhaps if you kill him, we will have nothing to deal with beyond his death rattles, which may be contained to this realm instead of the oceans of Earth. Though there are the Aesir and Vanir to consider as well."

"You mean Odin and all of them?" Mads questioned.

"Indeed. Jörmungandr is not wrong that Ragnarök is something *they* believe in. Odin foresaw it, and there are many signs of its coming. If you slay the world serpent, I do not know what they will do. They may start a Ragnarök themselves, or they may simply punish you for your actions."

"But I'm the Chosen of Freya!"

"And thus, Freya will likely take your side, but the Aesir can be cruel. They have offered her hand in marriage to various Jotun on multiple occasions. I cannot say what will happen if they decide your actions were wrong. Only that there will be consequences, and when it comes to punishment, the Aesir can be frighteningly creative."

"Or they'll see me as a hero," Terra returned. "When we revealed Fenrir to the world, Thor came to help. And when we defeated Hel's minions, Freya herself appeared. When we stopped Beatrice when she had Loki's wand, Odin and Freya came. I think…I think maybe we should do this."

She had a suspicion that if she tried to slay Jörmungandr, he would fight back, but so what? She could beat a snake of his size, even if he was still five times larger than the snake that attacked their ship. It would not be easy and likely not pleasant, but what other choice did she have than to cut off the proverbial head of the snake?

Jörmungandr had said many of his offspring were on the branches of the world tree even now. That the ones on Earth were the scouts, and the vast bulk of his offspring had yet to arrive. Could the Earth defend itself against thousands or even tens of thousands of serpents hungry for magic?

Humans had a great propensity for destruction. They might be able to stave off the overwhelming horde of serpents, but at what cost? They would suffer casualties. The only question would be if the world's governments could hold the casualties to the hundreds of thousands or whether they would spill into the millions. Or the billions. If the snakes could resist gunshots, any war against them would be much more difficult.

Or maybe the gods would get involved. Maybe Thor would unleash his full destructive might on Midgard. Maybe Odin and his wolves would crash across the countryside, destroying the snakes and anything else in their path.

Even Freya was a battle goddess. Would she help people survive the snakes, or would she treat them with disdain for running? Folkvangr was her domain and reserved for those who died in battle, not running from it. Perhaps the Norse gods would come to Earth and attempt to save humanity. Perhaps they would come and aid in its destruction.

Or cut the head off the snake.

She stepped toward the edge of the mountain overlooking the green water. Jörmungandr rose as if sensing she had come to her decision. He did not look as if he wanted to fight, to turn his last moments alive into a battle for the ages. He looked tired, confused, and ready to die. He raised his head above Terra, exposing his neck to her.

She had to do this. She had to stop the hordes of snakes from coming to Earth. She raised Freya's ax, willed the flow of *seidr* to spread through her body and into the blade. She would end this.

Even if it felt wrong. Even if Jörmungandr did not seem malicious or evil, only lost. He had not sent his children to attack the Earth. He had not even destroyed Midgard during Ragnarök, which had to count for something. But how could someone find purpose for a being that was supposed to play a part in the end of the world?

Then, everything clicked into place. Terra had an idea, or the beginnings of one. Maybe it wasn't the smartest choice, but decapitating this snake for being listless and letting his children flee from him didn't seem right, either.

She lowered her ax. Considered her words. Decided that perhaps bluntness was the best path forward.

"Those serpents all see you as their father and not as part of themselves, right?"

Jörmungandr eyed her with the massive slit of one eye. "That is true. They recognize that they are younger than me, less experienced. Children by any definition of the word."

"But they don't seem to like you very much," Terra added.

Jörmungandr nodded. "When I lost my first scales and saw what they could become, I tried to train them and make them a certain way, but there was no point. I let the others keep a will of their own so they could do what they wish. That freedom means they can hate me if they so desire. It is how free will works, is it not?"

"That's not true, though."

"Forgive me for not wanting to argue with a mortal about free will," Jörmungandr drawled derisively.

"I'm trying to understand you. You said many of them were born after Ragnarök. That you lost some scales when you were very angry, and the snakes that grew out of them have the same anger."

"Is that different from humans? Don't you find some of you have more anger than others?"

"We definitely have our differences, but we try to help each other get through them. From what I understand, that's part of what it means to be a parent."

"And part of being a parent is letting your offspring grow up. Sometimes, that doesn't work out."

"But you didn't give them a chance. You didn't help

them learn to control the anger that *you* put into them. You let them marinate in it, grow sick with it. You offered no cure, no solution, despite the problem coming from *you*."

"I am not perfect. I never claimed to be."

"I thought you would try to do better than those who came before you. That you would want your children to truly have free will instead of an anger problem and no ability to manage it." Terra kept talking. She had to get to her point, to show Jörmungandr he was wrong. And she had to get there before he figured it out, decided he didn't like it, and attacked her.

"Your apparent apathy fueled their rage, and now they are going to do what *you* are supposed to do. They are going to Midgard to rise from the oceans and destroy humanity. They are not free. They're pawns doing their father's bidding, even though they think they have free will. It's funny. You don't seem that different from Loki, really."

CHAPTER TWENTY-ONE

The realm of Jörmungandr

Jörmungandr rose from the water, growing higher and higher until he towered above Terra despite her standing on a mountain. The water streamed from his scales until Terra could see him clearly. This was not some nebulous serpent made of ideas or thoughts. This was a snake with scales like hard stone and eyes that flickered with malice.

And more of him was still hidden under the water, no doubt coiled and ready to assist Jörmungandr in crushing this tiny human who had dared speak such.

"I am *nothing* like my father. All he does is deceive. All he cares about is himself. We are pawns to him. My children are not pawns to me. No matter what you say or think, I did not put them up to this."

"So they're worth even less than pawns to you?" Terra threw back.

The waters hiding the vast bulk of Jörmungandr's body trembled and shook, but before the waves could crash upon the mountain, the massive snake lunged forward, jaws agape.

Terra roared a warrior's yell and swung her ax at one of the massive fangs.

The tooth and the ax clanged like steel, and Jörmungandr recoiled, flicking his tongue.

"It has been a long time since I have met a warrior capable of withstanding more than a single strike. I will enjoy destroying you."

"Hold that thought." Terra grabbed Leif, Mads, and Hildisvíni and teleported them from the mountaintop to another one in the distance. It was an impossibly far way to teleport, farther than she had ever gone before, but it did not matter as much in this realm. Time and space were more suggestions than hard and fast rules. Terra covered the distance easily and got her friends to safety.

"Here, take the feathered cloak. You two might need it to escape." Terra pulled the cloak from her shoulders, transforming her garb back into the slightly damp wetsuit.

"Don't be insane. There's no way you can stand against the power of Jörmungandr without your full armaments. Anything less would be suicide."

"But if I fail—"

"Luv, I don't need to be a demigod to see that if you fight that thing without every tool you have, you're going to lose, and we're all going to be stuck here. Which of course might be the better thing to happen if you lose. Seeing as how all that big snake's children are going to come for us."

On the horizon, Jörmungandr roared. A beam of energy shot from the snake's mouth, punching a hole in the sky. The stars and planets swirled around the hole like water. Then, Jörmungandr lowered his head and looked across the vast distance between them, directly at Terra.

Hildisvíni squealed, and Terra knew better than to try to leave the battle boar behind. She threw the cloak over her shoulders, mounted her hog, and teleported back to face Jörmungandr.

She reappeared in front of the mighty snake. He turned to face her, eyes glowing like suns on the verge of a supernova.

"You changed."

Terra looked down and saw her feathered cloak had given her armor for battle. She had heavy boots, steel shin guards, a battle skirt made of interlocking plates of metal, and coiled, twisted wires along her torso that allowed her to move while also providing protection.

Her breastplate fit so perfectly that it looked cast from a mold of her own body. Spiked pauldrons accented with eagle feathers covered her shoulders. Her bracers were the same, though now she also wore heavy gloves made of leather that might as well have come from Hildisvíni. On her head, she wore a helmet ringed in metal accents that made it look like a crown.

"You scared?" Terra asked. She shouldn't have. She knew better than to antagonize a deity that could destroy the Earth, but she had never felt such power. She had never felt capable of what she knew she could do at that moment. It didn't hurt that they were in this realm, and she was not exactly worried about collateral damage.

Jörmungandr lunged, and Terra swung herself onto the back of her battle pig. They teleported out of the way, and

Terra struck the back of the snake's head with her ax. Hildisvíni was not perturbed about jumping from one place to another. The battle boar seemed used to the technique. Rather than being surprised, he leaned his weight into Terra and added his strength to her blow.

Her weapon hit the back of Jörmungandr's head with such force that the snake hurtled downward into the mountain Terra had been standing on. The snake's face smashed through the rock, and the mountain collapsed into an avalanche. Stones fell into the green water far below them, and waves crashed across the world created as a prison for Jörmungandr.

Terra and her pig stayed high above the chaos. Hildisvíni pranced back and forth on thin air.

The victory dance was short-lived. Despite having his skull smashed through a mountain, Jörmungandr was far from defeated. He thrashed and recoiled, then struck at them.

But they were too high.

The world snake was too small. His body grew smaller as the end of his tail came closer to emerging from the water. Yet before it emerged, the world serpent's body swelled and seemed to thicken. Instead of the tip of his tail emerging from the water, the snake kept coming and coming.

Terra tried to evade, but Jörmungandr caught Hildisvíni in his jaws as he rose into the sky.

Hildisvíni squealed in pain, and Terra brought her ax down on Jörmungandr's nose with such force that she drew a spurt of the god's blood.

The snake released the pig, and they tumbled through the sky.

All sense of scale was gone for Terra. She couldn't tell if she was in space, above a planet, or fighting among the clouds.

Yet this realm of combat was not alien to her battle boar. Hildisvíni squealed, and the planets floating in the sky around them seemed to fix in place. Then the battle boar charged at the world snake.

He had already grown so much. He was as big as the sky, bigger than any lake could contain. Bigger than Fenrir. Bigger than a train.

And Terra was running right toward him.

She threw darts of energy from her bracers, a ball of fire, teleported this way and back, and was in the world snake's face.

She struck him again, and he flew back, crashing through a moon and breaking it into ten thousand pieces.

Even with the blow to his face, he fought on. The tip of his tail whipped out and snagged Terra across the chest. She went flying, somehow keeping her legs locked to the golden bristles of her battle boar.

They twisted and spun in the air as they tried to regain balance.

Before they could decide which way was up, Jörmungandr struck with his tail again, and they flew in a different direction. They struck a meteor, and the golden skin of the battle boar repelled it. They bounced off through space and crashed into another meteor and another, like a cosmic pinball machine.

Terra teleported behind one and caught her breath

while Jörmungandr slithered past. His massive bulk looked as comfortable among this asteroid belt as a garter snake would look among the pebbles of a garden pond.

"Little mortal. We are doing battle, not playing hide and seek."

Terra teleported out from behind the asteroid. Hildisvíni kicked off the front of it, and they crashed into the snake's belly. Terra felt her ax slice through his unprotected underside and into his flesh.

Then the snake was gone, its flesh no longer flesh.

"My children are not mine to control. They do as they wish. If that means destroying Midgard, so be it." The space around them vibrated with his voice.

"They won't destroy Midgard, though. Maybe it's been a while since you checked in on what we're doing on that blue marble, but we won't be beaten by a bunch of baby snakes who can hardly reason for themselves.

"We have guns. Missile launchers. Hell, we have nuclear weapons. Your children might kill thousands of my people. They might kill millions, but they won't kill them all. They're weak on Earth, with no magic to sustain them. You sent them to their deaths."

"I did not send them anywhere!"

Instead of a reptile covered in scales and powered by muscles, the world serpent became the cosmic version of himself. Larger. Vaster. But equally pissed off.

Two fangs made of the burning dust of supernovas came for Terra, and she sliced out with her ax. Her mortal brain told her this was the end, but she tried to defend herself and block the attack anyway.

Freya's ax protected her. It caught the cosmic dust and dissipated it to nothingness.

Terra could not see Jörmungandr, but she felt his presence. He was slithering through the ether, deciding when and how to reform his body. She had deflected his attack, but she had not done any damage. She thought she had hurt him when she cut into his belly, but apparently, she had only let him shed his skin and take on a new form.

She could not attack him until he took on a form. She could not battle that which she could not see.

But she knew Jörmungandr was listening.

"Your children. Are they not doing what you wished for on Midgard?" Terra asked into the void all around her. No answer came. Hildisvíni kicked his hooves, and together, they floated from the asteroid belt into a massive nebula that had not existed moments before.

Terra continued. "You always dreamed of Ragnarök as the end of Midgard, did you not? That's what the prophecy said, or at least the version I read. Your children going to Earth and wreaking havoc, that fulfills your goals, doesn't it? And if you lose in this battle, isn't that part of Ragnarök as well? This is all as you wished it to be!"

The nebula of dust swirled and coalesced into a version of Jörmungandr that burned like the sun. His eyes were motes of gravity and light. His scales reflected his inner power, but as he swam through the cosmos toward Terra, she saw his scales and fangs were formed from flakes of metal. He had taken the asteroids and used them to arm himself.

"I do not want my children to die!" Jörmungandr fumed

as he approached, faster and faster. Hildisvíni squealed and tried to run in the opposite direction.

Jörmungandr came up alongside them. They could not outrun him in this realm. They were both still thinking of space as space, but it was something different here. Something perhaps only Jörmungandr could understand.

"I'm only doing you all a favor by offering my life. This was not my plan."

"You said you wanted there to be an end to it. That mortality seemed sweeter because of the end," Terra repeated.

"That does not mean I wish my children to die!" Jörmungandr snarled, opened his jaws, and swallowed Terra and Hildisvíni.

One moment, they were in a mouth filled with shards of meteors for teeth. Then, they were down the snake's gullet into a stomach filled with the burning heat of suns. Hildisvíni squealed in fear, but Terra did not let herself panic. One of the first things she had learned to do was protect herself with her bracers.

She wove *seidr*, taking it from the bracers and spinning an orb to defend herself and her battle boar. The boiling stellar heat of the snake's guts tried to burn through the shield, yet it was not simple physics at play here but magic itself. Terra could stand against this cosmic deity because she had the vestments of a goddess. Jörmungandr could not swallow her and expect it to end the battle. Not while she still held every piece of Freya.

So, although she felt the heat of Jörmungandr's rage boiling away at her shield, she resisted. She pushed back.

The snake's innards burned hotter and brighter until nothing but white heat surrounded Terra and her pig.

Then, Jörmungandr went supernova.

Terra kept her shielding bubble around her and Hildisvíni as they tumbled through waves of dust and energy. Hildisvíni struggled against the currents. After a minute or a day, they stopped twisting and turning, and Terra regained her bearings.

Even with Jörmungandr's rage transforming him into a supernova, Terra knew he was not dead. She felt him lurking past her awareness. He was the guardian of Midgard. He had existed beyond what humans could understand for millennia.

He had moved from the shores of a cold land, past the horizons that had once been considered uncrossable, to the depths of the ocean, to this cosmic realm at the edge of the galaxy. He was a presence bounded by human understanding. And unfortunately for Terra, humans understood supernovas.

"If you don't want your children to die, you have to call them back, Jörmungandr! If you do not, they will perish! Every single one of them. You may not believe it, but they will. They lack magic on Midgard, and they don't know how to fight the weapons we have. I promise you that.

"You might have been telling yourself you were apathetic, but in your moment of rage, you spawned a brood of serpents who wish to finish what you were supposed to. You've made an army of pawns to carry out your will. If anything, you're a *better* manipulator than Loki."

"You will take that back!" Jörmungandr raged, and his

body was once more a giant serpent. A hundred feet of pure muscle, armored with scales that would make a crocodile jealous, the snake emerged from the void with fury.

He struck, and Terra parried, so he slammed his tail into the battle boar with such force that they were knocked from the sky.

Terra flew back, out of control, punching through a nebula, then a planet. Her shoulders shuddered from the impact, but somehow, she and Hildisvíni survived the ring of debris left in their wake. Her back grew hot as she reentered the atmosphere.

Jörmungandr emerged from the clouds and struck a second time. They rocketed through clouds, then above the green sea once more. Terra had the wherewithal to brace for impact before she and Hildisvíni struck the water's surface.

They shot down to the bottom. Waves crashed away from them in all directions, so instead of finding themselves on the seafloor, they were stuck in muck with walls of water moving away from them.

Terra pushed herself up from the mud, then helped Hildisvíni to his hooves. She leaned against the boar and felt him lean on her. All around her, feathers littered the mud. Her cloak has suffered in her fall. Her bracers were filthy with muck, and she felt grit between her skin and the cool metal. She reached for her neck and pulled more slime and mud from Brísingamen. Only her ax was undamaged from the blow, and she knew one artifact would not be enough.

Jörmungandr emerged from the receding water, slithering forward at a comfortable pace, flicking his forked tongue in and out of his mouth as if he delighted in the muck that covered Terra.

Terra understood what Jörmungandr wanted. The snake had all but bested her. He had kicked her from one end of the cosmos to the other. He wanted her to drop to her knees, to grovel for her life, to beg him not to do to Earth what he did to her.

Terra wasn't about to do that. Instead, she squared her shoulders, wiped some of the muck from her bracers, and looked him in his reptilian eyes.

"You should be proud. It's not many who outmaneuver their parents," Terra told him.

Jörmungandr rattled his tail and rose higher than Terra, ready to strike her with his fangs. She was not sure she could resist the poison this time.

"My wish was to have my place in Ragnarök. I was destined to end a great story, and that was all I desired! I did not seek to make my children do my work for me. I was robbed of my dream. They built their rights to Asgard on the promise of Ragnarök. They cannot have their paradise and deny us our part in the promised end."

Then, something occurred to Terra. She had goaded the snake enough. Perhaps now he could see he had choices to make, and those choices were based on the information he had or did not have. Could she use that? She had to try. It seemed a better shot than fighting this serpent in the muck before the tidal waves smashed back into them.

"Why is it that you believe Ragnarök is not coming?" Terra asked.

That got his attention.

He slithered toward them, encircling them so it was not

the bottom of the sea Terra saw but his muscular coils, taller than they were.

"Ragnarök came and went. I did battle and killed Thor, as it had been foretold I would. My brother killed Odin."

"Except he came back. They all came back," Terra countered.

The air seemed to grow heavier, and something rumbled in the distance.

"Yes..." Jörmungandr's head rose above his coils. His tongue flicked in and out as he tasted the change in the air with his tongue. It was the water. The water of this ocean had gone as far as it would go from Terra and her boar slamming into it. It had climbed out of its bed, found it uncomfortable, and was now rushing back toward them. Terra had less than a minute before it all came thundering back.

"How can you be sure it was the true Ragnarök?" Terra asked.

"Because it was so. Odin said it was so when he returned from the dead."

Terra's ears popped as the air pressure changed from the approaching water. Still, a planet-spanning tidal wave wasn't important right now. The rules were different here. Terra had been punched *through a planet* and come out the other side still standing.

She had no doubt the waves would hurt if they crashed upon them, but it would not be as devastating as Jörmungandr's children would be if left to do as they wished on Midgard. Terra would risk her own annihilation if she had to. It was the Viking way. She would risk it all to convince Jörmungandr to save their world. Because he was the only one who could.

So, despite destruction closing in on her from all sides, she stayed focused on Jörmungandr. He had to see. She had to change his mind.

"Odin said it was Ragnarök. Odin, the most deceitful of them all. Odin, who first understood the power of runes. He told you a story, and you believed it?"

Jörmungandr drew his coils closer around Terra and her war pig, and their world shrunk. The space they were in was now so small that they were touching Jörmungandr as he slithered around them. Terra felt for her ability to teleport and found it was still there. Jörmungandr had not taken it away, but should she use it?

"You are speaking down to one who could destroy you in an instant. Do you have a point, or do you simply wish for a quick death?" Jörmungandr filled the space above them, so all they could see was the distant sky and the face of the world serpent.

"My point is only that the gods are full of deception," Terra explained in a rush. The ground shook with the approaching tidal wave. "Your brother's imprisonment proves that as much as any other.

"They claim Ragnarök happened, yet you were placed in this realm. Your sister remained in her domain of the dead, and Thor took your brother back to his place of imprisonment. It does not seem as if the gods have truly forgotten the idea of Ragnarök. It seems as if something about the three of you occupies their thoughts."

"But Ragnarök passed. I killed Odin. My venom was in his blood, and his heart ceased to beat."

"Until it didn't. They *said* it was Ragnarök, and you believed them. You let your children believe them, but what if that was not truly the end? What if Odin knew he would come back to life, but he kept this from you so that you would not bother them for a time?"

"That is not how it was supposed to be. If you speak the truth, surely—"

The tidal wave crashed into them, and despite his great size, Jörmungandr was picked up and thrown around like a sock in a washing machine.

Terra shielded herself and her battle boar, but she had no doubt the only reason she survived the crushing waves was because they were wrapped in the snake's coils, and he did not yet wish them to die.

Suffer, though? He didn't seem to have any problem with that.

The waters of the realm crashed and thrashed, churning the mud at the bottom of the sea with the air that was supposed to be above it. For a moment, the three of them tumbled together—the insurance adjuster, the mechanical mythical beast, and the apocalyptic sea serpent—before Jörmungandr unwound himself, and Terra and Hildisvíni were thrown free.

Terra lost her grip on the boar, and he vanished into the crashing, churning waters. She swam, trying to reach the surface despite having no idea where the surface was. There were bubbles, rocks, and wisps of green slime everywhere, tumbling, crashing, and boiling about.

In the crashing churn of water, Terra saw Jörmungandr's coils, Hildisvíni's snout, then the face of the mighty serpent. His eyes were open under the water, rolled back in ecstasy. Was it because he had finally found a force in this place he could not control? Did he like being lost in the course of things? If he did, if he craved to be free of the planning and plotting, Terra's entire gambit might have been for naught.

She couldn't give up, though. She was still alive when Jörmungandr could have crushed her.

She could breathe underwater thanks to her control over *seidr*, but if she couldn't, would Jörmungandr have let her die? Had she done enough to make him see the story he had been telling himself and his children was not the full story?

The currents grew less intense, and Terra glimpsed the sun shining through the murk. She kicked for the surface, swimming past rocks tumbling down and green goo racing to keep up with her. She burst through to find the sea heaving and swaying.

A moment later, Hildisvíni burst from the surface and paddled over to her. She grabbed his golden bristles, and the battle pig shoved her onto his back with his snout. Her weight was not enough to make him even begin to sink.

The water calmed, and they were once more in a featureless sea of green water.

Only then did Jörmungandr resurface. His body stayed beneath the placid surface, no doubt ready to strike the moment the world serpent decided.

"It was an interesting idea," the world serpent casually remarked as if nothing had happened. "But I do not think it is correct."

Terra knew that despite his words, she had him. She only had to push him a little further.

"Does it not seem odd that first your brother, then your sister, and now your children have all come to Midgard in some form in the last year? Why would that be? Even if Loki did not give them orders, could he have planted an idea in their head, the way you might have planted the idea that you did want Midgard destroyed in the minds of your own children?" Terra asked.

"My father is a trickster. Not some master schemer. For him to have convinced us to all come to Midgard is beyond even him," Jörmungandr replied.

"Yet we have found pieces of him on Earth after they were gone for centuries," Terra pointed out. "Loki is planning something. Or at least that's how it appears to us. What would he be interested in that he would need his three children to be part of?"

"You misplayed your hand," Jörmungandr stated. "I do not want to be my father's pawn, even if I do not understand his motives. Or maybe, *especially* because I do not understand him. I will do nothing to make his plans come to be. I will not dance for him."

"But you have a choice," Terra insisted. "You have a choice right now. You can call your children back here. You can teach them to deal with their thoughts and feelings. Loki never did that for you, but you can do that for them."

"You wish me to be *your* pawn, then," Jörmungandr hissed.

"I'm only a human. I know I have these clothes from Freya, but I'm a regular person. I don't have pawns. I likely *am* a pawn. All we humans really have is free will, and many of us squander that.

"That's all I want for you. To have the same choice. You can let your children do what they will to the Earth, unthinking, with rage, or you can call them back here and try to help them. I don't want you to do the first, but if that is what you choose, at least my world won't die because of the apathy of a demigod. Or you could decide something different. You could train them. Teach them to be better than you. That's what parents on Earth try to do for their children."

"Help them prepare for the *true* Ragnarök?" Jörmungandr asked, though he sounded interested. "A Ragnarök that comes when *we* decide, not when the Aesir and Vanir deem it convenient."

"If that is your dream," Terra answered, trying to be comfortable with the thoughts she was putting in the world serpent's head. What if he decided to attack? What if, instead of only his children, he came as well?

"I suppose I already lived through one false prophecy," Jörmungandr mused, considering.

"And who is to say what will happen?" Terra added. "Prophecies always leave out details. We try to follow them, to make the events of our lives fit into what has come before and what we think should come to pass, but they are changeable. They are words, after all, and words are tricky things."

"That sounds like the words of the Vanir."

"My friend Leif had studied in the library at Asgard. I have learned much from him."

"They have been watching," Jörmungandr told her, and a mountain moved from the horizon to beneath where Hildisvíni was treading water. The mountain lifted them, and the rocks shifted, so they were once more standing with Leif and Mads.

"Bloody hell, that was a fight," Mads commented.

"Always interesting to see how these mortals think," Leif remarked.

"Do you want a choice?" Terra asked more gently. "Because if your children continue to attack Midgard, the Aesir *will* interfere. They believe in battle. If they have an excuse, they will attack your children. Then you will have to fight them, will you not? But if you act now, *you* can decide when you engage. You can teach your children what you think is best."

"And if I decide what is best is destroying Midgard with the full force of my thousands of offspring?" Jörmungandr flicked his tongue, tasting the air as much as he was tasting his idea.

"Terra, luv, we thought you were doing better than this," Mads intoned.

Terra tightened her grip on Freya's ax. This realm was rich with magic, and the ax knew it. She felt its power, even stronger than usual, but she knew it would not be able to defeat the world serpent. If they fought again, all she could hope to do was hold on long enough for the gods to arrive and herald the battle that would begin the end of the world.

"You can make that choice. I hope you don't, but you can decide. Your children can, too. They don't need to be controlled by their circumstances."

Jörmungandr considered for what felt like a millennium.

"It would be hasty to attack without my children

knowing the full extent of their abilities," Jörmungandr finally allowed. "I have neglected them too long. I have been indifferent. They could be truly great with my guidance."

"Worse than they are now?" Mads muttered. "Couldn't they stop magic?"

Despite Mads talking quietly, Jörmungandr heard him fine. "I watched some of how they fought. Of the numbers they lost. I did not care then, but now I see this was callous of me. I am not my father. I am better than him. I must be better than him. If my children are to attack Midgard, we will do it properly. You say you have weapons that can ensure the survival of humans over my young? I am not so sure about that." He smirked devilishly, and Terra saw something of his father's reputation in his eyes.

But Terra said nothing, only wondered at what she had done. Was this a victory? Had she bought humanity time or doomed them?

Jörmungandr did not wait for her to answer. He raised his head to the sky, and the stars and planets seemed to reform around him in a blink, giving him a silhouette that made it hard to tell where the reptilian body of the snake ended, and the cosmic version began.

He shook the tip of his tail, still hidden under the green water despite his head being in the stars, and the water shook and rippled. Rings of waves spread out from the tip of his tail, but while the earlier waves had crashed upon the mountains and brought destruction, these waves moved through the land, into the sky, and across the stars themselves.

"It is done," Jörmungandr announced, sounding self-satisfied. "I have summoned my children to return."

"And they will listen?" Terra asked. "In Midgard, children do not always obey their parents."

"They will obey. Most of them will come, but part of the message I sent was a reminder that their magic will not sustain them in Midgard. Those who choose to stay will be cut off from the supply they need from this realm. It is too harsh, perhaps, but most will listen. Most of them have always wished to listen. They will return to me and learn from me, and together, we will decide our place in the end of things."

"You wouldn't want to hang out here in this lovely domain of yours?" Mads asked.

"Perhaps that is what we will decide. I am not sure," Jörmungandr pondered aloud. "In a way, we are both the guardians of Midgard and its destroyers. As long as I exist in this realm, encircling Midgard, it is impossible for the Jotun or any other force from any realm to get past me.

"My children will take this role very seriously should we decide that is our plan. It would be satisfying to see my children battle the arrogant Jotun, who think we are nothing but legless lizards. Though it might be even more satisfying to send them out and watch what they could do to your world if they understood their true power. However, I think the most satisfying idea is that we can choose what our role will be."

"Do you think it will take long to decide if you're going to save humanity or destroy it, or is it the sort of thing you might have to go back and forth on?" Mads asked.

Jörmungandr chuckled, and the mountain beneath their

feet shook with his mirth. "I will have to speak to all of my children first. I will not force my will on them or trick them into doing what I wish, either. However, I do not think it will take long once they return. They are made of my scales, after all. The way we think is not so different."

"And how long until they return?" Leif asked.

"For all of them? A few millennia. Nothing longer than that. Not so long."

"You're certain?" Terra asked, daring to hope. "You're certain it will take that long for all your children to make it back here?"

"They left long ago. It might be only a few centuries if they do not get lost on their return, but the branches of Yggdrasil twist and turn. They will be here soon enough, though."

Terra did not feel it was necessary to point out that a few centuries was plenty of time for mankind to progress further than they were. Why, within a decade, Terra wanted to introduce the idea of magic to Earth. That alone could change how everyone would react to the arrival of the snakes. Jörmungandr might have felt he was making a threat, but that was fine with Terra. She would take centuries or millennia and claim it as victory.

"We thank you for our time here," Terra stated. "We did not know what to expect, and it was a pleasure to meet you and have this time to speak with each other."

"The pleasure was mine, Terra, Chosen of Freya. I still do not understand the lifespans of you creatures, but if you are around when my children and I decide what to do, I look forward to fighting with you against the Jotun or killing you with my own venom."

The two options seemed equally positive to the world serpent, a reminder that this monster was beyond mortal comprehension. How could defense and attack be the same? How could the end of Midgard equate to its preservation?

There was no time to discuss this, though.

The mountain beneath them began to shrink, then it was gone, and they were tumbling through the air toward the green sea. They clung to Hildisvíni as the boar kicked into the air, ready to fly them to safety, but there was no need.

Jörmungandr opened a portal, and they plunged through it into the sea of their own world.

Terra swam to the surface. Her head burst through along with Leif, Mads, and the huge head of her war pig.

"We got people overboard! Let's get a life preserver over there!" Romero shouted from the deck of Joana's ship.

Terra turned and waved for help, and a foam ring was tossed to them. How cute that humans could face the perils of a world serpent hungry for their death and still use something as simple as a life preserver for assistance?

"That'll do, pig," Terra intoned and patted the war boar's flank.

Hildisvíni shrank into a figurine, and Terra pocketed it. Then she grabbed the life preserver and let them pull her to the boat, back to the world she knew.

EPILOGUE

Keflavík, Iceland, Wednesday morning

Harris Barrow knew the moment Terra had succeeded. It was not so hard to figure out. The snakes had become such a problem that they were all over the news. There were thousands of them, primarily wreaking havoc on the ships and shorelines of Europe, but they had already spread to the east coast of North America and the northwest of Africa.

A few sightings in Asia had yet to be verified, but the news reporters covering those parts of the world were practically salivating at the prospect of the plague of serpents reaching their shores. People were funny that way. No one wanted to be left out, not even of the apocalypse.

There had been many of the serpents along the shores of Iceland. Harris Barrow had found a suitable home in the town of Keflavík. It was still secret to his team, but he longed for their company and would surely tell them where he had been hiding out sooner rather than later.

Though the snakes had made that a frightening proposition.

They had been attacking any boats that came in and out of coves around the town. Tourist boats had already given up on taking people out. Fishermen were a more stalwart folk and were still going out on the sea, armed with weapons alongside chum and nets.

Barrow had been watching one coming after a boat. They had little interest in the fish and instead seemed hungry for the power of the internal combustion engines. They struck with impunity, and even when one was killed, others would continue the attack. The local fishermen had been told not to go out, but of course, they would not listen to any bureaucrat tell them what to do.

So it was with great relief that Barrow watched the snake draw closer to the boat, then go rigid, turn back, and dive into the sea. He had never seen the behavior before, so when he turned on the news and saw that snakes the world over had given up on their attacks, he knew Terra must have played a part in their hasty retreat.

That made three demigods she had faced down. A pretty impressive resume, Barrow thought. He was glad to have her in his employ. It would be nice to focus on archeology again instead of whatever insanity the world had come to, though.

However, maybe those times were already past, Barrow mused as he looked at Captain Joana's incoming call. He had asked her to write up a report and to be as thorough as possible. She had already called once to ensure he really wanted *everything*, even if it sounded outlandish. He had assured her nothing she included would be outlandish to him.

She'd laughed and told him she would bet him ten percent of what he'd paid that she could surprise him. He had taken the bet, though he already felt guilty about it. After an army of death-worshipping cultists attacked his house, led by the half-corpse of a dead rival, not much remained on any branch of the world tree that could surprise him.

He answered her call.

After a few minutes of niceties and a bit about the billing for Barrow's odd requests, Captain Joana finally worked herself up to the meat of the matter.

"You've seen how there were snakes in the news," she began, trying to railroad him from the onset of the conversation. Surely, it wouldn't be so hard to imagine some of those unexplained reptiles that had been all over every news channel had appeared on her mission, right?

Barrow considered playing dumb and acting like he didn't know anything about anything. That he was a doddering old man who had buried himself in his books for the last week and hadn't watched television, let alone checked a news feed. But he couldn't do it. Even if it would be the easiest way to make sure the captain got the extra ten percent that Barrow was already convinced she deserved.

"Believe it or not, I saw some of them off the coast of where I'm staying. It beggars belief, does it not?"

Her sigh of relief was so heavy that it rattled the speaker. Barrow barely managed not to laugh. He didn't want to embarrass the girl.

"Well, we saw quite a lot of them. I was skeptical about the need for explosives, but one of them was quite aggressive," Joana told him.

"And the explosives did the trick?" Barrow asked.

"Not exactly. Truthfully, sir, I'm not quite sure how we survived. Terra and Leif went into the water in wet suits, and when they reemerged—this was more than a kilometer away, by the way—the big snake seemed to be gone."

"Terra is quite resourceful. That is why I keep her in my employ."

"To say the least, sir."

"And after that, it was relatively smooth sailing?"

"Not exactly. As we grew closer to your site, there were more and more snakes. They were all sizes, from a pencil to larger than any snake should have any right to be. When your team went down to the site, they swarmed us. Didn't attack, mind you, but there was a time when we were certain if the snakes came out of the sea, we'd be done for. There were simply so many."

"But they didn't come out?"

Captain Joana paused for the briefest moment, perhaps surprised that Barrow was not, then she continued.

"They seemed agitated, and we thought they were about to rise up and come for us. Then, all of a sudden, they stopped. They retreated beneath the surface, and we could not detect them after that. We didn't see any on the return voyage, either."

"I'd be interested to know exactly when this happened. It seems the snakes vanished from the world over at roughly around the same time. I wonder if your experience matches that timeline."

"I have timestamps in the ship's log. I'll check for you."

"That would be appreciated. After the snakes disappeared, you went and fetched my team?" Barrow had already heard from his team, so he knew they had survived and had the artifact in their possession, though he had yet to discover what it was. Apparently, Terra had sworn Leif and Mads to secrecy, and they were not about to break their word to the woman who'd saved their lives more often than not.

"Well, sir, that was the oddest part. Not long after the snakes vanished, a few minutes at most, your team fell out of the sky."

"Out of the sky?" That had to be the portal Leif had told them about. It had worked, then! Freya's artifacts had allowed them to travel to another realm. Amazing!

"Yes, sir. After they caught up to the ship, I wasn't that surprised, to be honest. It was what they had with them that caught me off guard."

Barrow felt himself leaning toward the receiver, eager to hear what sort of implement Terra had with her. "And that was?"

"They were riding on the back of a giant golden pig."

"Hildisvíni!" Barrow tried to say, but he was so shocked that he did little more than gurgle a response.

"You sound surprised, sir." Joana seemed pleased with herself. As well she should be. She had won her extra ten percent.

"A giant pig has been on your ship, and this is the first I'm hearing of it?"

"Well, that's the thing, sir. By the time we got them out

of the water, which was not long, only a few minutes, the pig was gone."

"Strange, indeed," Barrow replied. Though the battle pig being an artifact in the first place was more surprising than the idea that it could be concealed in some clever way. The feathered cloak had proven that things changing shape was a simple enough thing for the Norse artificers.

"I certainly thought so."

"Did they seem healthy enough when you brought them aboard?" Barrow asked. He already had his report from Mads, though his old friend had a propensity for sugar-coating how things went. He'd made it sound like they were fine and didn't even have to battle the world snake. Maybe the captain's impression of his team's return would give him a different idea of how their mission went.

"They seemed quite pleased with themselves, sir."

Well, so much for that theory!

"Although…" the captain continued.

"Yes?" Barrow pressed.

"They said they were successful, though I was not certain what that meant because it seemed like there were terms to their success."

"Did there?"

"They said it should hold for now. One of my crew can be nosier than I would like, and he asked what 'for now' meant to them. They said for at least the next few Ice Ages. I didn't know what to make of that."

"I don't always know what my team means, exactly, but we can certainly take that as good news."

"I had hoped so, sir."

"You did very well, Captain. I will happily pay you the

extra ten percent we wagered and would also like to offer to pay for some time off for you and your crew, if necessary. Working with the Barrow Company can be quite unusual, and if you need time to gather yourselves, I am willing to pay you for that."

"That won't be necessary, sir. Though I am curious about how nonchalant you seem about all this. These snakes... You have seen them before, I take it?"

"Not at all. However, compared to some of what I've seen, they don't seem all that unusual. Truly, you have done quite well. You had a reputation for having the mettle for a mission such as this, and I congratulate you for living up to that reputation."

"All in a day's work, Dr. Barrow. I was not expecting sea monsters, but you were quite clear that this mission would be far from typical. I came for the adventure as much as the generous pay package. If you ever need to take to the oceans again, please keep my crew and me in mind."

"I will, Captain Joana. Thank you."

Barrow said his goodbyes, hung up and returned his attention to the report Mads had filed.

Terra had the final piece of Freya, and it was the boar that often accompanied the goddess into battle. What a development. Barrow wondered what that meant for Terra's future. She had done what Freya had set out for her to do. She had gathered all the pieces of the goddess. She had as much power as a mortal could wield.

Did that mean the Norse legends would stop coming here, or that more than ever would try to enter this realm? Barrow thought they all deserved a break until he remembered their months of searching everywhere and finding nothing. Terra had not been happy then. Maybe she would prefer an incursion of Jotun.

He hoped she would stop short of wanting to see how it would all end. With the Norse gods, that was a big question with a bigger answer.

And to think it all began with a simple drinking horn.

Barrow put the report down, got up, and went to the horn. The lone ornament above his mantle. Most of his collection was still in storage after the attack.

He took the horn down and poured the rest of his tea into it. No sooner did he finish than the liquid turned gold.

Barrow took a sip. There was no denying the golden beverage was delightful.

Mead in hand, Barrow's mind could more easily wrap itself around the notes Mads made about Jörmungandr. The scale of the world serpent was something Barrow still couldn't fully understand. It was both big enough to eat Terra in a single bite and larger than the planet. It could hide beneath a shallow sea they had all waded through and was also bigger than the sky.

Barrow did not think he would have been able to conceptualize it at all, except for that brief moment years ago when he had looked into somewhere *else* with Beatrice. It had defied what he understood then, but now he felt the mortal mind could not fully understand the branches of the world tree. It was too much for them to see. Like the world snake, apparently.

What would happen if these other realms tried to spill into this one? Barrow did not like the thought, but he was also unafraid of that happening. If this world was in danger from beings from another realm, or because the beings of Midgard grabbed artifacts they should not, he would help defend it. He would provide what resources he could for Terra, and with her artifacts, she would protect this place.

One day soon, they would plan how to share magic with the world. They would build a future in which they did not have to hide the power they had discovered.

Barrow could not wait for that day.

Terra hoped today would never end.

Mads and Leif had agreed to come with her on vacation to Marstand, an unbelievably beautiful town in Sweden.

She had started the day with a cup of coffee and fresh bread, spent the morning sightseeing, had a lovely lunch, then dove into museums for the afternoon. She had just finished an early dinner with Leif and was now in front of a café, sipping a coffee that would surely keep her awake if she wasn't so tired. Mads, Romero, and Leif had already excused themselves to go on a bar crawl. Terra thought she'd had enough poison in her body for a good long time and had politely declined.

Besides, what could be better than sitting in front of a café with a good book about a rather interesting interpretation of the origins of Norse mythology? However, she could not help but wonder who would have the best time of the bar crawl. She knew Leif could drink a great deal of mead or ale, but when it came to hard liquor, he was not as hardy. Would the two humans have an advantage over the Asgardian's liver because they had more experience, or would the *seidr* in his blood give him the edge he needed to survive the evening?

She looked forward to hearing all about it but wouldn't bother trying herself. The bracers would cure her of the intoxication, so there was no point in trying to compete and automatically winning.

Plus, she was half expecting a visitor.

It was not that she needed approval. She knew Freya was proud of her. She felt it in her bones. However, she did not think it would be so bad to lay her eyes on the goddess of beauty and battle once more and to hear her soft voice say kind things. At the least, she wanted to know if she needed to feed the boar.

Yet as paragraph turned to page turned to chapter in her book, she forgot all about Freya as she fell into the version of history the author was trying to weave.

She hardly noticed when a stranger approached her table and asked if he could have a seat.

"Of course. Please, make yourself comfortable," Terra offered without bothering to look up first. The pleasant camaraderie of strangers was something she had come to enjoy about Europe. It felt odd to strike up a conversation with someone back in Ohio, but here, tables were made for sharing. Terra liked that. It did not hurt that no human on the planet could be a threat to her.

"Wonderful day. Do you recommend the coffee, or should I stick to mead?" the man asked once he was seated, and Terra put down her book to chat with him.

Her first thought was surprise that she had let someone so odd sit across from her without noticing. He wore a long purple jacket and a matching hat with a broad brim that covered his eyes. He had a way of moving his hands that made Terra think of a conductor or perhaps a magician who excelled in sleight of hand.

"The coffee is strong. I haven't tried the mead here. I don't think I saw it on the menu."

"It's right here." The man handed her a menu. Indeed, there was a section for mead written in golden ink. How had Terra missed it?

"Ah. I had not seen that."

"Some of these are quite good vintages. Though I'd prefer an endless supply to some old dusty bottle, eh?"

His eyes briefly twinkled under the brim of his hat, then she couldn't see anything but his smirk poking out.

"Are you from around here?" Terra asked. "I'm from out of town. Wondering where the best place is to see the entire city."

"I find the best place to see a city is from throughout it. When we stand above things, they seem like we can understand them. It's only when we're in the midst of it all that we truly get a feeling."

"That's fun advice," Terra replied. "Thought it could get me into trouble, I would think."

"You look as if you can handle quite a bit of trouble," the stranger suggested.

"What do you mean by that?"

"Only that if there's a branch of a tree, you look like you would climb it."

"I suppose I would." Terra sensed there was more to this man than it appeared. "I've been traveling quite a bit lately."

"Too many branches, so I've heard."

"You've been to some, then?" Terra asked. She felt as if she were tumbling deeper into this man's words.

"Oh, I've been to quite a few. Banished from some. Worshiped in others. I could not accomplish what you did recently, though. My children can be quite unruly. Sometimes, they forget they have been given so much, good and bad, and they should be thankful for all of it. I think you reminded them of that. And I thank you for teaching them that lesson."

"Wait. You're—"

"Loki. In the flesh. Well, we don't have flesh the way you do, precisely, and of course I can take any shape I choose. But still. I am here! Behold. I lift a glass of mead." Loki raised a glass to Terra.

"I can't help but wonder if you're here to start something," Terra intoned.

"Ah, so direct! What a refreshing way to be. I am quite accustomed to everyone talking around everything, but not with you!"

"Well?" Terra asked.

Loki chuckled. "Coming here to rattle sabers and bump chests has never been my style. Is it so hard to believe that I'm genuinely thankful? My children had forgotten their place. They had thought they had some right to Midgard. They are incorrect, of course, and they needed to be reminded of such.

"But it would not do for a father to discipline his children. You did a much better job, and they all got to stretch their willpower, which will make them much more… amenable. It can be difficult for a trickster like me to get his way. And this time, I did, with all three of them. So I thank you."

Loki stood and bowed to her with a flourish of his hat.

Terra did not know what to think about the trickster god being thankful. She could not imagine letting his children run amok on Midgard, but thinking she'd served as a deterrent like their father wanted was an odd idea.

Loki sat back down and slid a large silver coin across the table to her. "Consider your coffee on me. I would love to drink more mead with you, but my time is always in short supply. Are these modern times not busier than they've ever been? Honestly, I don't know how you people deal with it. All the messaging and social media and television. It's easier to trick your kind than ever before! But I digress. I have business to attend to."

"I hope it involves talking to your kids," Terra replied, but Loki was already gone.

It was an easy enough thing to disappear in front of a mortal. They were so accustomed to seeing with their eyes that if one made even the simplest illusions, they bought into them quite easily.

"What were you doing?"

Gods were always a bit harder to trick.

"I was making polite conversation, dearest Freya. Nothing more."

"Polite conversation with my Chosen."

"I suppose so, but I am hardly the first to do it! Thor came to this realm to bat my son around, and from what I hear, Odin made an offer to take one of your Chosen's friends to Asgard despite him being related to you! Quite the scandal, I would say. The arrogance of it, really, for Odin to attempt to take your own blood to Valhalla instead of Folkvangr."

"I'm not going to fall for one of your tricks, Loki," Freya replied coldly.

"I mean no trick, lovely Freya! I'm simply remarking that the world is changing. The Aesir and Vanir had not come to Midgard in quite some time, and now so many in such quick succession. Your Chosen has made quite the splash."

"What are you plotting, Loki?"

"I have only the vaguest idea myself," Loki replied before taking the shape of one of Freya's cats and vanishing into the evening.

The truth was, he had a hundred plots and a thousand schemes, all competing with each other, ready to be put into action. He did not know what would happen next, as foresight was not one of his strengths.

But he was quite eager to watch how this realm would change.

AUTHOR NOTES
MARCH 12, 2024

Thank you so much for reading our stories all the way to the end!

The Weather Made Me Do It... Or in other words... The British are Coming!

I sit here in London amidst the backdrop of the iconic London Book Fair, I'm struck by the profound influence that weather can have on a society.

Why? Because it's @#@#%@ COLD outside.

It's one of those cold, dreary days, with the kind of weather that chills you to the bone and cloaks the city in a shroud of mist, has got me thinking. It's easy to see how such an environment could stir a restless spirit, ignite the desire for exploration, and perhaps even the conquest of new lands.

Here are my top seven reasons why the Europeans might have been inspired to conquer the world, spurred on by their weather:

1. **The Quest for Sunshine**: Endless days of overcast skies could make anyone yearn for the warmth of the sun. Imagine the allure of distant lands where the sun shines brightly, promising vitamin D and a respite from the relentless gray.
2. **Cabin Fever**: Being cooped up indoors to avoid the biting cold could drive the most reserved person to dream of adventure. It's not a huge leap to think that this could translate into a desire to sail the seas in search of new horizons.
3. **Economic Aspirations**: The harsh weather impacts agriculture and living conditions. This could have motivated the British to seek out new territories with more hospitable climates for farming and trade, ensuring food security and wealth. In short: "The Spanish have gold…I wants some too." (I probably have my countries wrong, here.)
4. **Technological Advancements**: The necessity to adapt to and combat inclement weather may have spurred innovation. This drive to improve their lot could have led to the technological prowess that made long voyages possible. It was a type of 'keep up with the Joneses' but between (at that time) the world superpowers.
5. **Stories of Exotic Lands**: Tales from travelers who had braved the unknown and returned with stories of exotic, sun-kissed lands would have sounded especially appealing against the backdrop of a cold, wet European climate. In

short, a fiction-writer caused the whole 'Let's go conquer the world' aspect for the English.
6. **Strategic Advantage**: Rulers and nations may have seen the benefit of controlling lands with diverse climates as a way to ensure resources throughout the year, rather than being at the mercy of a single, often unforgiving, environment. Again – someone brought some good stories home – and the Queen or King said, "I want that. Go get it for me and plant a flag there."
7. **Cultural Enrichment**: The dreariness of a long, dark winter could have been the perfect catalyst for seeking out new cultures, cuisines, and experiences, enriching European societies with the spoils of their conquests. Hmmm…. Spices… All of those wonderful spices. Helps you understand the background of the DUNE stories.

While the weather here makes me appreciate the warmth of a good coffee shop and the company of fellow book lovers, it also stirs in me an understanding of the historical push for exploration. It's fascinating to consider how a simple change in weather can lead to world-changing events.

Or at least makes my over-active imagination create lies and damned lies as to the reasons.

So, whether you're enjoying a sunny day or braving the chill, remember that every type of weather has influenced someone, somewhere, to do something extraordinary, or at least they went and captured some land because it was always bitingly cold.

Ad Aeternitatem,
Michael Anderle

P.S. Don't forget to leave a review if you've enjoyed the journey so far, and stay tuned for updates and behind-the-scenes looks at this new series by subscribing to the MORE STORIES with Michael newsletter HERE: https://michael.beehiiv.com/

CONNECT WITH THE AUTHOR

Connect with Michael Anderle

Website: http://lmbpn.com

Email List: https://michael.beehiiv.com/

https://www.facebook.com/LMBPNPublishing

https://twitter.com/MichaelAnderle

https://www.instagram.com/lmbpn_publishing/

https://www.bookbub.com/authors/michael-anderle

BOOKS BY MICHAEL ANDERLE

Sign up for the LMBPN email list to be notified of new releases and special deals!

https://lmbpn.com/email/

For a complete list of books by Michael Anderle, please visit:

www.lmbpn.com/ma-books/

www.ingramcontent.com/pod-product-compliance
Lightning Source LLC
LaVergne TN
LVHW041748060526
838201LV00046B/943